CW00496817

LISZT:
MY TRAVELLING
CIRCUS LIFE

LISZT:
MY TRAVELLING
CIRCUS LIFE

David Ian Allsobrook

M

First published in the United Kingdom 1991 by
The Macmillan Press Limited
London and Basingstoke

Associated companies in Auckland, Delhi, Dublin, Gaborone, Hamburg, Harare, Hong Kong, Johannesburg, Kuala Lumpur, Lagos, Manzini, Melbourne, Mexico City, Nairobi, New York, Singapore, Tokyo.

British Library Cataloguing in Publication Data

Liszt: My travelling circus life.
  I. Allsobrook, Dr David
  920

ISBN 0-333-56360-3

Typeset by Wyvern Typesetting Limited, Bristol
Printed in Hong Kong

Contents

Illustration acknowledgments

We are grateful to the following for permission to reproduce illustrative material:

Ernst Burger, Munich figs.1, 3, 4, 6, 7
Hungarian National Museum, Budapest fig.2
Richard-Wagner-Gedenkstätte, Bayreuth fig.5
Devon Library Services, Exeter fig.8
Cheltenham Art Gallery and Museums fig.9
National Library of Wales/Trwy ganiatâd Llyfrgell Genedlaethol Cymru, Aberystwyth pp.136, 140, 153, 154, 157, 159, 161, 162, 164, 166
Illustrated London News, London pp.178, 190
Punch, London pp.194

FOR

WILLIAM SALAMAN

a friend generous with time and encouragement

and

MARIAN, DANIEL AND GUDRUN.

CHAPTER ONE

Liszt

> Musical biography has always tended to the diffusion of a romantic legend rather than to an impartial record of the sober truth. For the musical world is divided into clans, and each clan swears such unquestioning loyalty to its adopted chieftain that it is almost as much as the outsider's life is worth to hint that the Big Chief may have had a human as well as a heroic or a sacred side to him.
>
> (Ernest Newman, *The Man Liszt*, London, 1934, p. 1)

MORE THAN fifty years after Newman, the most respected critic of his time, wrote those words, it has to be acknowledged that Liszt remains a controversial figure. Argument certainly rumbles over his standing as a composer, though the scholarly, evangelical work of the musicologist Alan Walker and the composer Humphrey Searle has steadily consolidated a growing body of interest in Liszt's music, across the whole range of his career, from the early virtuoso transcriptions, through his mature works, like the two concertos and symphonies, to the intriguingly forward-looking pieces of his old age.

On the other hand, Liszt's reputation as one of the greatest keyboard players of the post-Baroque era has never been seriously doubted; though because of the failure of nineteenth-century inventors to create an effective recording device before the great pianist died in 1886, we shall never hear even a wisp of one of his performances. (Judging by what we can hear of Brahms's playing, this is probably fortunate.) He was, excepting Paganini, the most glamorous performing artist of the era before the gramophone; and it may be that speculation about the kind of pianist he was will continue to buzz simply because we have to rely upon accounts of his playing which, while they are usually adulatory, sometimes contain contradictions and poetical euphemisms.

The summary which immediately follows – of his career as pianist and composer – is not an attempt to add anything new to the accumulation of detail piled up by writers on Liszt in English, from Sacheverell Sitwell (also 1934) onwards: Sitwell's classic biography, and several of its successors – Ronald Taylor's recently published reassessment, for instance – must remain the chief sources of information for understanding the broad sweep of his career.[1] As with all biographical writing, each of the recent accounts has its weaknesses of bias, as well as of factual inaccuracy. There are still areas of Liszt's life which, despite the most painstaking research, will remain comparatively obscure. The account of his career offered in this chapter merely serves as a short preface to the fascinating story of Liszt's main encounters with Britain in 1840 and 1841. However, a detailed examination of a brief slice of his professional life – never dealt with before at length in one place – may throw light from a new angle upon the constantly changing edifice of one of the towering personalities of music in the Romantic era, while at the same time illuminating shadowy areas of early Victorian entertainment.

Liszt was born in 1811 on the estates of the noble Esterházy family, at Raiding in the Sopron region of Hungary. His father Adam, a bailiff and book-keeper, was well read, and gave the boy his first instruction on the piano and in the rudiments of a general education. From early childhood he was interested in folk music, and it was quickly discovered that he possessed considerable musical talent. He gave concerts locally and attracted the interest of wealthy patrons who subscribed to a fund which enabled him to go to Vienna for piano-teaching by Czerny and composition lessons with Salieri, the notorious rival of Mozart. In December 1821 he gave his first public concert in Vienna, and in the following year he received a celebrated kiss from Beethoven. Some commentators

1. Sacheverell Sitwell, *Liszt* (London, 1934); Alan Walker, *Franz Liszt: the Virtuoso Years, 1811–1847* (London, 1983); Ronald Taylor, *Franz Liszt: the Man and the Musician* (London, 1987).

have suggested that, at this time, Liszt was no more extraordinary than some other young players; but it is clear, from all the known reactions to the evidence of his ability as an improviser and sight-reader, and the poetic and brilliant qualities of his performances, that he was only a little beneath Mozart's divine level as a prodigy in musical execution.

The family moved to Paris in 1823, and that was to be Liszt's domestic and professional base for most of the next 20 years. He not only learnt French, but became French in all essentials. This was the first of a number of personal transformations during his busy, wandering life. He visited London three times in the mid-1820s, as well as touring very profitably under his father's management in Germany, the Low Countries and provincial France.

After Adam's death in 1827, he entered upon a crisis; he became ill, and the profound religious feelings engendered in childhood were intensified (along with political awareness) by wide reading. He became his own university. In the early 1830s he moved through Parisian friendships with Chopin, Berlioz, de Lammenais, Lamartine, Victor Hugo and Heine. During this phase of his career he was perhaps considerably in awe of Chopin as pianist–innovator and creator of very original piano music; but the Polish artist was never his competitor as a *public* performer, and the contemplation of Chopin's achievements was a spur to the further development of Liszt's genius as a player and, ultimately, as composer. It was at this time, too, that he encountered the other universal inspirer of contemporary young musicians – Paganini. The spell which the violinist cast over audiences helped Liszt in the creation of his own legend. Paganini had used the macabre facets of his personality in his publicity campaign as a performer; Liszt had no need for such dubious devices: he was slender, fair-haired, and romantically handsome, truly a matinée idol and a concert-promoter's dream.

Liszt's original compositions in the 1830s and into the 1840s were often wild in their novelty, like the *Harmonies poétiques et religieuses* of 1834, and the first versions of the Transcendental Studies (1838), or, as in the case of the *Années de pèlerinage*, had been nurtured by his feeling for Romantic literature and the awesome suggestiveness of landscape. But the bulk of his works for public performance consisted then of transcriptions and paraphrases, re-creations of the operatic, orchestral and vocal achievements of others.

His growing reputation as the outstanding pianist of this era was challenged in 1836 by the rise of Sigismond Thalberg, Swiss– Austrian by birth and, reputedly, an aristocrat. But their famous 'duel', at a charity concert in the Paris salon of the Princess Belgiojoso in March 1837 established Liszt, in the ears of the true *cognoscenti*, as the greater *artist*; though Thalberg subsequently retained the support of many who regarded him as the epitome of cool, finished accomplishment in piano playing.

In the late 1830s Liszt established, scandalously, a domestic ménage with his aristocratic mistress, the Comtesse Marie d'Agoult. She bore him three children, Blandine, born in 1835, Cosima (later Wagner's wife) in 1837, and Daniel in 1839. But by 1840 Liszt and Marie were moving apart; she became dissatisfied with her role as the handmaiden of a genius, and, perhaps in imitation of Chopin's mistress, George Sand, began to develop her own career as journalist and novelist.

Liszt, meanwhile, was winning the sometimes grudging admiration of German musicians: Mendelssohn, Schumann, and Clara Wieck, later to be Schumann's wife and herself an astonishingly talented pianist. He took his first steps in the direction of a serious interest in publicizing the works of Schubert and Scarlatti, and paid homage to Beethoven, first by magnificently true transcriptions of the symphonies, and later through his devotion to the cause of financing the erection of a belated monument to the composer, in Bonn.

The period from 1836 to 1848 is a phase in his career often called the 'Years of Transcendent Execution', or the 'Virtuoso Years'. He then travelled more widely than any other musician, reinforcing his reputation, from St Petersburg to Madrid, from Edinburgh to Constantinople. It is true to say that, during this phase, he tailored his choice of music to the tastes of the audiences he met. In Berlin, or Leipzig, he would play music from the 'serious' Classical and Romantic repertoires, while in London, or even Paris, he trotted out the flashy virtuoso pieces which he knew would excite and satisfy shallower listeners. He invented a new mode of presentation, the solo 'recital'. His life as a travelling performer was exhilarating and exhausting, astonishing in its geographical range and musical variety. This book is an attempt to capture, in a series of elaborate tableaux vivants, one part of those travels which has never been treated in detail: his two extended visits to Britain in 1840 and 1841.

By the mid-1840s he had decided to end his gypsy wanderings, choosing to settle in the Duchy of Weimar where, as court musician, after 1848 he devoted his energy partly to the composition and performance of his own works, but largely to the promotion of the careers of other artists, and to nurturing a new generation of pianists. Henceforward his influence upon the development of European music was immense. In particular he was the chief musical and psychological supporter of Richard Wagner; and, in addition, having rediscovered his own native origins in the late 1830s, he constructively encouraged the institutional growth of music in Hungary.

By 1844 Liszt and Marie had decided upon what soon became a permanent separation. Three years later in Kiev, during his second tour of Russia, he met the second of his 'muses', the Princess Carolyne Sayn-Wittgenstein. Although still encumbered by an aristocratic marriage, she decided to settle near Liszt in Weimar, and for the next 30 years their lives were inextricably intertwined. A legal divorce was ever imminent, but the increasingly spiritual communion between the ageing Liszt and the intellectual princess was paralleled by an ascending religious pilgrimage, which culminated in his taking minor Catholic Orders a year after Carolyne's husband died.

The period from 1848 until 1857 was musically the most fruitful of Liszt's career. Under his supervision, as conductor and impresario, Weimar became the preeminent European laboratory for musical experimentation. From this tiny, otherwise conservative, centre in Germany, Liszt made contact with a younger generation of composers represented by Borodin, Grieg, and eventually Saint-Saëns, Fauré, Debussy and Albéniz. His generosity to colleagues became legendary, and his unstinting assistance – in the form of advice and the publication of piano transcriptions and editions – was given at the very time when he was producing his own most significant compositions. Despite almost universal admiration for his exalted reputation, he never achieved a complete sense of fulfilment as a composer: he fought less vigorously for performance and acceptance of his own large-scale works than he did, for instance, on behalf of the early operas of Wagner.

As his star waned at Weimar in the late 1850s, so he began a triangular existence which encompassed travelling between Rome (where the princess now lived), Budapest (where he gave the first performances of his 'national' music), and Germany. The Weimar connection continued; but he also developed a Bavarian link with Wagner in Bayreuth. His teaching continued almost incessantly in Weimar, Budapest and Rome – though he never charged fees; and his students were drawn from Russia, America, France, Italy, Britain and Scandinavia.

In the last episode of his life Liszt became increasingly reclusive. He continued to travel, but his thirst for public adulation and the excitement of performance had been quenched. His own music became more intimate and reflective, inward-looking, yet more experimental.

Despite the critical success of his provincial tours of Britain in 1840 and 1841, and a further brilliant visit to London in the latter year, he had turned his back on the English Channel. He did not cross it again until April 1886, in the last year of his life, for the first British performance of his oratorio *St Elizabeth*.[2] In July, against the advice of his doctor, he went to Bayreuth to hear performances of *Parsifal* and *Tristan*. After *Tristan* he became severely ill and died of pneumonia on 31 July.

It would be controversial to argue that Liszt, of all musicians born in the nineteenth century, was the most many-sided, the most powerfully and variously influential. But he *was* a figure of monumental significance in musical history. At a time when British music was gradually moving from mediocre chaos towards rebirth and the promise of achievement – the period from the 1840s to the 1880s – Liszt was not only absent from Britain, but seems to have had little direct influence over its musical evolution. Some of the reasons for his staying away for over 40 years can be traced back to his experiences of British society and culture in 1840–41. In the

2. See below, Chapter Five.

following account there will certainly be a discovery of the human side of the young Liszt in Britain, and this might help to moderate the prejudice Ernest Newman revealed in his biased biography.

CHAPTER TWO

Liszt's London
Season, 1840

THE CITY to which Liszt reintroduced himself in 1840 was the most monstrous – and the wealthiest – that the modern age had seen. Foreign visitors simultaneously loathed and adored it. He must have retained memories of what it had looked, smelt and tasted like from his visits in the mid-1820s. On those occasions he had spent many weeks following a pattern of professional engagements which he was to repeat in 1840 and 1841. As a boy prodigy he had been taken up by the 'silver-fork society' of members of the aristocracy and gentry who infested the fashionable streets of the West End and the 'country houses' in the fields around Kensington. He had played at Windsor on two occasions for George IV, and at the home of the Duchess of Kent, mother of Victoria; and he had made the short social excursions from house to house in carriages supplied by noble patrons. He gave Hummel's popular A minor Concerto at the Philharmonic Society.[1] And he had even anticipated the later provincial tours of Britain by making a single foray in 1824 to Manchester, where he was severely outgunned as a prodigy by 'the infant Lyra', a miniature harpist reputedly only three years old.[2] He did not return to England during the 1830s which he devoted very largely to establishing his reputation as a pianist in Paris and, less frequently, in Italy, Germany and Hungary.

The quality of London's musical activity has begun to improve during his absence. Fashionable society was becoming more

---

1. Alan Walker, *Franz Liszt: the Virtuoso Years, 1811–1847* (London, 1983).
2. ibid., 107–9.

civilized in its generosity towards artists. In the 1820s Weber had been appalled by the indifference which greeted musicians who visited in the evenings for the purpose of entertaining the high-society crowd in their great houses. He wrote to a friend describing the kind of experience which Liszt would probably have remembered from his youth:

> At half-past ten I drove to Lord Hertford's. Heavens, what a huge company! Splendid rooms; 500 to 600 people assembled, all most brilliantly attired. Nearly all the stars of the Italian Opera company; also Veluti, the celebrated Puzzi, and the not less celebrated double-bass Dragonetti. Every kind of music was sung, but nobody listened to it. The din and noise of the throng were horrible. When I performed there was an endeavour to obtain a little silence, and 100 persons placed themselves sympathetically round me. God alone knows what they heard, for I myself didn't hear much of it. I bore in mind, however, my thirty guineas, and was resigned. At last at two o'clock they went to supper, from which I excused myself.[3]

Only the suave Rossini, it seems, had been able to break through the bad manners at such rowdy soirées; and later, in the 1830s, the massive and hugely talented Italian *basso*, Luigi Lablache, discreetly removed a barrier between performers and patrons when one evening he pointedly unhooked the silken cord which, like the bars in a zoological garden, segregated the vocalists from the 'listeners'. Visiting musicians often compared English lack of etiquette with their treatment in continental towns and cities where it was customary even for royalty to associate with performers and composers on a common ground of respect.

The singers and players who attended upon the soirée Weber described had probably arrived after an exhausting evening performing in the Opera House. The London musical season, from April to June, revolved around the Italian Opera. Stars from Paris – Lablache, Malibran, Grisi, Rubini, Tamburini, Persiani – would descend upon London like peacocks imitating vultures. Then, at the end of the summer, after a hectic period of professional plunder in

3. Julius Benedict, *Carl Maria von Weber* (London, 1881), 119–20.

town, they usually made a circuit of the main provincial centres, in Ireland as well as England and Wales. Even the astonishing Paganini submitted himself to that kind of commercial mauling in the early 1830s. Visiting musicians also engaged in what became known as the 'benefit concert'. These monstrosities were the means by which one artist could display his wares before a huge audience of potential patrons in a programme of excessive length, with most of the other items supplied by colleagues of equal or greater eminence. London concert-goers thus became accustomed to musical evenings which might last up to three hours, during which they heard as many as 30 separate pieces sung and played, singly and in combination, by ten or eleven performers. Contemporary English eating habits probably ensured that musical indigestion was accompanied by profound rumblings of intestinal protest.

One of the more sensible examples of this genre took place on 7 June 1836, for the benefit of Edward Schulz, a pianist whose fame proved to be ephemeral:[4]

PART I

OVERTURE (Midsummer Night's Dream)	F. M. BARTHOLDY
DUETTO, *Signor Tamburini and Signor Lablache*,	
'Un segreto' (Cenerentola)	ROSSINI
ARIA, *Madame Giuletta Grisi*, 'Dal asilo'	COSTA
FANTASIA, Pianoforte, *Mr. E. Schultz*, 'Montecchi	
e Capuletti' (first time of performance)	THALBERG
Air, *Signor Ivanoff,* 'O care imagine' (Zauberflöte)	MOZART
TRIO, *Signor Rubini, Signor Tamburini and*	
Signor Lablache (Guillaume Tell)	ROSSINI
SOLO, French Horn, *Signor Puzzi*	
(first time of performance)	PUZZI
ARIA, *Signor Rubini* (Adelaïde)	BEETHOVEN
POLACCA, *Madame Giuletta Grisi, Signor Rubini,*	
Signor Tamburini and Signor Lablache	BELLINI

4. Quoted in John Ella, *Musical Sketches at Home and Abroad* (London, 1878), 76–7.

PART II

TARTINI'S DREAM, for Voice and Violin,	
Madame Malibran and M. de Bériot	TARTINI
GRAND DUET for Two Pianofortes, *Monsieur Henry*	
Herz and Mr. E. Schulz	HERZ
ARIA, *Madame Malibran de Bériot*, 'La tremenda	
ultrice spada' (Capuletti)	BELLINI
DUETTO, *Signor Ivanoff and Mr. Balfe*,	
'La Marinari'	ROSSINI
SOLO VIOLIN, *Monsieur de Bériot*	DE BÉRIOT
ARIA, *Signor Tamburini*, 'Vi ravviso',	
(La Sonnambula)	BELLINI
TARANTELLA, *Signor Lablache*	ROSSINI
OVERTURE (Fidelio)	BEETHOVEN
Leader, *Mr. Mori.*	Conductor, *Signor Costa.*

In each short London season a merry-go-round of 70 or 80 such concerts would revolve, peopled by the same gaggle of supporting artists.[5] In their repetitiousness they were anticipations of the gramophone recording, since it ought to be remembered, in mitigation, that this annual handful of concerts provided the only occasions when bourgeois Londoners could enjoy the best performances of fashionable music. The rest of their musical experience depended upon hearing daughters, wives or mistresses play potted versions of the current 'hits' on their rapidly improving drawing-room pianos.

There *was* music-making on a more serious level. The oldest institution was the Concerts of Antient Music, established in 1776, under the patronage of George III. Membership was limited to 'the upper ten thousand', and its rules forbade the performance of music written in the preceding 20 years. Despite its high-minded constitu-

5. In the matter of the incidence of benefit concerts during the London season in the 1830s I acknowledge most gratefully the help of Christina Bashford, who is currently conducting research into early Victorian concert life in the metropolis. To her I owe references (i) to an estimate in the *Musical World*, XVIII, 2, 12 January 1843, 19–20; (ii) to the work of Joel Sachs, 'London: the Professionalisation of Music', *The Early Romantic Era, Man and Music*, vi (London, 1990).

tion, by the 1830s the programmes, as one amateur later recorded, had become 'dry-as-dust affairs ... with odds and ends ... some Handel ... slovenly performed and carelessly conducted'.

The steady decline of the Antient Concerts had been one of the reasons for the creation of a far more dynamic musical organization which has lasted with distinction until the present day. But of more pressing concern when the Philharmonic Society (now Royal) was founded, in 1813, had been the absence of a first-rate orchestra in London. The statement marking the establishment of the Society was signed by leading English musicians like William Horsley (father-in-law of I. K. Brunel), Henry Bishop and George Smart, but also by a group of influential foreigners working in London, among them the Cramers (F. and J. B.), Viotti, Clementi, and Philip Anthony Corri. Not for the first or last time, London's musical conscience was being shaken into new life by visitors from abroad.[6]

The Philharmonic Society gave its initial concert in March 1813, conducted from the piano by Clementi and led by Salamon (Haydn's impresario at the turn of the century). By today's standards the programme was somewhat macaronic; but it contained symphonies by Haydn and Beethoven, a Mozart wind serenade and one of his string quartets, and a Boccherini quintet. The Society's devotion to Beethoven was sealed when it commissioned from him in 1822 what was to become his Ninth Symphony. In the same year the members sought to promote the improvement of musical standards in England by helping Lord Burghersh to found the Royal Academy of Music. Eminent foreign visitors usually contributed to the Society's concerts: the boy Liszt in 1824, Weber two years later, and young Mendelssohn conducting his first mature symphony in 1829. After 1826 Moscheles, from eastern Europe (the leading pianist of his generation, and a protégé of Beethoven), began a 20-year connection with the Society, memorably conducting the second British performance of the Ninth Symphony. Of that 1837 occasion the critic of the *Athenaeum* said that it was 'greeted with an enthusiasm

6. Robert Elkin, *Royal Philharmonic: the Annals of the Royal Philharmonic Society* (London, 1947), 9ff.

we did not expect'; audiences had greatly improved in their understanding of such music.

Moscheles, a player of the old Classical school who lived long
into the Romantic age, is almost forgotten now; but it could be
argued that he, more than anyone – even Mendelssohn, whose
visits to London were intermittent – helped to nurture such
improvement in English musical sensibility as occurred during his
long period of residence in London. By the mid-1830s Moscheles
was participating in concerts which included large selections from
the serious Classical repertoire of both orchestral and chamber
music, as well as 'piano' music from Bach to Beethoven. In 1837,
he was associated with one of the 'Classical Concerts', a series
given at Willis's Rooms in St James's 'for the Performance of
Quartetts, Quintetts, etc., etc.' In February, outside the high musical season, Moscheles presided over a programme of Spohr's
Nonet, Haydn's English canzonets, a vocal duet in which Mr John
Parry took the baritone part, a septet of his own, a Mendelssohn
quintet, and a Beethoven quartet. Such rich food had surely rarely
before been advertised on one London menu. Moscheles's initiative
was taken up by native musicians: the previous year, the violinist
Henry Blagrove formed a quartet which devoted most of its
energies to performances of Haydn, Mozart and even Beethoven's
late, 'incomprehensible' quartets.[7]

In November 1837 it was announced that, at his 'Classical Soirée'
in the Hanover Square Rooms, Moscheles 'intends to illustrate the
development of the art of piano-playing during the last century, by
performing a selection of studies and exercises from the works of
Scarlatti, Bach, Handel, Woelfl, Dussek, Stiebelt, Clementi, J. B.
Cramer, Field, Hummel, Herz, Czerny, Potter, Chopin, Mendelssohn, Thalberg and Moscheles', with '"Grand Sonatas" by
Beethoven and Weber'. What heavenly length! But also, what
astonishing innovation! Two years later Liszt was to tell the
Princess Belgiojoso that he intended taking a novel step in music-
making, by performing completely alone, unaided by supporting
artists: the 'piano *recital*'. Though he did not ascend to the sophisti-
cation of inventing a new name for what he was doing, Moscheles,

7. *Athenaeum*, 18 November 1837.

it appears, had already discovered the solo-piano concert. Also, and equally remarkably, in order to make his 'historical' recitals more authentic, he blew the dust off an ancient instrument no longer fashionable, and played some of the earliest pieces on a two-decker harpsichord, long before the era of Landowska.

It is likely that the best musical performances in London at that time were given in the private salons of the leading professional players and in the homes of the musically well educated – music made in friendship and for pleasure. The Horsley household in Kensington Church Lane became a 'home-from-home' for Mendelssohn whenever he was in London. William Horsley, a celebrated organist and composer, and his talented daughters, also kept open house for Moscheles who had briefly been Mendelssohn's piano teacher in 1824.[8]

Moscheles's own home in London was a magnet for knowledgeable musicians. At one of his soirées in 1836, when he entertained 80 guests, Malibran and her second husband, the violinist de Bériot, arrived at eleven o'clock. Probably the greatest mezzo of the nineteenth century, she was then recovering from a riding accident in Hyde Park, and looked weary. But according to Moscheles 'she was soon herself . . . and sang two "Freischutz" scenas in German, a comic duet with John Parry, three Spanish, Italian and French songs, winding up with the duet "Cadence du Diable" for herself and de Bériot . . .'. When she had finished, Moscheles improvised. Finally,

> Young Parry amused us with his masterly parody of the scena in the Wolf's Glen in the 'Freischutz'. With a sheet of music rolled up, with one end in his mouth and the other resting on the music-desk, he produced the deepest horn or trombone notes; his hands worked the keys, and his feet a tea-tray. There was the 'Wilde Jagd' complete.[9]

8. R. Brunel Gotch, *Mendelssohn and his Friends in Kensington* (Oxford, 1938).
9. Charlotte Moscheles, *Life of Moscheles with Selections from his Diaries and Correspondence*, 2 vols (London, 1873), II, 9.

Thalberg, another Moscheles pupil, was present but unable to play because of a damaged finger. Later in 1836, however, he took part in an even more astonishing Moscheles evening:

She [Malibran] came at three o'clock; and with her Thalberg, Benedict and Klingemann [Mendelssohn's dear friend from the Prussian Embassy]. We dined early, and immediately afterwards Malibran sat down to the piano, and 'sang for the children', as she used to call it, the Rataplan and some of her father's Spanish songs; for want of guitar accompaniment she used, whilst playing, every now and then to mark the rhythm on the board at the back of the keys. After singing with exquisite grace and charm a number of French and Italian romances of her own composition, she was relieved at the piano by Thalberg, who performed all manner of tricks on the instrument, snapping his fingers as the obbligato to Viennese songs and waltzes. I played afterwards with reversed hands, and with my fists, and none laughed louder than Malibran. At 5 o'clock we drove to the Zoological Gardens, and pushed our way for an hour with the fashionables. When we had had enough of man and beast, we took one more turn in the Park, and directly we got home Malibran sat down to the piano and sang for an hour. At last, however, she called to Thalberg, 'Venez jouer quelque chose, j'ai besoin de me reposer', her repose consisting in finishing a most charming landscape, in water-colours [an art in which she was self-taught]. Thalberg played by heart, and in a most masterly way, several of his 'Studies', 'Allegri di Bravura', and my G minor Concerto. We had supper afterwards; then again it was Malibran who kept us all going. She gave us the richest imitations of Sir George Smart [the conductor], the singers Knyvett, Braham, Phillips, and Vaughan, who had sung with her at a concert given by the Duchess of C——; taking off the fat Duchess herself, as she condescendingly patronized 'her artists', and winding up with the cracked voice and nasal tones of Lady ——, who inflicted 'Home Sweet Home' on the company. Suddenly her comic vein came to a full stop; then she gave in the thorough German style the scena from 'Freischutz', with German words, and a whole series of German songs by Mendelssohn, Schubert, Weber and my humble self; lastly she took a turn with Don Giovanni, being familiar not only with the music of Zerlina, her own part, but knowing by heart every note in the opera, which she could play and sing from beginning to end. She went on playing and singing alternately until eleven o'clock, fresh to the last in voice and spirits. When she left us, we were all rapturous about her music, her languages, her painting; but what we liked best was her artlessness and amiability.[10]

The London seasons of the late 1830s were bursting with pianists of all shapes and sizes, like chorines at a mass audition. Each had his or her party trick which was displayed as frequently as possible on the new pianofortes of Erard, Broadwood, Collard and Pleyel. Alexander Dreyschock came to parade his rippling chains of octaves: his ultimate show-stopper was a version of Chopin's 'Revolutionary' Etude with octaves replacing the original single notes in the left hand. Theodor von Döhler came for the first time in 1836, but his career was meteorically short: in 1846 he achieved the apotheosis of musical mediocrity by marrying a Russian princess and immediately retiring from public performance. Henri Herz, another Austrian working out of Paris, was famous for prestidigitation. His music was of no consequence whatever, and he is now remembered, enviously by many musicians, not only as a craftsman who significantly improved the mechanism of his instrument, but as one of the few men to have made a fortune out of piano manufacture. Herz was the *arriviste par excellence* who cared almost as much for his personal appearance as he did for maintaining his technical accomplishment. When he visited the Horsleys, Sophy found his appearance more interesting than his playing:

> Herz played twice in the evening, first a duet of his 'Au Clair de la Lune' with Variations, the bass of which I performed, and to which his cravat, which I am sure must be lined with the stiffest of stiff muslin, creaked an accompaniment. I fear he wears that article of his dress much too tight, for Uncle John has observed that he never by any chance turns his head without the rest of his body.[11]

There were two leading lady pianists in London, both of whom enjoyed the boon of being, at various times, teachers of the young

10. ibid., 7.
11. Brunel Gotch, op. cit., 54.

Victoria and her children. Louise Dulcken had come to live in London in 1828, and achieved a sound reputation, giving the first English performance of Chopin's F minor Concerto. Lucy Anderson was the first woman to play in a Philharmonic Concert, though the *Athenaeum* described her 1839 performance of the 'Emperor' as 'lacking grandeur of touch ... expression ... gravity' in a work which, surprisingly for that time in England, was called a 'popular concerto'.[12]

As the stars of a new generation of prodigious technicians arose during the 1830s, Moscheles continued to cherish the older, purer tradition of Classical piano-playing. Yet he was still admired by the younger men, and in his turn showed respect, mingled with an amused tolerance for their finger-breaking achievements of innovation. In 1836, when Thalberg, his own pupil, conquered London, Moscheles wrote:

> I find his introduction of harp effects on the piano quite original. His theme, which lies in the middle part, is brought out clearly in relief with an accompaniment of complicated arpeggios which remind me of a harp. The audience is amazed. He himself remains immoveably calm, his whole bearing, as he sits at the piano, is soldier-like; his lips are tightly compressed, and his coat buttoned closely. He told me he acquired this attitude of self-control by smoking a Turkish pipe while practising his pianoforte exercises; the length of the tube was so calculated as to keep him erect and motionless.[13]

This stillness, while executing the most complicated technical feats, was what perhaps most endeared Thalberg to cool English audiences: he was a discreet engineer who concealed the physical tensions of performance; while, by contrast, Liszt 'acted' his music at the keyboard, to the embarrassment of many of his London listeners.

Moscheles's musical judgment was not unduly swayed by friendship with Thalberg. He confessed to his diary in 1836 that while

the proper ground for finger gymnastics is to be found in

12. *Athenaeum*, 15 June 1839.
13. Moscheles, op. cit., II, 12–13.

Thalberg's latest compositions, for 'mind' (Geist) give me Schumann. The Romanticism in his works is a thing so completely new, his genius is so great that . . . I must go deeper and deeper into the study of his works . . .[14]

Two years later, on holiday in Hastings, Moscheles wrote:

I play all the new works of the four modern heroes, Thalberg, Chopin, Henselt and Liszt, and find that their chief effects lie in passages requiring a large grasp of stretch and finger, such as the peculiar build of their hands enables them to execute. I grasp less; but then I am not of a grasping school . . . Just now the new manner finds more favour, and I endeavour to pursue the middle course between the two schools, by never shrinking away from any difficulty, never despising the new effects, and withal retaining the best elements of the old traditions.[15]

Moscheles the middle-European was more English than he knew. In 1839, rather like some of the London public, he was becoming just a little tired of his protégé's displays:

Thalberg is here, and after crowded concerts he receives as much blame as praise; but when one of the wise reviewers goes so far as to compare him with van Amburgh the lion-tamer, one can only laugh.[16]

Two years before, in Paris, Thalberg had crossed pianos and compositions with Liszt in the celebrated duel at Princess Belgiojoso's to decide who was the greater pianist. Whatever fashionable opinion declared, Liszt knew that he had been the victor. London critics, too, were beginning to distance themselves from Thalberg's continuing success. His repertoire remained limited to superficially brilliant compositions and transcriptions. Commenting on the 'calm and dignified grandeur of his style' in 1839, the *Athenaeum* reviewer remarked:

it is hard to believe that the man who can play everything as it

14. ibid., 19.   15. ibid., 44.   16. ibid., 54.

ought to be played, can write only according to one style. But we wish that he would give us proof that we are right in *this* judgement: his *fantasias* are very fascinating; but does he mean, all his life, to write or to perform in public nothing but *fantasias?*[17]

From our perspective we can answer, unequivocably, 'Yes'. But no one could have been sure that the two pianists whose reputations were pitted against each other in 1840 – Liszt was 29, Thalberg a year younger – would subsequently follow very divergent courses. Liszt moved far away from his role as maker of magical fantasias (while still using the medium as a means of introducing the music of his contemporaries to a new public). Thalberg continued for two more decades to plough his increasingly dull furrow. Perhaps he realized that something needed to be done in 1839 to rekindle English enthusiasm: he announced, in July, that this was to be his last London season; he would retire from concert-giving. He was not to fulfil this promise for a further twenty years. Nevertheless, *The Times* saluted his premature 'farewell' in suitably gracious prose:

> ... the gratification he afforded to his auditors was mingled with feelings of regret, excited by the reflection that it was *the last time* they could hope to hear the extraordinary performances of this great artist ... Thalberg's *name* is apt: we have the murmur of the distant mountain torrent, which at length ... rolls down like a resounding flood upon the plain, but still a flood of harmony.[18]

Liszt had been planning to come to London since 1838. He was certainly in need of money in the large quantities which he thought would be guaranteed by a successful season. And he may have wished to reinforce the connection with his English publishers, Mori and Lavenu. In January 1839 he had written to the Leipzig firm, Breitkopf und Härtel:

> As I have already had the honour of telling you, Mr. Mori had been previously engaged to print [my transcriptions of] the C

17. *Athenaeum*, 29 June 1839.
18. *The Times*, 10 July 1839.

minor and Pastoral symphonies [of Beethoven], and as the steps
you have taken have not been *crowned* with success, I will keep to
this first publisher, with whom I have every reason to be satisfied
up to now. My intention being to visit Vienna, Munich and
perhaps Leipzig at the beginning of next year (before going to
England in the month of April), I shall take advantage of this
appointment to let the Symphonies be heard at my concerts, so as
to give them a certain publicity.[19]

Liszt was to be a pianoforte *salesman* as well as a player in
England. The French firm of Erard, with the assistance of Henri
Herz, had recently made significant improvements in piano mechanism; on his English tours in the 1820s Liszt had been advertised as
playing 'Erard's New Patent Grand Piano-forte of Seven Octaves'.
Erards had built a London manufactory, and bourgeois Britain
offered a hugely profitable market for the drawing-room piano. In
Liszt's flamboyant brilliance the Erard company would have the
most effective travelling advertisement for their undeniably fine
instruments. The forwarding address in London which he gave to
his friends abroad was Erard's shop at 18 Great Marlborough Street.

At the end of April 1840 the town was agog to see and hear him.
Liszt was utterly confident of success. After he had settled down in
London he intended that Marie, leaving their three children in Paris,
should join him. His new reputation, he imagined, would be built
upon the earlier English visits. But there were not many in England
who, like Moscheles, could review a diary entry recording the
Philharmonic Society performance of the Hummel A minor Concerto by the 16-year-old Liszt on 9 June 1827: '. . . as to his playing,
it surpasses in power and mastery of difficulties everything I have
ever heard'.[20] The charm of those performances for the English
public in the 1820s, however, had consisted chiefly in his engaging
youthful spirit and unaffected openness. The Liszt of 1840 had
become a much more complex artist whose rhetorical posturings
might prove less attractive to English observers.

Liszt was uneasy about Marie's health when he left Paris. He

19. La Mara, ed.: *Letters of Franz Liszt* (London, 1894), I, 29.
20. Moscheles, op. cit., I, 141.

wrote to her from the steam-packet on the morning of 6 May about the eventful first part of his journey:

> ... we assisted at the scene of a dreadful fire on the outskirts of Beauvais, which consumed a whole village in less than an hour. Very few of the inhabitants were awake, and it is feared that several have perished, taken unawares by the conflagration as they slept. (It was half-past midnight.) You cannot imagine the silent stupor of several of the men trying to save their cattle and horses. It was a terrible spectacle. The lady next to me in the coach exclaimed to herself, 'Ah! How beautiful it is!' *I* saw nothing picturesque in the scene! ...
> In four hours I shall be in London. I was not sea-sick this time. I forced myself to sleep, and so things turned out well ...
> Write to me, especially if you should become unwell.[21]

He alighted at the Wapping quayside on 6 May. Thalberg was not in London. Indeed, there is some ground for thinking that he had purposely fled from the possibility of further direct comparison with Liszt in a country where he had made a good deal of money. Moscheles drew an apt conclusion: 'Thalberg intends to go to America. The clashing here with Liszt is, I suppose, too much for him.'[22]

Our images of Liszt are presided over by the later photographs of an old man with the profile of an eagle, few teeth and long white hair. The portraits of the 1830s and early 1840s reveal a very different figure – slender, with a dandified dignity. Alan Walker has quoted a description of him written by Balzac's mistress in 1843:

> Liszt is of medium height, thin, pale and drawn. He has the bilious complexion belonging to people of great talent and personality. His features are regular. His forehead is less high than they show it in his portraits. He is furrowed with lines ... His eyes are glassy, but they light up under the effect of his wit and

21. Daniel Ollivier, ed.: *Letters of Liszt and Marie d'Agoult* (Paris, 1933), I, 418.
22. Moscheles, op. cit., II, 62.

sparkle like the facets of a cut diamond . . . His best feature is the
sweet curve of his mouth, which, when it smiles, makes heaven
dream.[23]

Liszt went into the attack almost as soon as he arrived in London,
and he found an instant ally in the music critic of the *Athenaeum*,
Henry Chorley. In his article of 16 May, he called Liszt's return to
England 'the musical event . . . of the year', and he reminded the
public that, since his last visit fifteen seasons before, 'pianists of all
classes and colours, the classical, brilliant, the eccentric', had 'risen
up, flourished, and passed away'. Liszt's fame, by contrast, had
continued to grow: Englishmen had heard of his triumphs as the
votary of Romanticism in Paris and of his hugely successful journey
to Vienna. Chorley announced 'the re-appearance of the Poet of the
Pianoforte'.[24]

Liszt gave a concert of his own on 8 May at which he played what
were described in the *Athenaeum* as a grand fantasia on 'Rubini's
cavatina' and 'Grisi's *polacca*' in Bellini's *I Puritani*, another on
themes from Donizetti's *Lucia*, his 'Marche Hongroise', an unidenti-
fied 'Valse' of his own and the expected *Grand Galop Chromatique*.
Liszt was evidently satisifed with his reception. He wrote to 'dear
Marie',

> I had a great 'succès' this evening . . . My London business is
> nearly accomplished. There is no possible parallel save with
> Paganini, and that does not grieve me. I have been welcomed
> splendidly. Many people remembered 'Master Liszt'. I have seen
> nothing of Society. In revenge, I surround myself with publishers
> and artists . . . On Monday I play the Weber Concerto [*sic*] at the
> Philharmonic. That evening will decide matters once and for all.
> Below I've attached a programme and a short article from the
> 'Morning Chronicle'. I'll send you several papers during the
> week.[25]

The critics, he claimed, were having to invent new words to describe his playing.

23. Quoted in Walker, op. cit., 377–8.
24. *Athenaeum*, 16 May 1840.
25. Ollivier, op. cit., 429.

Two days later he appeared at the fifth Philharmonic Concert of the season, playing Weber's *Concertstück* with an orchestra rather doggedly conducted by Henry Bishop. Of this the *Athenaeum*'s opinion was that 'nothing could be nobler, more expressive, more free from caricature than the opening of the *adagio*'; while, in the Allegro his 'omnipotence over the instrument' was displayed, though in the passages calling for delicacy and self-restraint, 'nothing could be purer or more calm than his delivery'. The virtuoso sections of the last movement were given with 'a volcanic force'.[26]

At first, it seems, society *was* indifferent to Liszt. He relied for company on old colleagues who had known him abroad, like Moscheles, Batta, and Lord Burghersh, a renowned musical amateur; and he told Marie on 13 May that he did not really know anyone in London, 'except Mr. [Henry] Reeve, friend of Alfred de Vigny, whom I find charming. He has translated de Tocqueville into English'.[27] Gradually, however, the range of his social life broadened. He dined out with a Paris acquaintance, Polez, who was attached to the French Embassy. At first he refused to present himself at Lady Blessington's salon, but he soon capitulated; and there he was in his element:

> D'Orsay came to see me and invited me to their house (That's to Lady Blessington's). They long to know me. Probably someone had told them that I did not particularly want to visit.[28]

Marie had something in common with Lady Blessington: just as she, a countess, scandalized the *haute monde* by living openly with Liszt and bearing his children, so the Blessington–D'Orsay liaison, though without issue, continued to cause considerable embarrassment in London Society.

Margaret, Countess of Blessington, was a widow who had been condemned by her peers for setting up a joint establishment with her stepdaughter's stunningly handsome husband, the Count D'Or-

26. *Athenaeum*, 23 May 1840.
27. Ollivier, op. cit., 435.
28. ibid., 437.

say, formerly a close friend of Lord Blessington and their companion on European tours. The relationship, though blatant, was
ambivalent: she was a very beautiful, highly intelligent woman,
D'Orsay was the epitome of the Dandy; yet it probably lacked a
physical element, for he may have been homosexual, while she had
possibly been psychosexually damaged by the cruel treatment she
had received as a young girl at the hands of her first husband in
Ireland. Because of the public liaison ladies never visited her
London mansion, Gore House, but it became a brilliant place of
resort for eminent men.[29] Liszt explained matters thus to Marie:

> Lady Blessington is at loggerheads with Society here, but
> receives social lions and people of talent . . . D'Orsay adds to the
> tone with his waistcoats and cravats. Milady's attire and her
> furnishings are cited as models for others to imitate.[30]

By 17 May he could write:

> In the evening, to Lady Blessington's. By the way, she said a
> pretty thing about me to Reeve . . . 'What a shame to put such a
> man to the piano!' That recalls Bulwer's question: 'Why did M.
> Liszt not choose another occupation?' Lady Blessington, as that
> suggests, is charmed by my appearance, behaviour and tempera-
> ment. (I repeat what Reeve told me). She presented me to
> everyone without my asking it of her; to Louis Buonaparte; Lord
> Castlereagh, Chesterfield. Only men are admitted to this salon
> . . . [It] has given me much matter for reflection.[31]

In Lady Blessington Liszt was encountering not simply a fashionable novelist and compiler of literary anthologies, but the former
confidante of one of his great heroes, Byron. She had published a
famous account of her conversations with the poet in Genoa,[32] and
she enchanted Liszt by remarking that he resembled a combination
of Napoleon Bonaparte and Lord Byron.

29. Michael Sadleir, *Blessington–D'Orsay: a Masquerade* (London, 1933), 287ff.
30. Ollivier, op. cit., 435.
31. ibid., 433.
32. Ernest J. Lowell Jr, ed.: *Lady Blessington's Conversations of Lord Byron* (Princeton, 1969).

Liszt's telling Marie about her, at such length, was not very judicious. From Paris the countess retorted by implying that she was also enjoying a mild flirtation, and passed on some information of her own about life at Gore House. She told Liszt that she had dined out with Henry Bulwer Lytton, English diplomat and brother of the novelist and dramatist: 'I've heard about Lady Blessington's Salon from Bulwer. Lacking any vivacity, but by dint of money and shamelessness, it holds its place in the world alongside the Court.'[33] D'Orsay's sense of style provoked in Liszt a paroxysm of interest in the effect of his own appearance. He sent Marie a list of demands:

> Send me, through Erard: first, the Hungarian frock-coat with the fur (the Séké one), packing it carefully; second, the Hungarian dressing-robe, and the blue, sort-of-Turkish trousers, and some morning ones, in white, same kind (special material); third, my Bovy medallion (don't forget my portrait in dressing-robe, and the Dantan statuette, if you're able); fourth, my grey overcoat.[34]

She replied, with heavy irony, and in English – possibly prompted by her would-be paramour, Bulwer – 'Pascha, to hear is to obey!'[35] Liszt sent her also a copy of the *Athenaeum* article quoted above, with a request that she get it translated for publication in *La revue musicale*.

He concluded in his most pragmatic style:

> You ask for my impressions of London? You know how little susceptible I am to impressions ... One idea alone preoccupies me here – to get money. That's why I'm here: it's all I think about. As to the rest, enormous exaggerations are to be believed. Thalberg hasn't achieved a third of what is generally believed. I know the exact figures. They are far from being as high as I'd thought. He got only 20 guineas (at the very most) per concert. I get thirty, unheard of here. My success becomes more and more substantial. I intend spending two or three excellent seasons here.

33. Ollivier, op. cit., 436.
34. ibid.
35. ibid., 436.

He calculated that he would earn about 12,000 francs during the current London season.[36]

In the large spaces of time between his most important set-piece engagements, Liszt occupied himself by playing at a score of those 'miscellaneous' monster concerts which have been mentioned earlier. On 14 May he made a brief appearance at the cellist Mr Lidel's benefit.[37] With two of his fellow supporting-artists on this occasion he was to become thoroughly acquainted during his later provincial tours – the rising soprano Miss Steele, and John Parry, baritone comedian, entertainer of the Moscheles family, friend of the great Malibran, and pupil of Lablache. The very next day, in the afternoon, again at the Hanover Square Rooms, he played for Mr W. Cramer in a concert patronized by the Dowager Queen Adelaide, and repeated his Philharmonic performance of the Weber; John Parry again sang. In the evening Liszt made a splash at the joint benefit concert of Mrs Toulmin and John Parry.[38]

Then there was a brief lull before he appeared at Mrs Anderson's concert on the afternoon of the 20th in the Opera Concert Room. *The Times*, offering a 'puff' for this concert, noted that 'Liszt, the extraordinary pianist, will perform a Grand Fantasia and Duet with Mrs. Anderson, for two pianofortes'. It must have been rather galling for the beneficiary to have her thunder stolen by a guest. But in a review of the afternoon's events, the *Times* critic, while commenting on Liszt as 'the great attraction', and acknowledging 'his extraordinary power over the instrument, combined with a very delicate execution', gallantly emphasized that in the grand duet 'our talented countrywoman did not suffer by comparison'.[39]

In addition to his contributions to these formal concerts, Liszt probably pocketed his 30 guineas each evening by making a spectacular appearance in West End salons, suffering, assuredly, much less ignominy than Weber in 1826. But the most heartening news he had to tell Marie, even at this early stage, was that he had arranged with the young representative of his London publishers,

36. ibid., 439.
37. *The Times*, 16 May 1840.
38. ibid., 18 May 1840.
39. ibid., 22 May 1840.

Lewis Lavenu, to make a 'most fruitful' tour of the provinces later in the year. By the end of May he had signed a contract which guaranteed him 500 guineas a month, plus expenses for himself and his manservant Ferco: 'all of which amounts to 37,000 francs net. It is a splendid contract, especially in my first year here.' There was, however, a tone of desperation in the comparison which Liszt repeatedly made between his own anticipated success and the earlier, much less fruitful English commercial enterprises of other pianists, notably Döhler and Thalberg. 'In two words, my success, that is to say my position as a "Lion", is assured here.'[40]

He could also write that on 25 May, 'next Monday', he would play for the Queen and Prince Albert,

> which everyone regards as a great step forward, for she never usually summons instrumentalists. D'Orsay has arranged it, saying particularly that the Queen foolishly let herself become enthralled by Italian singers, ignoring the fact that there were artists of the calibre of me and [Ole] Bull in London.
>
> Thalberg only played [for royalty] in his second or third year here, and then only in the country, I believe . . .[41]

Liszt, very fortunately, had been requested to play for Victoria on her twentieth birthday; and she was not only deeply in love but had recently been told that she was pregnant for the first time. She was also, as D'Orsay had said, enamoured of female Italian opera singers. But, as Elizabeth Forbes has shown, her musical taste was changing, under Albert's influence: when they performed for her privately in 1840, the Italians were expected to include Schubert and Beethoven songs in their selections, alongside her beloved Rossini, Donizetti and Bellini arias.[42]

The Prince Consort, a gifted musician, had been appalled by his first encounters with the evidence of English musical taste and standards of public performance. In this 1840 season, just before Liszt's arrival, Albert had taken the unprecedented step of assuming the direction of one of the Antient Concerts – that is to say, he

40. Ollivier, op. cit., 441.
41. ibid., 442.
42. Elizabeth Forbes, *Mario and Grisi* (London, 1982), 45.

merely compiled the programme – and he included among the items, as a concession to English pride, a glee by Lord Mornington, Wellington's father, and, as a contrasting stimulant, Beethoven's 'Mount of Olives'. *The Times* of 29 April 1840 (marking a nice coincidence with the Antient Concert) contained an advertisement for

> Prince Albert's Songs and Ballads, correct edn., elegantly bound, with a Portrait of H.R.H., 12s.; Prince Albert's own Quadrilles, with the Royal Hussar Waltz, and the Tramp Gallop, as performed by Welpert's royal band at Her Majesty's balls, etc., 4s.[43]

The intimate Royal audience went well; Liszt told Marie:

> The Queen was almost alone with Prince Albert the other evening. I believe I had a success. She laughed beautifully (and quite spontaneously) when I said to her, 'that my vanity was not at all wounded by her not remembering me' [from 1825, when Victoria was six years old]. Her Mother approached and asked me if I had played in her house when I was fourteen.[44]

It is very probable that, on this occasion, the new royal taste would have been demonstrated by a discussion of Albert's admiration for Mendelssohn. In another letter to Marie, Liszt – perhaps seeking to prove that social indulgence and suspected flirtations were not eroding his capacity for serious work – wrote: 'I have *not* set aside revisions and corrections of proofs. I have also arranged some of Mendelssohn's songs.'[45] One of these was the beautiful transcription of *On Wings of Song*, an act of homage, perhaps, to the rising musical favourite at the English court.

Two days after thus balancing on the politest pinnacle of society, Liszt condescended to appear in a less demanding setting. Mme de Belleville Oury, 'Pianiste to the Princess Frederick of Prussia', announced in *The Times* that she was to give a *matinée musicale* at the mansion of Mr and Mrs F. Perkins, 26 Queen Anne Street,

43. *The Times*, 29 April 1840.
44. Ollivier, op. cit., 444.
45. ibid., 447.

Cavendish Square, at two o'clock. There would be an orchestra, conducted by Julius Benedict and led by her husband, which would perform with her chief guest, M. Liszt.[46]

Before he played at the Palace on the 25th, Liszt had been dealing with estate agents: or, at the very least, he had looked at properties for rent. He hoped to find a suburban love-nest in which the warmth of his relationship with Marie might be renewed. After house-hunting he told her – perhaps thinking of the phlebitis from which Marie was suffering and their earlier happiness in Switzerland –

> I went to Hampstead this morning to find you a *ratzenloch*. The scenery was charming and I think you would be happy there. The air is very healthy. It is the highest point on the outskirts of London: recommended for some invalids (but not for consumptives, of course, because it is rather windy). Send me the word, and I will rent a cottage for you where I am sure you would be happy. We could spend every day together. The employees in the house would look after you, and the cost wouldn't be too exorbitant. Once or twice a week we could make delightful excursions to Richmond, Greenwich, etc . . . I think the countryside would give you much pleasure. For myself I should start to appreciate those things once you were here.[47]

Beneath the technicolor surface of that enticing travel brochure Liszt was concealing a triple anxiety: about Marie's poor health, the future of their relationship, and – with his recently acquired knowledge of the Blessington–D'Orsay problem – about the way in which the English might react to news of his living openly with a high-born mistress, even in the suburbs.

Amid the toing and froing of his single life in London, and during his obsession with making money on the back of his English success, he was haunted by the prospect of her arrival. He wrote that he did not dread, on her behalf, 'the boredom of London'. But what he really meant to say was that he knew she would be appalled by society's treatment of her. In a more calculating mood he diverted Marie's attention from the topic of social embarrassment by discus-

46. *The Times*, 26 May 1840.
47. Ollivier, op. cit., 431.

sing the details of her journey to England. He advised her that, while travelling through Rouen, she should not omit to visit the cathedral. She told him more particularly that the Le Havre boat took two days to cross the Channel: 'Find out in London', she demanded, 'the day and the hour when it arrives . . . and send Ferco to help me with disembarkation.'[48]

In his emotional preparations for Marie's arrival, Liszt demonstrated the continuing paradox of his nature as musician and man. Throughout this phase of his life, until 1848, he showed day by day that he was self-obsessed: his first thought, spoken or written, was openly for himself. And yet there is also an undertow of evidence, often grudgingly revealed, that he consistently considered – and sponsored – the reputations of others. In the late 1830s he and Marie d'Agoult had cultivated (and been cultivated by) Chopin and George Sand. Chopin admired the bravura of Liszt's playing: indeed, he had once, in a hurriedly written letter, expressed the envious wish that he might rob Liszt of the way in which he was at that moment performing the op. 10 Etudes.[49] But the fastidious Chopin, who found large-scale concerts distasteful, began to see Liszt as a rather meretricious public performer; and Marie always, and quite reasonably, considered George Sand a competitor for Liszt's affections. While he was in England in 1840 the Countess supplied Liszt with a *staccato* sequence of ironic comments on Chopin and Sand.[50]

Yet Liszt's response was magnanimous. Despite preoccupation with his own success in London, his true appreciation of Chopin's genius remained in place. The London publisher Wessel had committed himself to the promotion of Chopin's works, but had been reduced to the expedient of inventing fantastical titles for pieces which might not otherwise have recommended themselves to a public which had not yet heard the composer play. In 1836, for instance, a group of his mazurkas had been advertised in the *Musical World* as 'Souvenirs de Pologne'. Liszt wrote to Marie, on 29 May,

48. ibid., 433.
49. Arthur Hedley, ed.: *Selected Correspondence of Fryderyk Chopin* (London, 1962), 117.
50. Ollivier, op. cit., 446ff.

On the subject of the publisher, Wessel, who has brought out the
Collected Works of Chopin, and lost more than 200 Louis: he
came to beg me to play several of those pieces so as to make them
better known here. No one so far has dared to take such a risk. I
will do it at the first good opportunity, perhaps at a Philharmonic
Concert, or at one of mine . . . It is a little service that I am
delighted to perform for him. I will play his 'Etudes', his
'Mazurkas', and his 'Nocturnes', all hardly known in London.
That will encourage Wessel to publish other manuscripts. The
poor chap is somewhat tired of publishing without selling.[51]

Then, in the same letter, Liszt reverted to type and told her that
D'Orsay had painted a portrait of him, 'which he is going to
publish'. Yet the shining moment of this account is Liszt's real
concern, despite personal irritations, for the promotion of Chopin's
reputation in England. Thalberg, Döhler, and Herz were far more
selfish; and we can speculate that, in addition to introducing Chopin
encores at his Philharmonic appearances and in his 'Recitals', Liszt
played the nocturnes and mazurkas as a matter of unrecorded course
at a number of soirées.

When Marie arrived in London on 6 June, she must have known
that Liszt's early optimism about the English venture had begun to
recede. After absorbing the first excitement of his euphoric reception, he had written to her, at the end of May, that he was by then
'not making much ground (all this between ourselves)'.[52] His
revised assessment of the prospect of earning sufficiently large
amounts of money here was based upon a triad of factors: first, he
considered he had arrived too late in the season; second, the season
was in any case comparatively limp; third, because of his large fees,
he had not been offered as many late-evening private engagements
as had been promised.

They abandoned the idyllic idea of living together, perhaps in a
Hampstead 'maisonette', and as it happened Marie found herself
stowed away in Richmond. Her temper cannot have been improved
by the conciliatory notes Liszt sent her:

I bid you good day; I also wanted to send you some flowers, but

51. ibid., 447.   52. ibid., 449.

I'm afraid Ferco isn't available tomorrow ... I had such an aristocratically splendid soirée at Lady Beresford's: it was by way of being a High-Tory reunion, with the Duchess of Cambridge (she told me she would be attending my concert), Lady Jersey, Lady Peel, etc ...

This evening I thought of giving you a surprise at Richmond, but along came the Duke of Beaufort, who will take up my time after the soirée. That earns me a score or more of guineas, for his Grace does not know my terms, and I don't know how to tell him the worst.

Adieu, my dear; there will be longer days.[53]

But even on days which were long enough for them to spend time together, they quarrelled. After one disagreement, probably provoked mainly by Marie's feeling of impotence about her exclusion from polite society, Liszt wrote,

'I can't do anything at present, and for the future, than live completely alone'. That is all you have to say to me! Six years of absolute devotion produces only that result. That is the sum of all your words! Today (to recall only one day), during the whole of the journey from Ascot to Richmond, you said no word which wasn't wounding – an outrage.[54]

She did attend several of his concerts; but her presence was a social and professional annoyance to him.

Against this emotionally strident background, and amid nagging doubts about his London success, the cycle of Liszt's musical activity continued. He played at Julius Benedict's monster concert on 29 May. Then on 1 June he undertook something new. Mr Eliason had announced in *The Times* that he and 'Mr. Liszt will perform Beethoven's celebrated Sonata for pianoforte and violin, dedicated to Kreutzer', at his annual concert. This was an extraordinary occasion in other ways: with George Smart conducting, Eliason also played the Beethoven Violin Concerto, then a much underestimated work, and the Chorus of the German Opera visiting London performed some excerpts from Weber. John Parry sang and, except for Tamburini, the Italians were significantly absent.

53. ibid., 451.   54. ibid., 452.

Liszt rounded off the concert by playing a 'grand Valse di Bravura'.
The Times afterwards called the event 'a concert of superior character', and this may have allayed some of Liszt's doubts, for the critic
also acknowledged that he was now 'the *rage*' of the season: 'a great
many celebrated pianists, including W. S. Bennett, Döhler, Litolff
and Kiallmark, were among the audience'.[55] And the *Athenaeum*
confirmed that, while some of the critics might not understand him,
'the musicians crowd to listen to him'.[56]
     As a flamboyantly noticeable listener, Liszt probably attended the
concerts of others. At the pianist Mme Huerta's benefit on 4 June,
he might have heard the promising young contralto Louisa Bassano, who was to be a member of both his provincial touring
parties.[57] The Italian Opera may have engaged some of his attention, and Taglioni – the ballerina of ballerinas – was in town for
most of June; but he would already have heard and seen many of
their performances in similar repertoire in Paris. It is probable, on
the other hand, that he visited the theatre to hear the German
singers in, for instance, *Fidelio*,[58] and to encounter the best examples of English contemporary acting. He had opportunities to compare the merits of Macready and Charles Kean, the latter in *Hamlet*
at the Haymarket, the former in Bulwer's *The Lady of Lyons* at the
same theatre (followed by *The Irish Attorney* and *My Wife's Dentist*),
and later, in *Richelieu*.[59]
     Macready certainly saw and heard Liszt. The actor was an excess-
ively self-indulgent diarist. On 31 May he wrote:

> Went to Lady Blessington's, where I saw the Fonblanques, Lords
> Normanby and Canterbury, Milnes, Chorley, Standish, Rubini,
> Stuart Wortley, an Italian – Count something, Mr. Palgrave
> Simpson, and Liszt, the most marvellous pianist I ever heard. I do
> not know when I have been so excited.[60]

55. *The Times*, 30 May 1840.
56. *Athenaeum*, 30 May 1840.
57. *The Times*, 5 June 1840.
58. ibid., 27 May 1840.
59. ibid., 29 May 1840.
60. Frederick Pollock, *Macready's Reminiscences and Selections from his Diaries and Letters* (London, 1876), 488.

As a performer Macready had the reputation of being cold and physically inflexible. His enthusiasm on seeing Liszt play at Gore House may have been tinged with the kind of envy he had felt when hearing Paganini in the early 1830s.

While Liszt was thus flying high in society, he must still have enjoyed social contact with those friendly musicians who could truly appreciate his achievements. With them he did not need to be meretricious, and he could exercise a charm which was remembered for ever. According to Mrs Moscheles,

> His conversation is always brilliant; it is occasionally dashed with satire, or spiced with humour ... The other day he brought me his portrait, with his 'hommages respectueux' written underneath, and, what was the best 'Hommage' of all, he sat down to the piano and played me the 'Erl King', the 'Ave Maria', and a charming Hungarian piece.[61]

In the larger game of concert-giving, Liszt had yet to play his trump. He chose London as the scene for publicizing his greatest innovation, the piano recital, or, as *The Times* more accurately put it, 'Recitals on the Pianoforte'. He had already given solo performances, notably in – of all places – Italy, where he had filled La Scala with one of the most insensitive audiences he could have chosen to entertain. Moscheles had also devised his own even more original form of recital, as we have seen, which anticipated Anton Rubinstein's great historical programmes given later in the century. Alfred Hipkins, the Broadwood technician who tuned the English piano used by Chopin on his 1848 visit, was also to give historical lecture-recitals whose ancestry could be traced back to Moscheles: indeed, at one of these, in 1886, Anton Rubinstein stepped up from the audience and assisted him by turning the pages.[62]

Liszt crowned his 1840 London season by giving two solo recitals. The *Times* critic added a pedantic footnote to his review:

We have heard the question more than once asked, 'Why does

---

61. Moscheles, op. cit., ii, 63.
62. *Grove's Dictionary of Music and Musicians*, 3rd edn (London, 1927), ii, 637–8.

Liszt name them "Pianoforte Recitals"?' and the choice of the
expression has been by some condemned as an affected
singularity. In the first place, it must be admitted that the term
concerts would be inapplicable to these performances. Liszt, we
presume, intends the word to be, as it really is, a proper transla-
tion of *Vortrage*. In Germany it is usual to call the performance or
execution of a piece of music, the recitation of a poem, *Der
Vortrag* ... The introduction of foreign equivalents for *Vortrag*
and the verb *Vortragen* are not, however, of a very recent date, for
Recitation and *Recitiven*, the Teutonic form of the verb, occur in
works of elocution, and may be found even in dictionaries of
some standing ... We hope that the alliance which exists
between music and Germany – in its results truly 'une belle
alliance' – will excuse these observations.[63]

The writer might also have referred, just as pertinently, to the
recent sensation created by the London performances of the great
French–Jewish actress Rachel, in public concerts: she had recited
excerpts from the plays of Racine and Corneille.

Liszt had advertised his intentions well in advance. On 22 May
The Times announced

Liszt's Pianoforte Recitals. —— M. Liszt will give at 2 o'clock on
Tuesday morning, June 9, 1840, Recitals on the Pianoforte, of
the following different works: – No. 1. Scherzo and Finale from
Beethoven's Pastoral Symphony. No. 2. Serenade by Schubert.
No. 3. Ave Maria by Schubert. No. 4. Hexameron. No. 5.
Neapolitan Tarantelles [probably Rossini's 'La Danza' arranged
by Liszt]. No. 6. Grand Galop Chromatique. Tickets 10 shillings.

Henry Chorley, writing in the *Athenaeum*, was enthusiastic and
analytical about the effect of this first recital; though he regretted
that, on the previous day, Liszt had chosen to grace Mme Dulcken's
morning concert with a 'flimsy' duet by Herz, 'garnishing all its
showy passages with freaks of execution which must make all others
despair'. Chorley revealed himself to be the most perceptive critic in
London, for while other listeners might have noted simply the
brilliance of Liszt's performance of part of the 'Pastoral', he drew

63. *The Times*, 11 June 1840.

attention to 'a wonderful transcript of a score, not merely preserving its notes, but also reflecting its dramatic colouring'. (These are precisely the features of Liszt's Beethoven transcriptions which the late Hans Keller noted.) He also dealt with the growing rumour that Liszt 'adjusted' some of the Classical pieces he played. Chorley claimed that 'many persons have been deceived by an enthusiasm of manner on the part of the performer . . . so as to greatly exaggerate the amount of innovation made by him'.[64] This controversy did not end in 1840; and it is clear, from the evidence of other reliable critics, that Liszt was never unwilling to embellish the printed notes with a few more of his own, even when playing Beethoven or Chopin.

At his second recital, in Willis's Rooms on Monday morning, 19 June, Liszt was not, strictly speaking, alone on the platform. It was announced that he would play 'No. 1. Fugue in E minor, Handel; No. 2. Overture to William Tell, Rossini; No. 3. Grand Sonata (violin obbligato M. Ole Bull), Beethoven; No. 4. Weary Flowers, Schubert; No. 5. Serenata e Lorgia [sic] (des Soirées de Rossini); No. 6. The Earl [sic] King, Schubert; No. 7. Grand Marche Hongroise, Liszt.' The *Times* critic noted that Liszt's programme had been chosen 'as if to refute the oft-repeated but unjust opinion that the great pianist excels only in the performance of his own compositions or those in which mechanical dexterity of execution is the chief characteristic'. In his observations on the performance of the Kreutzer Sonata he enlisted the support of Schindler, Beethoven's disciple and biographer who, while condemning all erroneous and imperfect interpretations of his master's works, had said that 'Franz Liszt has contributed more than almost any other instrumentalist of the present day to the just comprehension of Beethoven's music'. In the Schubert transcriptions, *The Times* recorded, Liszt had 'made the instrument sing'.[65]

Among musicians and critics who mattered, then, Liszt's recitals, along with his other frequent performances, were acknowledged to have been utterly successful. His partnership with Bull was a repetition of their appearance in a Philharmonic concert on the evening of

64. *Athenaeum*, 13 June 1840, 483.
65. *The Times*, 20 June 1840.

8 June, following Liszt's afternoon contribution to Mme Dulcken's benefit. And of course he had already played the 'Kreutzer' with Eliason on 1 June. It must have been a favourite work, for he introduced it to Dublin during his second provincial tour. He also used the remaining Philharmonic occasions not only to astound but also to flatter his musical friends. Moscheles wrote that, at one of the Society's concerts,

> He played three of my 'Studies' quite admirably. Faultless in the way of execution, but by his powers he has completely metamorphosed those pieces; they have become more his Studies than mine. With all that, they please me, and I shouldn't like to hear them played in any other way by him. The Paganini Studies [of Liszt – an early version of the set we now hear], too, were enormously interesting to me. He does anything he chooses, and does it admirably, and those hands raised aloft in the air come down but seldom, wonderfully seldom, upon a wrong key.[66]

The tickets for his recitals had been sold by two firms of publishers, Cramer and Lavenu. It will be remembered that Mrs Moscheles was charmed by Liszt's respectful visit to their London home. She had noted after that occasion, in some apparent confusion, that he intended, first, making an excursion to Baden-Baden; 'after that a tour of the English Provinces with Cramer (at £500 a month) and then on to St. Petersburg for recreation'.[67] She was correct about the English tour, but wrong in recording that Cramer was to be Liszt's manager. The pianist had entrusted his next British enterprise to Lewis Lavenu, the very youthful, inexperienced representative of his London publishers, Mori and Lavenu. In the hope of making money quickly, and basing his assumption of future success on the reputation he had made in the capital that summer and on news of Thalberg's profitable tours, Liszt looked forward eagerly to an assault upon the English provinces.

66. Moscheles, op. cit., II, 49.
67. ibid., 63.

CHAPTER THREE

The First Tour

Chichester — Portsmouth — Ryde — Newport
Southampton — Winchester — Salisbury — Blandford
Weymouth — Lyme Regis — Sidmouth — Exmouth
Teignmouth — Torquay — Plymouth — Exeter
Taunton — Bridgwater — Bath — Clifton — Cheltenham
Leamington — Coventry — Northampton — Market
Harborough — Leicester — Derby — Nottingham
Mansfield — Newark — Lincoln — Horncastle — Boston
Grantham — Stamford — Peterborough — Huntingdon
Cambridge — Bury St Edmunds — Norwich — Ipswich
Colchester — Chelmsford — Brighton[1]

As an experienced musical traveller in Europe Liszt must have
anticipated some of the difficulties which might attend a tightly
scheduled five-week tour. During his career as a child prodigy he
had collided with the opening of a new era at Manchester in 1824.
Alongside the review of his performance there, a local newspaper
reported the first work on George Stephenson's Liverpool and
Manchester Railway, the fitful beginning of a transport revolution
which would suit busy concert artists. Yet even in 1840, Liszt and
his touring colleagues still straddled the Ages of Horse and Steam.
Their journey through southern England and the Midlands was
sometimes by rail, but mainly by coach and horses, with a separate
van to carry Liszt's precious Erard piano, which could be mounted
on a railway waggon whenever necessary.

1. This information, and all the words of John Parry, are quoted from John Parry's
Diaries of Liszt's Tours of Britain, NLW MS 17717A and 17717B.
2. *Manchester Guardian*, 31 July 1824.

38

The London season had just ended and the concert party was seeking fashionable audiences in provincial, if not quite rural, pastures. Lavenu had arranged for their first concert to take place in Chichester, and the English musicians drove down on 16 August, but without Liszt. His chief anxiety seems to have been about cash and presents reaching Marie in France while he was away:

> I have arrived in London and depart in three hours. My Company has already cast off. Tomorrow at noon our first concert is in Chichester. The crossing was ghastly: six hours behind time! I was terribly ill today; but it's no use dwelling on that now. I am somewhat perturbed about your having to deal with Customs. If you should need anything before the end of September, write.[3]

News of a gigantic storm had reached London from Aldeburgh in the east, and its force was to wreak damage also along the south coast during the first week of the tour.[4] Liszt's illness proved to be a more enduring problem. It seems he had been suffering for some months from what would now be called a virus infection;[5] and at various times in 1840 he had recourse to anaesthetics like laudanum and alcohol. When the tour began he was quite ill, and was not to recover for a fortnight.

Another early letter, however, suggests that at first he was approaching his problems with equanimity:

> My travelling-circus life begins today, or rather I embark upon a new mode, a change of career which I have bravely embraced in the last eighteen months. This morning, then, there was the Chichester Concert: 50 or 60 in the hall; this evening a Concert at Portsmouth (I will bring back printed views of each town), the audience about 30 people. But Lavenu was ready for this sort of thing, and he treats these two concerts as preliminaries. The programme of each concert, all the same, is well arranged, and I

---

3. Daniel Ollivier, ed.: *Letters of Liszt and Marie d'Agoult* (Paris, 1933), I, 418.
4. *The Times*, 27 August 1840.
5. Alan Walker, *Franz Liszt: the Virtuoso Years, 1811–1847* (London, 1983), 349.

enclose a specimen for curiosity's sake. All this week we give two
concerts on almost every day.[6]

The outline of this phenomenal tour can be traced from a number
of sources. Liszt's infrequent and vaguely dated letters to Marie give
one angle of view; and there is the irregular occurrence of accounts
in the local press wherever he played. But a continuous overall
record is provided by the diaries of one of his constant companions,
the singer and pianist John Orlando Parry. This document, which is
a treasure of great significance, falls into two parts, the first dealing
with the August–September tour, the second with the longer circuit
of England, Ireland and Scotland which lasted from November 1840
to January 1841.

Thirty years of age in 1840, Parry was a bright little black-haired
entertainer who was then building his considerable reputation as a
singer and composer of the popular songs with which he was to
delight audiences until his retirement in 1877. His father, also a
musician, had come to London from Denbighshire at the beginning
of the century after an apprenticeship as a militia bandmaster and
instrumentalist.[7] John Parry senior used his versatility, and the
popularity of Celtic folksong in that era, to make a career in
metropolitan musical and theatrical life. He arranged Welsh traditional tunes, composed vocal pieces of his own, and included both
species in the operas and dramatic works he produced for Drury
Lane and Covent Garden. His success in these enterprises coincided
with the revival of the Eisteddfod in Wales, and he frequently
returned to his native country in the 1820s and 1830s to direct
concerts at Eisteddfodau in the major towns, under the patronage of
the Anglo–Welsh nobility and gentry with whom he rubbed
shoulders in London. He was Secretary to the great Westminster
Abbey Handel Festival in 1834 and the charitable Society of Musicians. He must have made a steady income from the publication of
his popular folksong arrangements with verses translated into
English by the fashionable poetess once much admired for the
wrong reasons by Shelley, Mrs Alicia Hemans. He became an

6. Ollivier, op. cit., II, 15.
7. *The New Grove Dictionary of Music and Musicians* (London, 1980).

author, publishing a traveller's guide to the scenery and inns of his native North Wales;[8] and in the last phase of his career, after 1839, he wrote music criticism for the *Morning Post*. But all these achievements were to prove ephemeral when compared to his greatest production, the career of his only son, John Orlando, initially known as John Parry junior.

Writers on Liszt's English tours, perhaps being misled by the 'travelling-circus' metaphor, have sometimes claimed that his colleagues were artists of mediocre talent and accomplishment. Given the relatively impoverished condition of English musical culture at the beginning of Victoria's reign, that kind of judgment might appear plausible. But on closer examination Parry, at least, is a more striking musical personality than the superficial evidence suggests. Born in 1810, a year before Liszt, he received a sound musical training from his celebrated father, and from Sir George Smart, the Philharmonic Society's emissary to Beethoven. As a boy treble he had sung with the greatest executants of the day – with Parry senior's friend the tenor Braham, for whom Weber had written the part of Sir Huon in *Oberon*;[9] with the horn player, Giovanni Puzzi, the Dennis Brain of that age; and with Miss Stephens, a leading soprano who had played her social cards immaculately, becoming countess to the ageing Earl of Essex a year before he died. Parry also developed considerable facility as a harpist of the traditional Welsh school, studying with the morally notorious Nicolas Charles Bochsa, professor at the infant Royal Academy;[10] and the accompaniments to his song settings demonstrate a command of pianoforte effects sufficient to have earned practical acknowledgement from Liszt himself.[11]

As an adult singer he made his début with 'Arm, arm, ye brave!' in Mr F. Cramer's Concert at the Hanover Square Rooms in May

8. John Parry (Bardd Alaw), *A Trip to Wales, Containing much Information that Relates to that Interesting Alpine Country* . . . (London and Caernarvon, [?]1840).
9. *Grove* (1927 edn).
10. ibid.
11. ibid.; also, C. B. Andrews and J. A. Orr-Ewing, *Victorian Swansdown: Extracts from the Early Travel Diaries of John Orlando Parry* (London, 1934).

1830; and he developed a baritone voice promising enough for his astute father to send him to Paris and Naples for brief periods of study with the greatest *buffo* bass of the nineteenth century, Luigi Lablache, whose admirable musical taste, impressive size and immense vocal power caused his having a hand in creating roles in new operas of Donizetti and Bellini.

Parry's ambition, by the mid-1830s, was to become an operatic baritone, or at least an oratorio singer. But before he left Naples he had discovered the perfect line for his career, though he did not seize on this new course completely for some time: at an entertainment in Posilipo patronized by the great Neapolitan impresario and artistic tyrant, Domenico Barbaia, the most successful item was Parry's *Buffo Trio* in which he imitated in turn the three leading opera singers of the day, Lablache, Malibran and Ivanoff.[12] Malibran, a friend since she had first appeared at the Italian Opera in London in 1831, suggested to him that he become a singer of humorous songs. And so when, on returning to London, he discovered gradually that the small size of his voice would never enable him to challenge Lablache's reputation, he started to take engagements as a singer of comic pieces, setting to music the arch, innocent words of Albert Smith and Dubourg. This new career suited him and the public ideally. He seems to have been a 'camp' performer of the highest professionalism; moreover, he had chosen an appropriate moment for assuming this new role.

Middle-class taste, under the influence of Evangelicalism and the early Temperance movement, was hardening against what was considered to be the increasing vulgarity and salaciousness of entertainments in the old taverns and the infant music-halls. So the prosperous realm of genteel bourgeois diversions became Parry's sphere, with one short break, for almost 40 years. His trimly plump figure and dark hair, with kiss-curl, were depicted in the public prints, merry black eyes anticipating the song's punch line with a wink, and his elbows alongside the keyboard ready to nudge the audience into uproarious appreciation of words which, as the years passed, they must have known by heart already. Parry was no intellectual, but he could write wittily; he painted, and drew clever

12. ibid.

1. *Anna Liszt*

2. *Adam Liszt*

3. *Liszt in 1824; lithograph by
François de Villain after a drawing
by A X Leprince*

4. *Thalberg in 1838; lithograph by Josef Kriehuber*

5. *Marie d'Agoult; oil portrait by Henri Lehmann*

6. *Liszt in Hungarian Costume (1838); watercolour by Josef Kriehuber*

pictures to illustrate the diaries he kept on all his major tours; and he spoke German, Italian and French fluently. He loved his father, and adored his wife, Anne, and their two little daughters. Many diary entries were devoted to the getting and sending of letters between him and his family, and to receiving pictures from and buying presents for his infant daughters. Parry's account of the events of 1840–41 is valuable, not only for its reflection of Liszt's English experience, but as a record both of a leading Victorian entertainer's professional life and of current musical taste. His artistic ability was out of the ordinary even at a time when sketching and painting were widely cultivated accomplishments. The *Dramatic and Musical Review* commented in 1843:

> He draws beautifully, particularly comic subjects, and during his visit abroad, he completed two volumes of various curious costumes . . . All the lithographic titles to his songs are from designs and drawings of his own, which will give an idea of his talents as an amateur artist.

The *Morning Post*, in an encouraging review of a London concert in 1837, combined praise of his musical and artistic skills:

> In Italian music he has no equal among native performers. He is also a very clever artist, and his sketches of life for breadth of humour and graphic accuracy are worthy of Cruikshank or Seymour.

Liszt, often the subject of caricature throughout his career, was in 1840 a relative stranger to English life and culture, separated as he was by language and experience from the world immediately outside the coach, the hotel and concert room: his letters to Marie often seem like cries from a deep abyss. Parry, on the other hand, knew the English travelling life well, and had already visited many of the towns where they were to play; and he responded, gaily or rhetorically or mock-tragically, to the information he received from outside the sealed tube of their journeys. The contrast between Liszt and Parry adds a sharp savour to this tale of the unsuccessful attempt by the Jupiter of pianists to descend upon English provincial society and rapidly fleece it.

Parry and the other musical journeymen aboard Lavenu's coach
were sketched by Liszt in an early letter to Marie:

> The company is composed of Mlle. de Varny who is going to
> marry the editor of a new French journal, *L'Alliance*. She is more
> good than bad: French in appearance and manners ... *Prima
> Donna assoluta*, which is to say, absolutely detestable. Miss Bas-
> sano (who has nothing in common with the Duke[13]) is a pleasant,
> unpretentious woman. Mori and I reckon on buying her a cloak,
> for her present one is hideous. John Parry, whom you met in
> London, is our Grazioso. Then there are Lavenu and Frank Mori.
> (The latter asked for news of you, which makes me the more
> interested in him.) ... for the rest, we have a splendid carriage,
> and the post-boys take us along in fine style: this is a pleasure
> which I relish all the more for its being the only one I have. On
> Sunday we have promised ourselves to play Whist all day. We
> sigh for Sunday ... Tell me what *Les Mouches* [their three chil-
> dren] are doing, and kiss them for me.[14]

Frank Mori, aged 20, Lavenu's brother-in-law and business partner,
was a competent pianist and later a successful conductor.[15] He
seems to have joined the party mainly as genial hanger-on keeping
an eye on the financial side, for his only musical function was to
partner Liszt occasionally in piano duets. Lavenu was their conduc-
tor-accompanist, directing the band in the few places where one was
available, but mainly playing for de Varny and Bassano. As
impresario he was in charge of all the prior publicity, the booking of
the halls, and the last-minute making of decisions. Liszt foresaw
that the tour might be punctuated by hitches of various kinds: after
all, Lavenu, in his early twenties, was still learning the trade. But
the eminent pianist surely did not anticipate how ragged, exhausting
and financially unsatisfactory his English engagement might turn
out to be. For the moment however, at the beginning of the tour,
he seemed content that, having left Ferco (his Hungarian servant)

13. The Duc de Bassano was briefly Prime Minister under Louis Philippe in the
mid-1830s.
14. Ollivier, op. cit., I, 12.
15. *Grove* (1927 edn).

in London to conduct his business there, he was well cared for wherever they went. Liszt's responsibilities were simple: to draw the crowds and to advertise Erard's undeniably remarkable pianos.

Parry's tasks were equally clear. Whenever he had a spare minute in each town, he dashed to the music shops to check how many copies of his songs had been sold. The most important items in his diary, therefore, were his notes respecting the number of encores his songs elicited, for those repetitions gave a fair indication of how numerously the song sheets might sell.

The two ladies of the party must have been aware that with Liszt aboard, their contributions would be delivered from a deck below the highest. They were certainly not the 'stars'. Mlle de Varny, however, would probably have disagreed with this assumption: she had already enjoyed some success at La Scala, the Paris *Opéra Italien* and the London licensed houses in the operas of Rossini, Donizetti and Bellini, though she was not of course in the same division as Malibran, Grisi and Persiani. She sang duets with Miss Bassano, who was the ballad singer of the party; and John Parry joined them in trios. Louisa Bassano, who by many accounts had the makings of an impressive contralto voice, was only 17, and must at first have found the experience of touring in such company both exciting and terrifying.

The form each concert took was quite conventional. Liszt's innovation, the solo recital, was completely abandoned – indeed, it is clear that he wished to avoid the strain of such performances during a long tour – and each of the concerts was to be in two parts, or 'Acts'. The ladies usually prepared the way for Liszt with items from their respective repertories of arias and Scottish and English ballads, accompanied by Lavenu. Then the young demigod emerged from the green-room to shower the fashionable assembly with perhaps fifteen minutes' worth of astounding pianism. Finally, Parry gave his comic songs, presumably in order to restore good-humoured equanimity in an audience which had been bewildered by prestidigitation and passion. After the interval the formula was strictly repeated. The concerts were 'Morning' – that is to say, at one o'clock in the afternoon – and 'Evening', at eight o'clock or thereabouts; and the time before or after was filled with eating, travelling hectically, and disturbed sleeping, on the coach as well as at hotels and inns.

Of the first concert, at Chichester, Parry wrote: '180 present; great wind; genteel company. *Musical Husband* for the first time – good. (*No* encores.)'. At Chichester, too, despite the remark about 'genteel company', a precedent was set for other places on the tour. It must have seemed to Lavenu on some occasions that the most fashionable portion of his potential audience was fleeing ahead of him: before this first concert the Duke and Duchess of Richmond had left nearby Goodwood for the shooting in Scotland, and Colonel Wyndham had decided to visit his Irish estates.[16]

It is clear, from a later letter, that Liszt had visited the cathedral; given its cosy central setting, he would have found it difficult to miss. But it is an unlikely speculation to suggest that he was told of the presence there of the remains of one of the greatest English Jacobean composers of liturgical music, Thomas Weelkes, whose rough-and-ready appetite for life Liszt might then have found very engaging.

The *Musical Husband* – a soubriquet which suited Parry himself neatly – was one of his comic songs. His other standby on this tour was *Wanted a Governess*. And occasionally he might insert as a *tour de force* the *Buffo Trio*, perhaps a consciously conceived contrast with the serenity of Mozart's *Soave si' al vento*, from *Così*, which he sang with de Varny and Bassano. On the evening of this first day they were in Portsmouth for a concert at the Green Row Rooms. The 'great wind' which Parry had noted was developing into a hurricane and pursuing them along the south coast. In the great naval township, however, they might have felt reasonably secure. Parry reported, '80 present. Bad light. Wind dreadful. "Governess" encored; Liszt ditto. Two men drowned sailing for a Prize.' Since he had begun to keep a touring diary as a young boy on the road with his father, Parry had always expressed a delighted anxiety about natural disasters and the hazards of coach travel. He often wrote detailed accounts of the overturning of coaches and recorded the unreliable behaviour of post-boys who lost control of their horses.

16. *County of Sussex Agricultural Express and General Advertiser*, 8 August 1840.

In Chichester Cathedral, indeed, he might have seen the toga-clad stone statue of William Huskisson, MP, whose fatal accident at the opening of the Liverpool and Manchester Railway in 1829 stood as a reminder of the perils of the latest means of conveyance for concert artists.

Lavenu had shown some percipience in booking two concerts on the Isle of Wight, at Ryde and Newport, during the Regatta, which had become an event of fashionable significance under the patronage of George IV. But it is doubtful whether much yachting took place that August, for the storm was howling its worst when the little party set out for the island from Portsmouth on the morning of the 18th. They crossed in either the *Duke of Buccleuch* or the *Princess Victoria*, Her Majesty's Post Office steam packets.[17] The beach at Ryde sloped very gently, and so it was advertised that the passengers would be landed at Ryde Pier (half-a-mile long, and begun in 1817)[18] without the inconvenience of ferrying the passengers in rowing-boats. The packet left Portsmouth each morning at nine, arriving at quarter-past eleven. Lavenu, with his usual extravagance, would surely have booked the best aft cabins for the party, at two shillings each, with stewardesses to attend upon the ladies. But these splendid comforts seem not to have protected the travellers against assault from elemental furies: everyone was violently sick during the crossing, except Parry. More crucial to the concerts' success, however, was the fact that, because of the storm, the precious Erard had to be left on the mainland. In consequence, before what Parry described as 'gay company', numbering 200, Liszt had to perform on an antique square piano, against the background of a roaring wind.

The storm was causing distress in other places too. In the wake of Louis Bonaparte's unsuccessful *coup* near Boulogne, Louis Philippe and the Royal Family had decided upon a visit to heal and settle north-eastern France; but near Calais their ship was driven aground and they were lucky to survive.[19] Even in London the extreme

17. *Portsmouth, Portsea and Gosport Herald*, 8 August 1840.
18. A. Temple Patterson, *Hampshire and the Isle of Wight* (London, 1976), 158.
19. *County of Sussex Agricultural Express . . .* , 22 August 1840.

weather caused havoc. All navigation above Tower Bridge came to a halt; the Thames diminished to a trickle, and it was possible to walk across near Blackfriars; the stumps of Old London Bridge appearing above the muddy stream.[20]

Meanwhile, for our musical tourists the comforts of the Star Hotel in Ryde provided little compensation; and when the party travelled over the island's rough, rutted roads to Newport, they found there was no space for their luggage. Parry left his dress-clothes behind and had to sing, as he said, *en déshabille*. Liszt demonstrated the adaptability of his touch by playing at the evening concert in The Green Dragon Hotel on a cottage piano. The technical refinements of Erard and Broadwood had evidently not yet reached the Isle of Wight. But the fair audience – about 150 – had what one local observer described as 'certainly one of the greatest treats the lovers of music in Newport have enjoyed for many a day'. The critic could not decide to whom the palm should have been awarded: to Mlle de Varny for her 'animated, sonorous and melodious warblings', to the 'rich, deep tones of Miss Bassano', to Parry for his 'exquisite taste and fine voice', or to the 'wizard-like touch of M. Liszt on the piano'. Each had reached 'the summit of perfection', yet Liszt received 'rapturous shouts of applause' for his performance of the *Grand Galop Chromatique*. Miss Bassano, the juvenile, was granted a glowing compliment on her good taste in an age of continuing vocal extravagances: '. . . it is somewhat refreshing to hear a plain and graceful melody uninterrupted by Cadences [cadenzas], which, by their frequent intrusion, only produce annoyance'.[21]

Next day, the 19th, they left for Cowes at 5 a.m., and crossed to Southampton where Parry was overjoyed to meet his wife at the York Hotel. The concert was at one o'clock in the Royal Archery Rooms. Liszt was encountering Southampton, very briefly, at the end of its short phase as a fashionable spa town. The railway had just arrived and was to transform what had been a sleepy port, living on memories of medieval eminence, into a thriving commercial centre where modern docks overwhelmed the elegant Regency quarter.[22] Southampton never rivalled Bath or Brighton,

20. ibid.   21. ibid.
22. A. Temple Patterson, op. cit., 40–41.

but it had its polite entertainments. In the month when Liszt arrived, the local press was advertising a series of Promenade Concerts at the Royal Victoria Rooms, Portland Terrace, morning and evening. The attractions included 'Beautiful Cosmoramic Views, a Fancy Bazaar, and Salon de Danse, superbly illuminated every evening'. All purchasers at the Bazaar were entitled to join in the Quadrilles at the concerts.[23]

One local newspaper described Lavenu's concert as 'Mori's', and as taking place at the Victoria Rooms. Mori, it was said, following the example of his famous father, who had died early in 1840, 'introduced to the provincial public the musical lion of the season'. The meteorological happenings out of doors seem to have inspired the Southampton critic's depiction of Liszt's performance:

> ... at one moment the most delicate and silvery tone steals over the sense; and at another, a torrent of magnificent sound, which has never been heard from the instrument before, – even thunder seems to roll across the keys and then subsides into the breathing tones of an Aeolian harp.[24]

In addition to *Musical Husband* and *Governess* Parry sang his ballad *The Inchcape Bell*, perhaps in deference to the storm blowing itself out around them. The words of the song, unusually, are Parry's own:

> The storm had passed, and the winds had sung,
> On the ear scarce a murmur fell,
> Save the warning toll from the iron tongue
> Of the desolate Inchcape Bell.
> The rock where it stands in the deep doth lie,
> And around it the seabirds lave,
> But the Bell still warns though no hand be nigh,
> For 'tis rung by the passing wave.
> When mists arise o'er this treach'rous ground
> And the shoals their victims crave,
> 'Tis then that the mariner blesses the sound
> That saves him a wat'ry grave.

23. *Hampshire Advertiser*, 1 August 1840.
24. *Portsmouth, Portsea and Gosport Herald*, 22 August 1840.

The Southampton reviewer proffered a tasty mouthful of information about Miss Bassano. He said that she sang the pieces allotted to her with fine taste and purity, and that Crevelli's [her celebrated teacher's] prophecy that she would, in a year or two, become the leading English singer, could soon be fulfilled. 'She is as amiable as she is gifted, being the support, at the early age of seventeen, of a mother, and brothers and sisters to the number of ten, we believe.'[25] Singers, perhaps because of the dramatic setting of many of their performances and the rich meanings of the words they sang, seized the public imagination more tightly than instrumentalists. It was probably no accident that, in his novel *Béatrix*, reflecting the real relationship between Liszt and Marie d'Agoult, Balzac had made his Liszt-figure, Gennaro Conti, a *singer*-composer. And just before Lavenu's party left London, *The Times* had reviewed, at some length, the fictional tale of a young, exploited opera singer. Mrs Grey, it was said, had written 'a simple, powerful story', *The Young Prima Donna*. All the sensibilities of her readers must have been stimulated by this novel about a young lady, patronized by a noble family, 'herself and her mother being in narrowed circumstances'. The heroine was taken up and exploited by an Italian bass singer, who then married the mother. After a brilliant début the virtuous and religious songstress had to endure many abuses, 'the whole concluding with her death from a pulmonary complaint'. The depiction of her character, thought the *Times* reviewer, was 'exceedingly beautiful and original'.[26] Only a year earlier, the public prints had been full of the duel fought by the Vicomte de Melcy and Lord Castlereagh over the soprano, Giulia Grisi, de Melcy's 'wife'.[27] Such fictions and actual events encouraged a very broad – and hardly musical – appreciation of leading vocalists by the public, in the provinces as well as the metropolis. Audiences might find the personal details of the English Miss Bassano's private life more engrossing than the performances, however remarkable, of a foreign pianist, however flamboyant.

After the morning concert in Southampton, on 19 August, the

25. ibid.
26. *The Times*, 12 August 1840.
27. Forbes, op. cit., 102.

players travelled, in the comfort of first-class railway carriages, to Winchester for their evening performance at St John's Rooms. The tickets, available from Mr Bracewell's Music Shop in the High Street, were at the usual rates for the tour: family tickets, admitting four, 21 shillings; single tickets, 6 shillings. Having captured the shore-bound yachtsmen at Ryde and Newport, Lavenu was a week early for the Winchester race-goers. And he had a further problem: Liszt was becoming rapidly more ill, his feverish condition possibly aggravated by turbulent seas, jolting coaches and Parry's incessant good humour. Lavenu had to announce the circumstances before the Winchester concert began, but the pianist did not disappoint the audience of 200. The *Hampshire Chronicle* commented:

> M. Liszt ... notwithstanding that he was severely indisposed, delighted the audience by his wonderful execution; nothing can surpass the agility with which he performs the most intricate passages.[28]

Mr Parry junior 'as usual, made the audience as merry as himself', and Mori played the *primo* part in a duet with Liszt, probably the arrangement of episodes from Mozart's *Don Giovanni*.

Everywhere they went, it seems, Parry was well known already, and of course he was to continue touring the provinces very successfully for at least ten years more. For instance, he was due to return to Hampshire in little over a month; a local newspaper announced that, under the direction of Mr Corri,[29] Parry, his good friend Joey Richardson the flautist, and the violinist Blagrove would perform in October next at Salisbury and Romsey, supported by the vocalists Misses Woodyatt and Dolby (though the Romsey concert had to be cancelled because of one of Parry's coaching accidents). Liszt's tour, then, was not an exceptional occurrence: in the autumn the main provincial centres were visited by famous English and foreign performers with concerts which provided a confectionery and set relatively high standards for regular events featuring local singers and musical societies. At Southampton in 1840 the Salisbury

28. *Hampshire Chronicle and Southampton Courier*, 24 August 1840.
29. *Grove* (1927 edn).

Philharmonic Society, under its conductor, Mr C. W. Corfe, was advertising winter subscription concerts, with season tickets at 14 shillings and family tickets at £2.[30] And in October the Southampton Sacred Harmonic Society arranged a performance with items from Parry's teacher Lablache, Miss Birch (then the leading English soprano), Lindley, doyen of the cello, and Dragonetti, the bass player whose virtuosity was renowned throughout Europe and who – on the few occasions when the work had been performed in England – played the double bass recitatives in the final movement of Beethoven's Ninth as solos. The conductor in Southampton was a Mr Truss, perhaps the original 'tenor's friend'.[31]

Local reviewers were thus in the habit of commenting, almost as a matter of course, on a frequent passing parade of the best international musical talent through their concert rooms during autumn days and nights. At Salisbury, however, the appointed critic undertook his task in a markedly offhand way. He reported the occurrence of Liszt's morning concert, at the Assembly Rooms, to an audience of about 120; but then his enthusiasm collapsed:

> Our Southampton correspondent has in the preceding column favoured us with so able a notice of this gentleman's efforts, that we have nothing further to add, than to call our readers' attention to that portion of local news.[32]

Much more space in the Salisbury paper was given to a report of the Grand Dahlia Show: 'most of the great growers in England having entered for the competition'. Parry's impressions of Salisbury confirmed this local indifference to Liszt's visit:

> Stupid audience – dreadful. *Laughed* in 'Soave il vento'!! No encores. Gave Lady Craven a copy of the 'Inchcape Bell'. Good dinner.

The party was late in arriving for the evening concert at the Bastards' dignified Blandford Forum: in fact they leapt off the coach

30. *Salisbury and Winchester Journal*, 28 September 1840.
31. ibid.
32. ibid., 24 August 1840.

at 9 p.m. to find that only eighty had bothered to wait, for over an hour, in the Assembly Rooms. Parry thought the Crown Hotel was 'nice', though he seems to have quarrelled with a man named Hoyle. A year earlier John Parry had entertained the citizenry of Blandford at an evening concert with the pianist Thalberg as part of a more leisurely tour. On that occasion the local press had paid most attention to Parry, noticing his tendency to find amusement and inspiration in the behaviour of members of his audience:

> At the window, nearly opposite the singer, sat, in wonderful self-approbation of his own personal attractions, an *Exquisite* of the first water, sweetened with all the perfumes of Arabia, with long-flowing glossy ringlets of raven hue, an irresistible pair of love-ticklers, and a sweet little imperial on the dimple of his under-lip – a chain and waistcoat that beggar all description. To heighten the effect of his performance, Parry, in mimicking the enamoured Signora, threw the most bewitching glances from his large rolling eyes on this hairy Adonis, which drew forth peals of laughter. The youth, thoroughly devoted to himself, was wholly unconscious of the amusement which he afforded to the company.

On this 1840 tour through the same countryside, Parry was developing too much respect for Liszt to permit his making that 'exquisite' the butt of his professional humour.

Next morning they made their way – 28 difficult miles – to the fashionable seaside at Weymouth. This was the fifth day and they had already played eight concerts. Their régime was fast turning into an imitation of the forced marches of a Roman army; and Liszt, stricken by fever, must by now have been playing like an automaton. In this respect he may be said to have met his match in Weymouth, for the *Dorset Chronicle* had recently advertised:

WONDER OF THE WORLD!!

The Queen of Pianists – a piece of mechanism never before equalled in the world, representing a lady PLAYING THE PIANO with that surprising rapidity and brilliancy of execution not to be surpassed by the most celebrated living performers. It is indeed indicative of the advanced state of art and invention, as she not only selects the music, but *turns the pages of the music* before her

with the greatest ease and grace ... She places her foot on the
pedal, and adjusts her music book, while the pleasure she feels is
evinced by the palpitation of her bosom! When she has concluded, she *arranges her hair*, and prepares for another performance. The figure is raised from the table, set in motion by clock-
work, and is so natural in appearance, as to startle the spectator
... It plays four beautiful airs, as follows:— 'Fortune
Galopade', 'Marche Triomphale', 'Walse de France' [*sic*],
'Quadrille de Authier' ...

Performance Gratis at

THE MUSICAL PROMENADE AND FANCY BAZAAR
8, Chesterfield Place, Esplanade, WEYMOUTH ...

Doorkeepers in attendance from six o'clock to prevent the intrusion of improper persons to the Music and Promenade in the
Evening ...

By Authority, ABRAHAM ROSENBAUM,
Licensed Hawker, No. 1647A.[33]

Weymouth Races had taken place a day or two before, and the
fresh, neat town was still packed with 'fashionables' and gentry,
some of whom had sailed in their private yachts through the
improving weather from the Isle of Wight. Among the arrivals at
Luce's Hotel were the banker, Baring, and his wife; Lady Craven's
son; Lord Grimstone; Lord and Lady St John; the Earl of Jersey's
son, Lord Villiers, MP; Mr R. B. Sheridan, son of the playwright
and seducer of heiresses; Bishop Sumner of Winchester and his
family; Count de la Stork [*sic*], and Mr and Mrs Clutterbuck.
Melcombe Regis Cricket Club were playing an end-of-season match
against some local gentlemen, and, at the theatre, under the
patronage of the Steward of the Races, A. W. Horsford, Esquire,
there were performances of Bulwer's *The Lady of Lyons*, which Liszt
was also to avoid seeing later, in Cork.[34]

The morning concert, attended by an encouraging audience of
220, drew the sort of bland review which suggests that the
newspaper writer was simply choosing from a musty store of

33. *Dorset Chronicle and Somersetshire Gazette*, 23 July 1840.
34. ibid., 27 August 1840.

second-hand epithets: 'The fingering of M. Liszt, though suffering severe illness, was most astonishing, and elicited distinguishing marks of intense admiration.'[35] Parry's view of the occasion was abrasively more critical. He reported that Lavenu had made an inelegant apology to the audience on Liszt's behalf, at which everyone had laughed. But his chief complaint was that, having been rewarded by a large assembly at the morning concert, Lavenu had lacked the foresight and acuity to promote another in the evening – such knee-jerk reactions were evidently expected of impresarios. So, for the first time, the party was unengaged, and Liszt probably spent the evening asleep.

Next morning they interrupted the 27-mile journey by taking breakfast in Bridport. Travelling down the hill into Lyme Regis Parry noticed the 'lovely view' and the 'splendid bay'. At the morning concert there they played to 120, and *Governess* was encored. Four horses were needed to drag them up out of the town towards their next venue, the London Hotel at Sidmouth, where they again arrived late, at 8.15 p.m.: 'People tired of waiting.' Parry met some old musical acquaintances, had a dull tea, then watched a firework display, refreshing himself with lemonade, an exceptional event on this tour. Next day, Sunday 23 August, they drove the ten miles to Exmouth, and Parry stayed at Rosebank Cottage with his friend, Mr Green. He dined, made a sketch of Green's home, and enjoyed 'a nice drive, lovely'.

Liszt's indisposition had made it impossible for him to write to Marie as frequently as she might have wished and he had promised; but the enforced idleness of Sunday provided an opportunity for a languid letter:

> Thanks to British religiosity, I was able to stay in bed all day, and I am feeling better. I believe – rare thing – that I have found a reasonably good doctor who has promised to get rid of the fever without using extreme methods. He seems a man to be trusted, and I do believe I'm improving.[36]

He certainly possessed enough strength to write at some length; and

35. ibid.
36. Ollivier, op. cit., II, 14.

he also uttered, for the first time, doubts about young Lavenu's
competence as a concert promoter:

> Lavenu is losing a fair amount of money at present. The over-
> heads are huge. For the past two days we were equipped with
> four horses and two postillions. Everywhere we stay at the best
> hotel. In this respect nothing could be more satisfactory. But I am
> sorry he has not been able to handle the business side more
> efficiently. To be fair, we have been only in minor places up to
> now (with the exception of Southampton), and he is counting
> upon Bath, Exeter, Plymouth, etc., to recoup. The countryside
> through which we have passed recently is charming. Sidmouth
> and Exmouth, whence I am writing, seem especially fine.
> Everywhere there are admirable parks ... For myself, I simply
> enjoy the pleasure of rapid travel, and fortunately we have only
> the very best postillions.[37]

Monday 24 August was, according to Parry, 'a lovely day,
beautiful', and in Exmouth they gave their concert to seventy souls
in Ewan's Beacon Hotel. Parry was delighted with their Devon
cream tea. For the second engagement of the day, at Teignmouth,
instead of toiling around the estuary of the Exe, through Exeter,
they drove across the sands, when the tide was favourable, and saw
an enormous beached fish – 'all mouth', said Parry, who made a
sketch of it. As a consequence of examining closely this marine
phenomenon, perhaps, they were late for the concert in the Assembly Rooms. Teignmouth provided an interesting coincidence: or
was it in some way prearranged? Liszt was due to tour in central
Germany later in the autumn: one of his concert appointments was
to be in Ems; and he told Marie that in Teignmouth he had received
a letter from 'Parish' who had written from Ems.[38] This was
undoubtedly Parish Alvars, the greatest harpist of the day, whose
virtuosity was deeply admired by Mendelssohn and described at
length by Berlioz in his *Memoirs*.[39] Moreover, Parish Alvars's play-

37. ibid., 15.
38. Ollivier, loc. cit.
39. Ernest Newman. ed.: *Memoirs of Hector Berlioz* (New York, 1966), 291–2.

ing had inspired the 'three-handed' effect which gave to much of
Thalberg's style a peculiarly interesting quality. The coincidence –
if such it was – lay in Liszt's receiving a letter from the harpist in
Alvars's birthplace, Teignmouth. This might have proved some
consolation, for Liszt was again very poorly; so ill, in fact, that their
next concert, in Torquay on Tuesday afternoon, was cancelled,
though only about thirty had to be turned away, and it was the only
occasion, through 50 scheduled engagements, that Liszt failed to
appear. No evening concert had been arranged, so they pushed
forward to Plymouth where good receipts were expected.

Parry's last contact with Plymouth had taken the form of a dis-
astrous miscellaneous concert in December 1838. On that occasion
the local musical critic had praised his performances. But the comments then made on the skills of the local orchestral musicians may
well have accounted for Lavenu's decision to do without a band in
1840. The 1838 concert had begun with Rossini's *Barbiere* Overture
which had been 'indifferently played, with the stringed instruments
anything but in tune'. And when it came to a Handel vocal duet, in
which Parry was involved,

> a more miserable failure on the part of the orchestra we never
> before witnessed – it was more like a rehearsal ... Mr. Parry was
> obliged to stop the orchestra for the purpose of pointing out the
> time of the movement to the Leader ... We would seriously
> recommend ... having an efficient leader, or conductor, at the
> pianoforte.

In 1840, however, their first concert at Plymouth went well;
according to Parry, there were

> 280 present. Very fair concert, about £40. 'Musical Husband'
> encored – not 'Governess'!! Bazaar in the morning – 40,000
> people.

When Liszt arrived in Plymouth the town was nearing the end of
a remarkable period of new building. In 1840 it was a shining young
monument to the recent work of two architects, John Foulston and
his student and disciple, George Wightwick. The stuccoed Classical
brilliance of the new town centre made it one of the gems of early

nineteenth-century urban planning, and it was to retain its dignity until German bombs blew it away in the 1940s. The nucleus of Foulston's work, in its early stages, was the group of Royal Hotel, Theatre, and Assembly Rooms. He died in 1842; but in the 1830s he had already seceded the management of Plymouth's physical development to Wightwick. His pupil was an extraordinary man: at one time, according to J. C. Trewin, he had thought of deserting architecture for the stage, and gloried in the friendships he made with contemporary theatrical luminaries, notably Charles Mathews, one of Parry's heroes (for whom Wightwick designed a memorial in St Andrew's Church, Plymouth), William Charles Macready, and Kean. If Wightwick was in Plymouth when Liszt appeared, he would surely have attended the concert, for dramatic flamboyance always appealed to him, even in others. He was a playwright, and probably fancied himself as a rival to Shakespeare. In the Prologue to his own *Richard I, a Romantick Play in Five Acts*, he wrote:

> Shakespeare for Richards Number Two and Three,
> Has done, what none could do save he;
> And now to make amends for what's undone,
> We come to do our best for Number One.[40]

The beautiful concert room in which Liszt played was designed by Foulston; and it would be wonderful to find that Wightwick was there to enjoy the occasion.

The 'Bazaar' which Parry had mentioned took place on a pastoral stage across the water from Plymouth, in Cornwall, at Mount Edgecumbe, the park of Lord Edgecumbe who had inherited title and estate from his father, a celebrated amateur of music, in the previous year. The occasion was a fête in aid of the Devon and Cornwall Female Orphans' Asylum, whose buildings in Lockyer Street were planned by Foulston and Wightwick. For two days, Wednesday and Thursday, 26 and 27 August, Mount Edgecumbe was open for the pleasure of everyone. The chief formal attractions were his Lordship's Italian, French and English Gardens. At eleven o'clock each morning, wrote the correspondent of *Trewman's Exeter Flying*

40. J. C. Trewin, *Portrait of Plymouth* (London, 1973), 91.

7. *Liszt in Polish Fur Coat (1840); lithograph by Josef Kriehuber*

8. *Mount Edgecumbe, Plymouth*

9. *The Montpellier Rotunda; by J. W. Hance*

Post, the populace were admitted to 'the noble avenues and clustered woods of the park (which) was glowing under the brightening influence of a glorious sun, tracking its way through the deep azure of a cloudless sky'.[41] The circumstances of Liszt's visit are unknown; but he was considerably moved by the experience, and communicating it to Marie, reflected on their sojourn by the Italian Lakes, two years earlier:

> In Plymouth I visited an impressive park belonging to Lord Edge-cumbe. Imagine the Villa Serbelloni, or rather the hill at Bellagio outlined in a park, with splendid groups of trees, waves of grass such as one only sees in England, exotic plants and beds of flowers scattered pleasingly here and there, all flanked by the sea, with a view of the harbour and Plymouth below. It is really a very beautiful conceit, and I thought, sadly, how much more I should have enjoyed it, had you been there.[42]

After the first successful concert, Lavenu optimisitically planned a second. But another popular event in Plymouth, more hectic than Edgecumbe's Bazaar, threatened to damage attendances. Local newspapers celebrated an occasion which stimulated a patriotic fervour not seen since Nelson's time. On Thursday evening booths were erected on an extensive scale in the Port, and the Naval authorities permitted the public to witness the launching of the *St George*, a ship of the line of 120 guns. Because of Admiralty economies it had lain on the stocks for 13 years, and the tension of waiting was probably released when the bands blared *Rule Britannia* that Thursday. The launch took place soon after five o'clock 'amidst the astounding cheers of the multitude'.[43]

Liszt was amused by the aggressive conjunction of the launching and his second concert. He told Marie,

> Yesterday . . . a pleasant diversion occurred. We were at Plymouth where we had earlier given a very fair concert. Lavenu

41. *Trewman's Exeter Flying Post and Plymouth and Cornish Advertiser*, 3 September 1840.
42. Ollivier, loc. cit.
43. *Trewman's Exeter Flying Post*, 3 September 1840.

had announced a second, for one o'clock in the afternoon; but at a
quarter-past one there were only about four people in the room.
Over ten thousand people meanwhile were elbowing their way to
the harbour for the launching of a vast ship . . . What an attraction this was for all classes of society!

Lavenu did not give in and ran immediately in search of seven
men and bedecked them with huge placards announcing the post-
ponement of the concert till evening. These seven fellows walked
up and down the town and through the port all day. At eight
o'clock the Room was lit, but no one came. Eventually, after a
good half-hour of waiting, there arrived about half-a-dozen
people, to whom money was refunded at the door, much to their
chagrin; and the concert was cancelled for a second time. In
fairness, and to console ourselves, we heard that Thalberg had
only twenty for his concert here.[44]

By this time Mlle de Varny's suitor, the editor M. Lemoine, had
joined them and Liszt found little reason for liking him. He was
about fifty years of age, 'bloated and vitriolic', wore spectacles and,
'having lived for some time in Brussels, has manners finished to
perfection'. Poor man: he was twice the age of everyone else in the
party. But Lemoine did have one mildly appealing feature in Liszt's
eyes: '. . . he is only a little less insufferable because we were
waiting for someone to supply a fourth for Sunday whist'.[45] And in
Plymouth, on a Thursday evening, they played cards in lieu of an
abandoned concert.

Next morning at eight they started for Exeter – Parry riding
outside on the box seat – and, skirting Dartmoor, breakfasted on
cream at Ivybridge. The weather was fine and the journey went
well. Lavenu had advertised two Exeter concerts, at the Royal
Clarence Assembly Rooms near the cathedral; the first on the evening of their arrival, Friday the 28th, the other next morning at two
o'clock. Tickets could be purchased from Mr Pilbrow's Pianoforte
and Harp Warehouse. For Parry, at least, the first was a 'bad
concert', though both his solo songs were encored and there was a
respectably large audience of 180. Perhaps it was a sort of 'flat'
affair which all performing artists fear, and one reason for the lack

44. Ollivier, loc. cit.   45. ibid., 16.

of elation may have been that Lavenu was now ill; so Parry probably had to take on the role of accompanying the other vocalists as
well as playing for his own songs. Next morning he went to Pilbrow's to practise. The second concert – audience 160 – was as bad
as the first. But afterwards Parry had a 'nice dinner', Liszt played
studies and in duets, and they walked out and visited the cemetery.
They whiled away Sunday with whist and cribbage, and Liszt,
recovering, certainly strolled about the Close admiring the cathedral
and its setting. At five o'clock they mounted the Taunton coach,
arriving at ten.

His improving health, the relaxation of card-playing and the
comparative leisure of two days in Exeter did not mollify Liszt's
attitude to his companions:

> I will say no more about the invincible boredom I feel every hour,
> every minute, not just deep down, but running through my whole
> being. The singular thing is that, among six so diversely assorted
> individuals, not one piquant incident occurs, not a single word is
> said which is worth repeating. Each day is like the one before and
> the one after: a line of water-jugs removed one by one from the
> table after dinner.[46]

Taunton was a flourishing market centre, truly a county town.
The energetic promotion of agriculture in Somerset and north
Devon, by local gentry and nobility as professionally active as the
musical Aclands and the Earl of Devon, and by the work of the Bath
and West Society, had revitalized Taunton. The town which Liszt
might have seen in summer twilight was growing rapidly. They
stayed at The Castle Hotel which stood on the square Castle Green,
bounded on the west by ruins, on the east by the Free Grammar
School, and on the south by the Winchester Arms. The mock-
Gothic hotel, under its landlord, James Fackerell, at least provided
them with what Parry called 'a capital breakfast' next morning. The
recent growth of Taunton had stimulated middle-class occupation of
new quarters like South Street (formerly Holway Lane). The local
hospital was in course of rebuilding, and a new church, Holy
Trinity, was rising above domestic terraces. The Market House

46. ibid.

enclosed not only a concert room but a library and museum. Taunton was also on the lip of its leap towards becoming an educational centre of some significance: Parry's enigmatic reference in his diary to an 'Academy' suggests that there may have been some connection between the overnight guests at The Castle Hotel and the Revd Thomas Crotch's grammar school at the side of Castle Green.[47]

The local newspaper described the concert on Monday as 'an extraordinary musical treat'. The attendance was thin, but those present included 'the most distinguished of our county families'. A 'Prince' was there, and according to Parry this eminent person 'laughed at "The Governess"'. But who he was it has been impossible to tell: was Nikolaus Esterházy, currently the fiancé of one of Lady Jersey's daughters, staying in the country near Taunton at the end of August 1840?[48]

Most of the reviewer's remarks on this occasion were devoted to a comparison of Liszt with Thalberg, and to a brief discourse on the nature of genius. Liszt was 'more wonderful than Thalberg, but we do not think him so pleasing'. Surprisingly, given what is known of Thalberg's characteristics as an executant, Liszt's performance recommended itself 'to the mind, but it does not touch the heart' as his rival's did. The critic was on firmer ground when he compared the appearance of each artist. Thalberg's bearing was 'mild, pensive and sensitive'; Liszt's was 'the very *beau ideal* of those German students who figure in the old German tales of *diablerie*, contemplative, stern, abstract, mysterious'. Both, however, were men of genius; and since members of that species were 'nature's nobility, holding their patent from divinity', comparisons were ultimately pointless. Parry's contributions to the Taunton concert were warmly appreciated: he delighted the company with *Musical Husband* and *Governess*. The distinguishing features of his performance were that 'he makes humour graceful' and 'sings a comic song like a gentleman; how difficult this is may be judged by its rarity'. Liszt's accompaniment of Parry's rendering of *The Inchcape Bell* 'told the story in his music'.

Liszt's genius did not protect him from the perils attending physi-

47. Dr William Crotch, a celebrated composer, died at his son's grammar school in Taunton in 1847; see *Grove* (1927 edn).
48. *Burke's Peerage.*

cal frailty: at The Castle Hotel he cut his hand on a broken glass. The concert at Bridgwater in the evening was a disaster: there was an audience of 30, and Liszt played with a bandaged hand. Parry recorded that their performance was shorter than usual, and Lavenu seems to have used the relaxation provided by failure and brevity for developing his affair with Miss Bassano. The Bridgwater concert may have reminded Liszt of the intense commercial rivalry between piano manufacturers: on one hand, the *entente* of the classic Broadwoods – with Beethoven and Chopin among their past and present clients – and the Pleyels based in Paris; on the other, Erards, comparative upstarts, but nevertheless beginning to make inroads on their rivals' markets, aided by Henri Herz's technical improvements and Liszt's patronage.[49] The MP for Bridgwater, from 1837 till 1852, was Henry Broadwood, whose chief interests were London brewing and parliamentary politics, rather than the real family business. He had used a considerable portion of his share of the Broadwood inheritance to purchase the votes which enabled him to defeat R. B. Sheridan, rapscallion son of the playwright, at the 1837 Election. But it is possibly fanciful to conclude that, in 1840, Broadwood also bribed his constituents to refrain from hearing Liszt's Erard.[50]

On 1 September Liszt and Company moved on 43 miles to Bath. Nearly fifty years earlier Haydn had made a private visit lasting five days. He had stayed with Rauzzini, the famous castrato, dedicatee of Mozart's *Exultate jubilate*, and teacher of Parry's friend Braham. Haydn was there early in August when he had written that the city was empty: '... for the people taking the baths don't come till the beginning of October, and stay through half of February'. In the proper Bath season there was an influx of 25,000 people. While he had been there the Pump Room was under construction; but what had most impressed him was, half way up a hill, 'a building shaped like a half-moon, and more magnificent than any I had seen in London'.[51]

49. David Wainwright, *The Piano Makers* (London, 1975), 56, 77, 78.
50. David Wainwright, *Broadwood By Appointment* (London, 1982), 138.
51. H. C. Robbins Landon, *The Collected Correspondence and London Notebooks of Joseph Haydn* (London, 1959), 295.

Haydn had visited Bath near the end of its golden era, when music and the theatre provided stimulating diversion of the highest quality, and when the town itself was still a theatrical mechanism for social display. In 1840 it was becalmed. As an epitome of the elegant eccentricities of English town planning and social organization it remained attractive, but its bloom was fading. Nevertheless, rather like Lady Blessington, even the evidence of its decay was magnificent. The indigenous musical life of the place was certainly in decline; the age of the Linleys had passed, and the shade of Haydn would not perhaps have been impressed by the performances which were served up to visitors as a matter of course. In the 1830s and 1840s Bath's musical vitality depended upon ignition generated by the brief visits of artists like Liszt and Thalberg, Grisi and Lablache; and, as corollary, the success of Lavenu's tour now required the response of Bath's fashionable residents to what had been transmitted beforehand of Liszt's exciting reputation.

At most of their concert venues there must already have been some knowledge of Liszt's London triumphs, culled from *The Times* and the *Morning Post*, for which Parry's father wrote articles, and from the primitive musical journals of the day. Some of the members of each élite audience in the larger provincial centres might well have earlier attended one of Liszt's London concerts. But Lavenu tried to stimulate local appetites by inserting 'puffs' in the press before almost every concert: a week in advance, the pro forma paragraph about 'the eminent Pianiste, Monsieur Liszt' would appear in the papers, surrounded by trivial items of news, reports of cricket matches and accounts of lurid crimes and catastrophes. Liszt's flamboyant public manner was positively advantageous; but at this stage in his career his 'legend' consisted strictly in his startling abilities as a pianist. Paganini's English promoters in the early 1830s, on the other hand, had a truly Faustian myth to work upon; and the violinist's publicity was couched almost exclusively in unambiguous references to Niccolò's contract with 'Old Nick'. For instance, before Paganini visited Liverpool in 1832, the *Albion* had described him as an optical illusion:

> The outward and visible sign of Signor Paganini is no Paganini at all – flesh, blood and bones in appearance (though marvellously

little of them, to be sure), but, in reality, 'the spirit of the fiddle' –
one

'Doomed for a certain time to walk the night
'And by day condemned to – bow and scrape!!'[52]

Before he played in Chester, the *Chronicle* printed the following
'poem':

The Two Nicholases.

A famous fiddler of old
Signor Tartini, we are told,
Once dreamt he heard the Devil play
In so miraculous a way
On his Cremona, that he woke,
And in despair his fiddle broke,
Because, forsooth, Professor Scratch
In fiddling was above his match.
But should the wizard Paganini
Have such dreams as woke Tartini,
Or if Old Nick should dare pretend
With Nick, his namesake, to contend,
To sixpence I would bet a guinea,
He'd prove no match for Paganini,
Whose flourishes and rich adagios,
Staccatos, cadenzas, and arpeggios,
Shakes and harmonics, double, single,
Where pizzicatos intermingle,
Would make old Scratch's ears so tingle
He'd well nigh burst with envious spite,
And, in a flash of fire, take flight.[53]

The candle-lit, cadaverous figure shuffling on-stage in the Chester
Theatre was a personage of great Romantic potency. In 1840 Liszt
could not yet embroil the public imagination in such a way. But in a
Bath newspaper just before his visit, a poem appeared which, while

52. Quoted in *Chester Chronicle*, 20 January 1832.
53. *Chester Chronicle*, 3 February 1832.

it might have made Keats wince, must surely be seen as an effective part of Lavenu's advertising strategy:

> Lines on hearing the celebrated Liszt at Chichester
> by F. Champion, August 17th, 1840.
>
> The Piano of Liszt.
>
> How beautifully wild that fairy touch —
> Like pebbles gently dragging down a stream,
> Then warbling as the lay of some stray bird
> Of Paradise. Scarce reaching sound, the tones
> Swim rippling, gliding, whispering along;
> As one could dream, embark'd on floating leaves,
> The watery spirits hail the rising sun.
> The rapid bass now rumbling on the ear
> Portrays an earthquake struggling to be free;
> And then with sudden rush of tenfold power
> The mingling notes resume the torrent's roar.
> Again they sweetly, gently murmur, fleet
> As the wild lama bounding 'cross the plain
> The pliant fingers fly. I dare not breathe,
> Lest one soft note of joy's ecstatic time
> Be lost. A thousand harmonies prevail —
> Each note a word, each word a song of bliss.
> The soul, entangled by its silken chain,
> Is led to rapture's last abandonment.
> I have felt the power of sound approaching pain:
> By turns (enslav'd by harmony) have wept,
> Have sung, have danc'd, have trembled at her feet:
> But here's the soul, the poetry of sound —
> A vivid painting hanging on each tone;
> Here joy and hope and love are all display'd
> In Liszt's piano's all-eclipsing power.[54]

The 'sudden rush of tenfold power' rescues the verse from its otherwise deserved obscurity; but, even entangled by its silken chain, it may well have propelled a fair proportion of the audience of 280 towards Liszt's first concert at Bath's Theatre Royal on Thursday evening. And Liszt himself almost certainly read and

54. *Bath and Cheltenham Gazette*, 25 August 1840.

appreciated the 'Champion' verses, for he wrote to Marie, from Bath, 'I am sending you hereafter an excellent specimen of English "puff" '.[55]

There was, however, a diversion in Bath which even Paganini might have found difficult to counter. When Lavenu and party arrived the town was *en fête*, not for Liszt, but for Isambard Kingdom Brunel who, on 1 September, was staying at the White Hart Hotel preparing for the opening of the Bath–Bristol section of his Great Western Railway.[56] He and Liszt were contemporaries who spent their creative energies in distinctly different ways. But Brunel was a polymath among whose ancillary gifts – drawing, water-colour painting, conjuring and insomnia – musical sensitivity manifested itself.[57] In 1836 he had married Mary Horsley, grand-daughter of John Callcott, MusDoc (pupil of Rauzzini), and daughter of William Horsley, leading London composer and organist, at whose house in Kensington Brunel had met Moscheles, Henri Herz and, above all, the most treasured Horsley family friend, Mendelssohn. Perhaps, then, Brunel attended Liszt's first Bath concert, accompanied by Sir John Josiah Guest, ironmaster and chairman of the great engineer's first railway project, the Taff Vale, who was also ensconced at Bath.[58] Brunel was in a state of considerable excitement: a Bristol newspaper reported that he had wagered £1000 on the notion that, when the GWR was complete, it would be possible to travel from Bristol to London in two hours.

The *Bristol Mirror*, describing the opening of the Bath–Bristol section, declared, 'we doubt not but that this great line will possess and maintain the position which of right belongs to it, that of being ... the first railway line of the empire'. The new railway received much heavier coverage, of course, than did Liszt's appearances at Bath and Bristol. The comforts awaiting passengers were especially stressed:

The carriages are admirably built; those of the first class being

55. Ollivier, op. cit., II, 22.
56. *Bath and Cheltenham Gazette*, 1 September 1840.
57. L. T. C. Rolt, *Isambard Kingdom Brunel* (London, 1970).
58. *Bath and Cheltenham Gazette*, 1 September 1840.

fitted up with an attention to comfort which royal vehicles cannot surpass. We were surprised at the luxurious ease imparted by these *somniferous* vehicles, which, we have it on good authority, contain work that coach-builders are not in the habit of putting even into gentlemen's carriages! The wants and desires of every possible description of travellers seem to have been consulted – the sociable and the retired, the valetudinarian and the robust. The second-class carriages also afford accommodation which may be sought in vain on the top of a stage-coach . . . I have spoken of the warning noise the engine makes. It is impossible to describe it. It may be likened to the loud and prolonged snort of an irritated elephant, driving in his ire a current of air impetuously through his straitened trunk.[59]

A year before, in August 1839, Liszt's chief rival had given a morning concert in the Assembly Rooms which was advertised as 'being positively Mr. Thalberg's last appearance in Bath'. He played his Grand Divertisement on Airs from Mozart's *Don Giovanni*, the Andante in D flat, some of his Etudes, and the Grand Fantasia on the Chorus of Bards from Rossini's *La donna del lago*. One of his supporting artists was the Irish baritone, later a successful composer, Michael Balfe.[60] But Thalberg's appearance seems not to have merited a critical notice in the Bath papers. A few weeks before Liszt's concert in 1840, another rival, Julius Benedict, who had been schooled in the early German Romantic manner by his teachers, Hummel and Weber, appeared in two concerts at Bath, accompanied by the operatic 'stars' Grisi and Tamburini. The local critic had agreed that Benedict's performance of a grande fantasie was 'a fine triumph of art', but, with a turn of phrase which might have reflected the public attitude to pianists in general, he added, '. . . it struck us as being too exclusively calculated for the gratification of advanced proficients in music to be fitly placed in a concert intended for the general public'. It would be profitable, thought the writer, if impresarios bore it in mind that 'all who may be expected to come are not scientific musicians, and that other requisites than the achievement of musical difficulties are necessary to please mixed

59. *Bristol Mirror*, 5 September 1840.
60. *Bath and Cheltenham Gazette*, 27 August 1839.

audiences'.[61] So much, then, for any mildly adventurous attempts to raise the level of musical taste in fashionable Bath.

For Liszt's three concerts Lavenu brought up reinforcement in the form of the flute virtuoso Joey Richardson, and his arrival delighted John Parry who always enjoyed the flautist's jokes and games. Richardson provided obbligatos for de Varny's excerpts from Donizetti and played solo fantasias of his own making. He was a frequent, almost constant, companion of Parry on his provincial tours for more than ten years.[62]

Public enthusiasm for the Bath concerts seems to have been dampened by the shower of excitement accompanying the railway opening. A newspaper critic acknowledged that they were not so well attended as might have been wished – only a total of 260 for the second and third – but he was undoubtedly impressed, borrowing for his review some of the poetic sentiment exuded by 'Champion of Chichester':

It seems to us that we have never heard pianoforte playing until Tuesday night ... He appears to deal with the piano as if it were a living and intelligent creature – sometimes persuading, sometimes chiding, sometimes urging the music forward with greater and greater rapidity, as a horseman urges a fleet and spirited steed ... The listener never once thinks of *wires*, but of liquid breathings of instruments not before heard excepting in some by-gone and beautiful vision. Sometimes Liszt pauses and toys with the keys, as if irresolute what tones of loveliness he shall next call forth, and soon there comes upon the ear a flood of the most ravishing melody – or rather luxuriant showers of notes, which makes the hearer forget instrument, player, and everything else but the most unearthly strains which dance, like *aurora boreales*, around the magician whose will has created them ... There is meaning in every note – an eloquence which finds a response in every bosom. It is impossible to imagine a more forcible development of the poetry of music.[63]

61. *Bath Chronicle*, 27 August 1840.
62. *Grove* (1927 edn).
63. *Bath Chronicle*, 3 September 1840.

Such a eulogy, coupled with Champion's paean, gives some indication of why Liszt in his prime was once called the 'Piano-Centaur' –
half superman, half piano. There is no doubt but that, in the eyes of
his contemporaries, he, above all other public artists, was the piano
personified.

The Bath critic noticed two other facets of Liszt's professional
behaviour: his delight in the act of performance, and his generosity
to his fellow-artists. He recorded that Liszt slid quietly into
Lavenu's place at the piano to accompany Parry in *The Inchcape
Bell*, 'which he did in a beautifully simple, touching, and effective
manner'. Parry described Liszt's accompaniment as being 'beautiful
– Storm and Calm !!'; and so moved was he by this repetition of the
gesture first made at Taunton, that he rushed to the shops and
bought the pianist a seal with a bell engraved upon it. Liszt played
the *Bell* at all their Bath concerts, and he also extemporized there for
the first time on this tour. His natural ebullience was returning. But
underneath this evidence of revived well-being, he seems to have
been nurturing his boredom. He wrote to Marie,

> I don't drink much coffee, and I smoke very little. In self-defence,
> I took a fancy to Porter, which will make me fat I suppose . . . My
> exterior life continues to be the most monotonous in the world.
> Everywhere I make a tremendous impression, but the receipts of
> the concerts are less than satisfactory.[64]

On Thursday 3 September the company set out on the new
Railway for their next concert in Clifton, at the Royal Gloucester
Hotel. The trains ran on the hour from 9 a.m. till 9 p.m. on
weekdays, and the first-class fare was half-a-crown.[65] Three locomotives were in service: *Fireball, Lynx* and *Arrow*, the last-named
manufactured in Bristol by Messrs John Stothart. It was advertised
that the train took only eighteen minutes to cover the twelve miles
from Bath. Parry declared the railway to be 'pretty'; and he and
Richardson had second-class seats in the open air, at one shilling
and sixpence each. Lavenu would surely have ordered covered,
first-class accommodation for the rest of the party. As a theatrical
and musical centre, Bristol was almost as volatile as London,

64. Ollivier, op. cit., II, 21.   65. *Bristol Mirror*, 22 August 1840.

though the mob in the riots of 1831 had refrained from sacking the Theatre Royal. When Paganini had appeared at the theatre the management offered tickets at the unprecedented rates of ten shillings, seven shillings and three shillings and sixpence – an increase of more than one hundred per cent over normal prices; but after the threat of a public 'demonstration', reductions had been hurriedly arranged.[66]

Before the evening concert Parry 'ran about the rocks' with de Varny at Clifton – where he might have seen the anchorages for Brunel's unfinished suspension bridge. Newspaper comment was again very favourable, and the performance was called 'a lyric feast of richest harmony'. Liszt's *Marche Hongroise* was 'like a magnificent organ producing one volume of sound'.[67] Each artist's contribution was praised in some measure. But in a town whose Madrigal Society was taking a leading role in the rediscovery of the treasures of Tudor vocal music,[68] a reservation was expressed, not for the last time during this tour: a flickering foreshadowing of the development of sound musical taste:

> . . . we may be permitted to suggest, that immediately after the extraordinary and interesting music of Liszt, which raised the feelings of his audience to the highest enthusiasm, it was not well judged to introduce the comic songs of Mr. Parry, however amusing they might be under different circumstances.[69]

The following day, by coach this time, they covered the 41 miles to the next in their sequence of spa towns. If Bath had lost its sparkle, Cheltenham was effervescent with confidence in its social position and the fitness of its new buildings, public and private. Lavenu's party put up at the George Hotel. Nearby, at the more venerable Plough in High Street, the Bishop of Bath and Wells, Sir Michael Hicks Beach and their respective families were in residence.

66. Kathleen Barker, *The Theatre Royal, Bristol, 1766–1966* (London, 1974), 106.
67. *Bristol Mirror*, 5 September 1840.
68. H. C. Colles, *The Mirror of Music, 1844–1944* (London, 1947), II, 44.
69. *Bristol Mirror*, 5 September 1840.

General Wolf (no relation) was at the Imperial. A local newspaper
registered the names of over a hundred distinguished visitors in one
of its editions.[70] Through August and September this kind of high-
toned throng was being entertained at a series of Promenade Concerts by a band of 30 players, led by Mr Butt, 'our talented towns-
man'; by Musical Galas at Pittsville, which featured Mme Rossini
(completely unrelated) and Mr Chapman on the *Corde Tendue*, and
by the aerial flight of Signor Joel Il Diavolo, as Mercury, from the
dome of the Pump Room.[71] Benedict, in two earlier concerts, had
had the temerity to play 'selections from the works of Thalberg,
Döhler, Liszt and Chopin'. The Promenade Concerts ('thronged
with company every evening this week'), at seven o'clock in the
gardens of Promenade Walk ('the Pump Room if wet'), were far-
ragos of ballet music by Adam, Strauss waltzes, and arias, trios and
quartets from Italian operas.[72]

Earlier, in the spring, Cheltenham music-lovers had received
news from the Metropolitan front. The high-spirited correspondent
of the *Cheltenham Looker-On*, a journal of tittle-tattle, one 'Tom
Crotchet', having heard of Liszt's triumphs in May at Parry's and
Mrs Toulmin's London benefit concert, made up his mind 'to slip
my ropes and run up to Town'. His physical description of Liszt in
concert is the most complete of any offered during the 1840–41
tours:

> I took my seat near the Orchestra, so that I had a full view of the
> Wizard's doings! When he entered the Orchestra, he was loudly
> applauded; his appearance wears a touch of eccentricity; his hair,
> which is very thick, is cut straight along the back of his head,
> from cheek to cheek; he is tall and very thin, with a wildness in
> his manner which bespeaks something out of the common. He sat
> down, and never did I hear such astounding effects from the
> pianoforte, different from Thalberg's performance, insomuch as
> there were so many fanciful flights; and the energy with which he
> played rapid passages in octaves with both hands was
> overwhelming.[73]

70. *Cheltenham Free Press*, 5 September 1840.
71. ibid., 15 August 1840.
72. ibid.
73. *Cheltenham Looker-On*, 1840, 847.

This whetted the appetite; the meal quickly followed:

> A scene took place towards the end of the Concert, which created a good deal of mirth. Liszt was announced in the programme to play his Chromatic *Galop* the last piece but one; and young Parry was to follow him with his Buffo Trio; but Liszt having heard much of Parry's power of imitation, etc., requested he would sing before *he* played, which he did, and was loudly encored; when Liszt took him by both hands and planted him in his chair, amidst the loudest plaudits of the whole room, and he sung his 'Singing Lesson' instead of the Trio to the delight of Liszt, who, after the conclusion, appeared to be quite elated, and he performed his *Galop* at a rail-road pace, which was loudly encored, and he played instead some Waltzes with a most extraordinary brilliancy of effect.

Two Cheltenham concerts had been arranged, the first at the old Assembly Rooms, on Friday the 25th, the second next day at the Rotunda. Neither, even after Crotchet's long-distance 'puff', was the success which Lavenu was looking for. According to the *Cheltenham Looker-On*, the Assembly Rooms concert was 'not so full as we had expected to have seen it from the high celebrity of its principal performer', though there were 250 present. Liszt had 'the happy knack of throwing a spell over everything he does', executing with supreme ease 'thirds, sixes [*sic*], octaves, tenths, nay, occasionally, twelfths'. But the critic was evidently not bewildered by sparkling brilliance, for, he recalled 'many eminent professors have been heard to say, that he is greater in the cantabile style, than in bravura'. Liszt played the *Guillaume Tell* Overture as his chosen 'recital', to great applause. But Mori, too, was given his due: the critic reported Liszt as having said that 'he never wishes to take a part in a duet with any performer in preference to his young and highly talented coadjutor'; they played an arrangement of themes from *Lucia*.[74] Parry found the first concert very long – over three hours; but this must in some part have been due to the large number of his own encores.

In his opinion the second concert next afternoon in the beautiful

74. ibid., 563.

Rotunda of Montpellier Spa (now Lloyd's Bank) was better. Liszt again accompanied him in the *Bell*, and this may have swayed his judgment. The reviewer for the *Cheltenham Free Press* admired all the performances, but noted that the audience – in fact about two hundred and twenty – was not numerous. The problem, as he saw it, was acoustical: '. . . no one ever expects to hear music to advantage in the Rotunda, and if they do, they are sure to be disappointed'.[75] Immediately after the concert Frank Mori departed for London, presumably on business. The remainder of the party promenaded through the elegantly furnished streets of the burgeoning town, played cards at their hotel – Parry lost money to Joey and Lewis – and, after toasted cheese, retired to their beds.

On Sunday they travelled towards another – though less celebrated – gem of Regency town planning, Leamington, where they stayed at The Crown. Of their journey Parry wrote, 'Shakespeare – Warwick!'; and while Liszt left no account of what was surely a loquacious luncheon at Stratford, he must have shown some enthusiasm for the birthplace of one of his literary deities. However, although his friend Berlioz was inspired to composition, and to courtship, by Shakespeare, Liszt made only one English songsetting, quite late in his career, and that was of Tennyson's *Go not, happy day*;[76] and among his orchestral programme music there is but one work on a Shakespearean theme, the symphonic poem *Hamlet*, of 1858, which Humphrey Searle considered one of the most successful pieces in that form. During the first and second tours of 1840–41 Liszt's relationship with Marie d'Agoult was slowly but quite perceptibly deteriorating. By the time he came to write *Hamlet* they had long parted; but his musical representation of the personalities of Hamlet and Ophelia might be seen as a reflection upon the radical weakness in his relationship with the countess who, in 1840, was beginning to aspire to a separate career for herself as an author. In 1858 Liszt wrote of Ophelia,

> Yes, she is loved by Hamlet; but Hamlet, like every exceptional person, imperiously demands the wine of life and will not content

75. *Cheltenham Free Press*, 12 September 1840.
76. Humphrey Searle, *The Music of Liszt* (New York, 1966), 120.

himself with the buttermilk. He wishes to be understood by her without the obligation to explain himself to her . . . She collapses under her mission, because she is incapable of loving him in the way he must be loved, and her madness is only the descrescendo of a feeling, whose lack of sureness has not allowed her to remain on the level of Hamlet.[77]

In this brief discourse Liszt may have been recollecting the tragic tensions in his own affairs which were turning him away from Marie who, in 1840, was already metamorphosing into the writer, Daniel Stern.

At Leamington on Monday afternoon, Parry the comedian reckoned, they had a 'good concert', with 108, and a sufficient number of encores. But, frantic correspondent and diarist that he was, he spilt ink in his coat pocket on the coach. Their evening concert was in unpromising Coventry and, having enjoyed the historic and literary associations of romantically ruined Kenilworth *en route*, they found a 'poor hotel' with 'rum servants', and a 'bad concert' – only 30, no encores. Next day there was a tedious drive to Northampton, though they were musically entertained by a 'Cornet à Piston' on the coach. Remarkably, Mori had dashed back by the railway from London to rejoin them, and he and Parry spent most of the journey arguing in the open air on their box seats. The Northampton concert, at The George Hotel, a commodious coaching inn near All Saints' Church, was the only one that day; but it was a very flat affair. The local newspaper simply remarked that the county families had not deigned to attend, and we have no account of what Liszt or the others performed there. To pass away a frustratingly inactive evening the artists seem to have sampled a good deal of local beer – perhaps it was the product of Phipps' brewery – and next day Parry wrote tersely, 'Ale – queer – Oh!' When they set off towards Leicester on Wednesday he added, 'Head-ache for six – conscience'. The afternoon Concert in Market Harborough was a disaster, with an audience of barely forty, none of whom had the courage to applaud; though Parry – and, no doubt, Liszt – noticed 'a pretty girl'.

77. Quoted in Searle, op. cit., 74.

The concert in Leicester was among the most important of the first tour. The town was passing through its most Radical phase, sustained by an energetic combination of lower-middle- and working-class political and economic activity.[78] Industrial Leicester – more architecturally attractive than some of the larger English commercial centres – was then taking shape and prospering; yet the town stood at the heart of a traditional, agrarian – even feudal – county. When Lavenu and party arrived it was the first day of Race Week, under the stewardship of E. Bouchier Hartop, Esquire; the place was bustling and the hotels were full of the families of gentry, clergy and yeomen. The most lucrative race was Her Majesty's Plate, for three-year-olds with a hundred-guinea prize.[79] The evening entertainment for punters was surprisingly sparse: apart from the theatre, the chief rival attraction was van Ambrugh who presented a dramatic performance, with live lions, tigers and leopards, which young Victoria had recently witnessed at the Theatre Royal, Drury Lane.

Parry's account of their Leicester concert was typically brief and titillating: 'Concert in Mechanics' Institute – Mummies, Bloody coats – Statues – Lambert's breeches!! Audience in midst.' This calls for a lengthy exegesis. The formal movement for the education of artisans had begun in the 1820s when an aristocratic and gentry group, led by Henry Brougham and Lord Lambton, took control of a new self-help institution for working men in London. With the encouragement of the Benthamite *Society for the Diffusion of Useful Knowledge*, the London model was imitated by the founding of similar Mechanics' Institutes in the provinces, where artisans might attend improving lectures on social topics and learn the scientific principles which formed the bases of their trades. Usually each institution had an assembly room and library – probably their most useful feature in the age before the Public Libraries Act of 1850.[80]

At Leicester, in August and September 1840, the Committee of

78. H. Temple Patterson, *Radical Leicester: a History of Leicester, 1780–1850* (Leicester, 1954).
79. *Leicester Chronicle*, 29 August 1840.
80. John Lawson and Harold Silver, *A Social History of Education in England* (London, 1973), 231.

the Mechanics' Institute had established an Exhibition of Paintings, Statues and Historical Artefacts by which they hoped to raise funds to pay off the debt on the recently constructed New Hall of the Institute. In this room the concert took place, amid a Victorian clutter of mummy-cases, relics of the Civil War, and the trousers of Daniel Lambert, a Leicester citizen earlier famous for his grotesque corpulence. An advertisement had appeared in the *Leicester Chronicle* at the end of August: the Committee had 'determined on providing an entertainment deserving of the high patronage under which they are permitted to announce it', and they had secured the talents of M. Liszt, 'the extraordinary pianist, whose performances have been the wonder of the Royal Concerts and the Philharmonic, during the past season'. The tickets, at the very reasonable price of five shillings each, were restricted to those who were willing to purchase in advance.[81] So Liszt was appearing at a benefit concert for a provincial education institution; but for once on their long tour the party was assured of a packed house.

The local newspaper critic emphasized that the concert was 'most numerously and fashionably attended, comprising the nobility and gentry attending the Races, and most of the principal inhabitants of the town and its neighbourhood'. Between 400 and 500 persons were comfortably seated, 'with scarcely any disarrangement of the beautiful specimens of art which adorn the Exhibition, and which, combined with the gay and elegant dresses of the ladies, formed a splendid *coup d'oeil*'. He was sure that this was the most superior concert Leicester had enjoyed 'since Paganini some years since astounded us by his wonderful vagaries on the violin'. Liszt was certainly the equal of Thalberg, he thought. The people of Leicester ought to have been grateful, for the concert 'has not only increased the funds of the Exhibition, but at the same time agreeably filled an evening in the race-week, which is generally a blank, so far as public amusements are concerned'.[82] Liszt was indeed a rare and eccentric amusement. But in Leicester one member of his audience was an equally extraordinary character for whom the eminent pianist was not merely an ephemeral feature in a passing social show.

81. *Leicester Chronicle*, 29 August 1840.
82. ibid., 12 September 1840.

William Gardiner's fascination with Liszt far exceeded the thrills
which van Ambrugh's lions excited in the middle classes.

Gardiner was a local hosiery manufacturer and Dissenter who
devoted all his intellectual energy and much of his wealth to the
pursuit of his chief passion, music. Like many of his middle-class
contemporaries, he enjoyed Handel's music; but he became extraordinary because he was probably the first Englishman to idolize
Beethoven. Indeed, as Jack Simmons has recently pointed out, as
early as 1794, in Leicester, Gardiner had organized and taken part
in positively the first performance in England of a Beethoven composition, the Piano Trio op. 1 no. 1. For the rest of his life he
publicized all the Master's works except for the late quartets, which,
like many other music-lovers of the time, he claimed not to understand. In 1848 he was to travel to Bonn to attend the unveiling of
Beethoven's statue which had been paid for largely from the profits
of Liszt's recital tours. Gardiner had heard Paganini in London as
well as Leicester, and in 1840 this extraordinary English votary of
great music was present to hear Liszt play.[83]

The *Leicester Chronicle* sensibly – and for us, fortunately – allowed
Gardiner room to comment on Liszt's performance in detail:

> The performance of Liszt on the piano is truly astonishing. He
> attempts not to win your attention by captivating passages or
> pretty melodies: he begins incoherently, without any apparent
> design, as if a child dashed its hands upon the keys. Presently, a
> degree of arrangement ensues, promising something like intelli-
> gent music, when, at once, he overpowers you, by a flash of the
> most exquisite and luminous tone.

It is clear that Gardiner disapproved of Liszt's duetting with Frank
Mori:

> This Artiste should never be coupled with another performer
> upon the same instrument. His imagination has not enough room
> to play. He requires the whole range to himself. Like Beethoven,
> he describes the grand evolutions of nature by the power of

83. Jack Simons, *Leicester: the Ancient Borough to 1860* (Gloucester, 1980), 178.

sound. He can raise a storm about him, which he finds in the *hurly-burly* of the instrument, so frightful, that he is obscured and lost; but as it dies away, he reappears through a mist decked in the most radiant colours. The rapidity with which he showered down a succession of minor thirds, through all the semi-tones, from the top of the instrument to the bottom – resembled the fall of a cataract into an abyss – producing whirls of thunder, on the lowest depths of the scale. This stroke of sublimity was strikingly shown in the elevated aspect of his countenance.[84]

It has to be admitted that, if Liszt spoke to Gardiner at Leicester, he would probably have found the encounter less memorable than the experience of having played for an audience studded with members of the nobility and gentry. The Duke of Rutland and Sir John Manners were present, with Earl Howe, Baronets Palmer, Hazelrigg, Fowke and Heygate, and the county and borough MPs, and their assorted ladies. And they all dallied in the New Hall until midnight. Liszt's already massive ego blossomed in such assemblies, and his desire to become an aristocrat, or at least to become ennobled, marked a weakness in his nature of which Marie d'Agoult was ironically aware. He could express disgust at the manners of the aristocracy on one occasion, and on another fawn upon noblemen like any *petit-bourgeois* tradesman. He came nearest to gaining a pedigree in his native Hungary; but it may seem strange that the presentation to him of the 'Sword of Honour' in January 1840 by the Hungarian nobility[85] meant much more than the sum total of all the reports of his playing – like those at Taunton and Leicester – which ranked him in the aristocracy of genius.

The next few days of the tour must have seemed an anti-climax. On Thursday morning they travelled by the railway to Derby. At the station Parry was 'diddled out of twelve shillings'. Perhaps after celebrating – too well – the artistic and financial triumph at Leicester, Lewis Lavenu was temporarily indisposed, and Parry had to accompany the ladies' songs at the afternoon concert. Only 80 came, and then there was a row at The King's Head about two horses. Eventually four beasts were brought from The Bell, and

84. *Leicester Chronicle*, 12 September 1840.
85. Walker, op. cit., 327.

they proceeded to the evening concert in Nottingham where they were greeted by a 'stupid audience'. For their morning concert in Mansfield on Friday Liszt was again 'very ill indeed'. But he had to please only 30 customers. Parry thought that the concert was 'Horrible work – a Bagatelle!'; though he did make a favourable comment on their journey: 'Went to Newstead Abbey (Lord Byron) on our way to Mansfield – beautiful spot – very hot.'

Liszt may have been feeling very poorly, but he insisted on the chance of meeting the ghost of Byron. In London he had already sat at the table of Lady Blessington who, as a young woman, had faithfully recorded her daily conversations with Byron in Genoa. Now, in a late English summer, the ill-assorted party of entertainers paused for the pianist to relax in surroundings which must surely have had a powerful effect upon his fervid imagination. Writing a few days later from Peterborough, he told Marie:

> At Newstead I lay in the grass under a huge sun; a flock of crows cawed overhead. Then I went into the apartments. I was shown the cup which Lord Byron had fashioned from a monk's skull, and his hound's grave. As I moved outside, the moaning of the forest pines awakened the harmonies of my soul, and I sang and mused quietly amid the sounds of nature. One day I shall write about it all. I know not whether it was the expansion of my spirit, or indeed the sun and the warmth of the turf on which I lay outstretched for so long, but, in a word, the fever seized me again an hour afterwards. Quinine was ordered for me, morning and evening. From the very next day I felt better. But I bided my time so that I would be completely recovered for writing to you. One of my companions also made me consider that I had been most imprudent in leaving my flannel in London.[86]

By this time Liszt was yearning more than ever for the companionship of friends who understood and respected him. He wrote to Franz von Schober in Germany that he had just renewed 'an unfortunate engagement' which would effectively keep him in England until the end of January. He wanted to invite von Schober to accompany him on that second leg of the British tour, but

86. Ollivier, op. cit., II, 26–7.

England is not like any other other country; the expenses are enormous. I really dare not ask you to travel with me here, for it would almost ruin us. Moreover, we would hardly have time to be together, for I have three or four *compulsory* companions, from whom it is impossible for me to separate.[87]

To Marie, on the other hand, he communicated some of the benefits of tedium:

One of the good aspects of this artistic tournament is leisure for reading. Between each set of pieces at a concert I read a dozen pages; the same in the carriage. I got through my huge Villemain volume in under five days.[88]

Liszt had told von Schober that he was thinking of spending the following winter at Constantinople. His experience in England had made him tired of the West:

I want to breath perfumes, to bask in the sun, to exchange the smoke of coal for the sweet smoke of the nargileh. In short, I am pining for the East! O my morning land![89]

Yet to Marie he expressed a longing for the warmth of Italy, perhaps inspired by his communion with the soul of Byron; he recalled earlier Italian journeys with her:

What are we going to do in Italy? Florence, Venice, Rome, Naples! On this tour I am seized by an extreme longing for Italy, which I know you have felt for the past four years.[90]

For the moment, however, the ailing pianist had to labour through the Friday evening concert in Newark. On the way there, Parry's spirits had been raised by the sight of 'the most wonderful Rainbow – Two Rainbows! Bright as Gold.' But at the concert

87. La Mara, ed.: *Letters of Franz Liszt* (London, 1894), I, 46.
88. Ollivier, op. cit., II, 23.   90. Ollivier, op. cit., II, 27.
89. La Mara, op. cit., I, 47.

there was a 'Stupid audience! Horrid!' At Lincoln, after a 'lovely ride', they toiled up to their hotel at the top of the old town. The little closed community of clergy wives, fertilized by a sprinkling of gentry ladies, cannot often have seen a phenomenon such as Liszt. Perhaps prior news of his illness induced diffidence, for, despite its being the only concert they gave that day, a mere 80 turned up, and Lavenu, as in Winchester and Weymouth, made a speech of apology for Liszt beforehand. The heavily liturgical surroundings of their weekend visit may have suggested to Liszt that some gravity was needed in order to balance the customary flashiness of his *Morceaux Choisis*: he included for the first time on the provincial part of the tour Handel's Fugue in E minor. For the rest, Parry simply recorded: ' "Governess" flat. Bah! Cathedral. Great Tom! Moonlight.' It seems unlikely that, given his fragile condition, Liszt would have clambered the 347 steps to Great Tom with Parry and Joey Richardson; but perhaps the quinine inspired a parallel ascent of a spiritual kind. In any case, Liszt invariably took notice of the treasury of English ecclesiastical architecture whenever he encountered specimens from it. Earlier in the tour he had favoured Marie with descriptions accompanied by philosophical reflections:

> The cathedrals at Chichester, Winchester and Salisbury are remarkable. At Salisbury I went to sun myself among the tombs which surround the cathedral.[91]

And he added later that Chichester, Salisbury and Exeter were 'beautiful':

> They are completely surrounded by magnificent trees and large open spaces. In France, when we have a handsome monument, we are constrained to smother it under a pile of workshops, pokey little houses and vile masonry. Witness Notre Dame, the cathedrals of Lyons, Metz, and so on. Here, the majesty of the building is respected. Its grandeur preserves it from vulgar interference. I have several times compared the finest monuments of France and Italy, surrounded by wretched shops which back on to them, to the great men of every age, of every country, always

91. ibid., 15.

encumbered, harassed and exploited by the most infamous riff-
raff who are guided by the vilest motives.[92]

Perhaps, in his current circumstances, Liszt was thinking as much of
Lavenu, Parry and Mlle de Varny, as of the corrupt politicians of
Louis Philippe's France.

Prim Lincoln, or rather those who lived within the bail on the
medieval hill, took little notice of Liszt and his enthusiasm for
cathedral cities. Even the local newspapers virtually ignored him,
and gave space instead to news that the Lincoln Harmonic Society,
six days after his appearance, had held 'a very numerous and convivial meeting at the Plough Inn' to celebrate 'the opening of a very
fine-toned new pianoforte, which had been purchased for the
Society'.[93] Presumably the instrument was *not* an Erard. Lincolnshire indifference triumphed even over a splendid 'puff' for the
pianist in the *Lincoln, Rutland and Stamford Mercury*, on Friday 4
September. This was a very long extract, chosen perhaps by
Lavenu, from an article in the *Musical World*:

> The power which Liszt possesses of *dividing* himself, as it were,
> into two, or sometimes even three performers: the feathery deli-
> cacy of his touch, at one moment, and its enormous forte at
> another . . . In that kind of sleight of hand which addresses itself
> to the ear, we think he even transcends Thalberg . . . in seeming
> defiance of the restrictions of nature.[94]

Yet his concert at Lincoln captured 'only a very thin audience',
and the newspaper critic castigated local folk for their 'cold reception'.[95] On Sunday afternoon they travelled eastwards into the
Wolds to Horncastle. Around the Early English greenstone of St
Mary's Church, the little town was in a confident phase.[96] It was the
week of the great Horse Fair which then rivalled even that of

92. Ollivier, loc. cit.
93. *Lincolnshire Chronicle and General Advertiser*, 25 September 1840.
94. Quoted in *Lincoln, Rutland and Stamford Mercury*, 4 September 1840.
95. ibid., 18 September 1840.
96. Nikolaus Pevsner and John Harris, *The Buildings of England: Lincolnshire*
(London, 1964), 276–7.

Northampton. At the inn on the Market Square Parry noted 'painted passages' and 'sham Chambermaids'. Lavenu, recovered from a brief indisposition, went fishing at seven o'clock in the morning (though Parry may herein have been encoding more scandalous information). The midday concert, before 65 'funny people' in the Assembly Rooms, at least produced some encores. But the image of Liszt, on a morning stroll, elbowing his way through a milling crowd of wily horse-dealers, tawdry prostitutes and drunken farmers in Horncastle is indelibly fascinating. What did they all make of the tall, slender, exotically dressed figure, with his dreamy manner and flowing fair hair?

They galloped 34 miles to Boston for the evening concert through very wet, cold weather. The Peacock and Royal was pleasant – recent Georgian, and the epitome of a good market inn – with a most accommodating 'Boots'; and the Assembly Rooms, by Parry's estimate, a 'fine hall', with long windows illuminating a large space. But the 60 'stupid (asses) the people in the room' accorded them 'No encores – no laughter – no nuffin !!' They stayed overnight. Parry broke the boot-seat door as they boarded the coach at half-past nine on Tuesday for the long pull to Grantham. There they played a morning concert to great applause from a decent audience of 110 – Parry was encored twice – in the Town Hall. Unusually there was no evening concert that day.

This unwonted pause for recuperation afforded Liszt an opportunity for reflecting on the tour's progress. Even in the West Country, after the first week, he had begun to doubt Lavenu's ability as an impresario; by the time they reached East Anglia he was convinced that his young English manager had bungled the strategy of their venture. Liszt knew that he was enjoying a great critical success. 'The public and the English newspapers are unanimous in their eulogies of me,' he had written to Marie from Bath. 'I have the honour of being encored everywhere'; and he continued ironically, and in English, 'and all the people are very much pleased'. But 'receipts are invariably mediocre'. He was not making the fortune he had expected – or rather, Lavenu was not making the profits he had anticipated: '. . . there are twenty reasons for this; but next year will be superb, everyone tells me. This is a country on its own, as I have often told you: nothing to prove, nothing more to achieve.'[97] There was, however, one particular reason, among others, for the low receipts.

In the eastern counties Lavenu's party was again upstaged by the same groups of rival performers which had taunted them on the western wing of their tour. At Bath, early in September, Liszt had outlined the problem:

> Unhappily we are now subject to two coincidences, Grisi and Tamburini on one side, Persiani and Rubini on the other, who injure Lavenu – who is, besides, still unknown to the public as an impresario, which makes a big difference to the success of the enterprise.[98]

At their earlier venues, as far as Northampton, Lavenu's performers had been pursued by the vocal 'stars', aided by the horn virtuoso Puzzi. In eastern England they were again caught in the Italian pincers. Grisi's and Tamburini's advertisements in local papers were larger and more glamorous; tickets for their concerts were more expensive; with a financial acumen based upon the conventional greed of all operatic artists, they managed their tours themselves as customary profitable speculations in the lull between European operatic seasons. Persiani never ventured into the snakepit called Horncastle. But at Newark, she, Rubini and Puzzi gave a well advertised concert three days after Liszt's; at Stamford they sang and played the day before he appeared, and in Peterborough only two days afterwards. And so it went on.[99] Of course, Lavenu's party had vocalists too; but Mlle de Varny and the inexperienced Miss Bassano could not possibly compete with the Sutherland and the Caballé of their day: English provincial audiences believed all that they read in the national press of Persiani's triumphs in London, Paris, Milan and Naples; and by 1840 they had become used to attending the autumn concerts of the touring Italians. Persiani and Grisi separately do not appear to have been any more successful than Lavenu's artists – certainly not in size of audiences – but their

97. Ollivier, op. cit., II, 22.
98. ibid.
99. e.g. *Norwich Mercury*, 4 July 1840.

almost continual proximity was a grating descant to Liszt's progress through southern England.

Stamford, a town of perfect eighteenth-century style, was in its architectural heyday when Liszt played there on 16 September.[100] It was still one of the great coaching centres: the railway was not to arrive till 1848. The Corn Exchange, built as recently as 1839, to the design of a local clergyman, represented the continuing opulence of Stamford's agrarian prosperity. The large hall of the Assembly Rooms, where the party performed, was early Georgian. Parry and Mori seem to have had some fun beforehand: they busked a 'Grand March' with Parry accompanying the other on the drums. The dinner at the inn was 'bad', with 'marmalade'. And the concert was chiefly memorable for the squealing of pigs outside during the ladies' singing. At the Peterborough concert in the evening the audience was small – only 60; but so was the room where they played. An old gentleman, perhaps a clergyman, sitting in the front row, made Parry laugh so much that he could not sing. But all 60 'roared' at *Musical Husband*. Everyone had a good tea, and they spent the dark hours after the concert at whist and écarté. 'Joey,' said Parry, 'read me to sleep.'

Next morning they 'Left at $\frac{1}{2}$10 after having to see the Cathedral', according to Parry. Liszt evidently persisted in his cathedral-crawling. At Huntingdon they gave a morning concert. Parry thought the audience 'very stupid ... no encores'. The local newspaper commented that Lavenu's concert was attended 'by many of the families of the county'; but it appears that the artists had begun to gossip about the failure of the tour so far, for the reviewer added, 'we fear that the company (about 90) was not sufficiently numerous to repay the conductor the expenses he must have sustained'.[101] After dinner they left for Cambridge and put up at Hoo's Hotel. There were only a hundred at the concert, but, although Parry described it as being 'so, so', he was encored twice, 'tremendously', and so was Liszt.

100. Nikolaus Pevsner and John Harris, *The Buildings of England: Lincolnshire* (London, 1964), 656 ff.
101. *Cambridge Chronicle*, 19 September 1840.

On Saturday morning they left Cambridge at eight, for, extra-
ordinarily, there were to be two concerts that same day in Bury St
Edmunds. The weather was fine and, interrupting their journey
across the cantering heath, they breakfasted in Newmarket. Bury
was famous for its delightful theatre; but the town also continuously
attracted at this time the best of English and European vocal performers. Lablache, for instance, was a regular visitor to the concert
room, presenting arias from *Le nozze di Figaro* and Rossini's *Otello*
and *Barbiere*; Frank Mori's father had usually led the band
accompanying the performances, supported by leading English
players like Lindley and Richardson, and the singers Miss Birch and
Miss Fanny Wyndham. Thalberg's cool brilliance had impressed the
town and neighbourhood.[102]

The local critic on this occasion in 1840 devoted a single review
to the two concerts. Thalberg notwithstanding, he awarded to Liszt
the title of 'the first pianoforte player in the world'. But such
judgments were probably more the product of word-juggling and
lexicographical pin-sticking than of sensitive, reflective listening.
The review, in the *Bury and Norwich Post*, bears the imprint of the
writer's having read superficially in the London musical journals:
his comment on Liszt's 'wonderful combinations and *divisions of
himself* ' comes rather too close to the Lincoln 'puff' from the *Musical
World*. Even today we know how the judgment of well-oiled critics
can be influenced by post-concert largesse, verbal as well as alco-
holic. Yet the closeness of Bury to a current change in metropolitan
musical taste was expressed in the reviewer's comment on Parry's
comic songs: '. . . the public have grown rather tired of these performances in a concert room'. Perhaps the contrast between Parry's
humour and the other items in the programme had been heightened
by Liszt's again accompanying *The Inchcape Bell*, the only 'serious'
piece in Parry's vocal repertoire on this tour. In the newspaper it
was noted that 'the attendance in the morning concert was very
fashionable and numerous [180]; in the evening it was scanty
[80]'.[103]

Parry mentioned that he was in 'bad voice' for the *Governess*; the

102. *Bury and Norwich Post*, 23 September 1840.
103. *Norwich Mercury*, 26 September 1840.

local critic commented on his 'hoarseness', which might almost have been expected by this point in their rigorous itinerary. He had again encountered a 'stupid audience', with no encores. Between concerts they had a good dinner, during which there was 'a great row in French', presumably between Liszt and de Varny. Joey Richardson had been encored at the second concert; then he rushed off to London by the mail. Lewis lost some money at écarté ('silly fellow!').

After breakfast on Sunday morning they left for Norwich. There was 'a great mob' to see them start; then a fight on the road with a sheep-driver; Parry summarized: 'great brute – bloody noses', so the encounter cannot have been a sham affair, and the passengers in their grandstand coach must surely have treated the event as an unscheduled delight enlivening a flat, bumpy journey. They arrived at 5 p.m., had dinner, and, after their exhausting 53-mile haul, went to bed at the unaccustomed hour of nine o'clock. 'Rushlight! Letters!' wrote Parry. Equally remarkably, he was up next morning by half-past eight, and he spent the early hours studying two new songs, perhaps purchased at Messrs Fish and Trowlett's music shop, *The Younger Son* and *I never believe what I hear*. There were to be two concerts that day, one at the Assembly Rooms in the afternoon, the other in St Andrew's Hall at eight o'clock.

Norwich was a city of considerable musical pretensions, and of substantial recent achievement. The great triennial Musical Festival was its cultural jewel, though the sparkle produced since its inauguration in 1770 had been fitful. The last meeting had taken place in 1839, and had included the premiere of Louis Spohr's *Calvary*, as well as 'an oratorio founded upon the Requiem of Mozart', and selections from the works of Gibbons, Purcell, Haydn and Beethoven. Among the singers were Persiani, Tamburini and Balfe. The comments on each of the vocalists in the local newspaper were expansive and polished, reflections of a highly developed individual taste. Writing of Persiani the critic asked why her reputation stood below those of the 'supreme singers' like Grisi and Malibran. His answer was that her force was sometimes too dramatic, leading her into coarseness of delivery 'incompatible with refined polish'. Those qualities – refinement and polish – were, it seems, what the most knowledgeable provincial critics expected of the best artists, whether singers or instrumentalists.[104] The provincial public, too, apparently wished to remain undisturbed by passion and drama in concert performances, and despite the excitement which he aroused everywhere in England, Liszt was probably treated as a temporarily acceptable manifestation of the exotic, before audiences settled back to enjoy once again the cool finish of players like Thalberg, Moscheles, and the successful ladies, Mrs Anderson and Mme Dulcken. For the moment, however, at Norwich in September 1840, the 'coarseness' of Mme Persiani provided competition for M. Liszt. On the very day when the pianist played two concerts in Norwich, Messrs Howlett and Trory, owners of a music warehouse in the city, were staging a Persiani concert in neighbouring Great Yarmouth.[105]

Liszt's Norwich concerts were nevertheless reasonably well attended: 130 in the morning, and 200 in St Andrew's Hall, the traditional venue for Festival concerts. The morning event was typical of the tour so far: a very fashionable audience had come as much to admire itself as to hear Liszt. But the evening concert broke new ground. At Leicester the Mechanics' Institute concert had devoted its proceeds to the promotion of the adult education movement for working men. In Norwich the local critic identified the St Andrew's Hall concert as a new kind of musical occasion; there was only one price for tickets, and they were much cheaper than was customary, in the hope that members of the lower middle class, even artisans, might be attracted to attend.

This socially innovatory kind of concert was acknowledged enthusiastically by the critic of the *Norwich Mercury* in his account of Persiani's concert:

> Ten years ago, had it been said, that two of the finest Italian singers in the world – the finest horn player in existence – and a third singer of character, could be brought down to Norwich, and a concert given, with a band, in St Andrew's Hall, for the admission of three shillings and sixpence, it would have been represented as impossible or a ruinous speculation.

104. ibid., 21 September 1840.
105. ibid., 4 July 1840.

But he stressed the social and moral implications of the new venture:

> It is of immense importance to *morals*, as well as to happiness, that the *general mind* should be trained to intellectual pleasures. Temperance and anti-intemperance societies may do much in one direction, but the wise institutions see also the advantage of blending amusements of one kind with forebearance from sensual pleasure of another sort, which they purpose to extinguish ... Therefore, we rejoice to find the principle of extending such entertainments *to the many* at a cheap, instead of indulging them to *a few* at a dear rate, established. We hope it will diffuse itself in many other directions.[106]

The Mechanics' Institute at Leicester provides one clue for tracing the roots of a social and educational movement to which the Norwich critic was drawing attention. The *Society for the Diffusion of Useful Knowledge* since the 1820s had sought to spread proper cultural appreciation among the masses – or at least among the aristocracy of labouring men – using the new institutes as their chief agencies of dissemination. The Education Committee of the Privy Council was established in 1839, with the aim of advancing the cause of popular education in the elementary schools and in evening classes; and its first Secretary, James Kay-Shuttleworth, counted among his priorities the policy of using the soothing powers of musical education to quieten the children of the masses during the period of Chartist political agitation.[107] Around 1840, the possible alliance of musical with social harmony was therefore seen by some as a matter of public policy; and in Norwich the conjunction was represented in private musical enterprise, as well as in publicly sponsored educational practice.

Writing of Liszt's and Persiani's concerts – those given at a cheaper rate in St Andrew's Hall – the newspaper critic returned to his social theme, the democratization of musical performance. He had recently been reading, he said, some lectures given by Dr

106. ibid., 19 September 1840.
107. Bernarr Rainbow, *The Land Without Music: Musical Education in England, 1800–1860* (London, 1967), 43 ff.

Channing to apprentices at a mechanics' institute, in which he had noted especially the following sentiment:

> In this meeting I see, what I most desire to see, that the masses of the people are beginning to comprehend themselves and their true happiness; that they are catching glimpses of the great work and vocation of human beings, and are rising to their true place in the social state.[108]

The Norwich critic considered that the Liszt and Persiani concerts were evidence of Dr Channing's principle at work, for representatives of 'all grades of society' had been present in St Andrew's Hall.

The groundwork for such a broad public response in Norwich had been prepared assiduously in previous years by a dynamic local figure, whose place in the history of British musical education has never been properly recognized. Born in 1786, Sarah Glover was the eldest daughter of a Norwich rector, and had received her earliest musical training from the cathedral organist, Dr Beckwith. In her twenties she took charge of the music at her father's church, and the quality of the children's 2-part singing helped to attract large congregations. She did not overestimate her own musical abilities, but saw herself simply as an evangelizing teacher; by training other teachers she became the centre of a network of musical enthusiasts and practitioners in the elementary schools of Norwich and its neighbourhood. Her aim was simply to improve standards of congregational singing; but in the process, through her version of sol-fa teaching, she considerably enlarged opportunities for the labouring classes to gain access to music of the most elevated kind. In an important sense, therefore, the audience for Liszt, and the later audiences at Norwich triennial concerts, were partly her creations.[109]

Probably Liszt never met Sarah Glover; but since she was an accomplished pianist, it is possible that she attended one of his concerts, though the substance of what he played was hardly to her liturgical taste. Liszt had, in the recent past, shown more than a

108. *Norwich Mercury*, 26 September 1840.
109. Rainbow, op. cit., 52.

lightweight interest in music-making among the masses. Bernarr Rainbow, in his study of music education in this period, has described the pioneering work of the German vocal teacher, Joseph Mainzer, among the Paris workers in the 1830s. The critic Henry Chorley's account of Mainzer's singing classes and societies in the poorer suburbs of Paris was published in the *Athenaeum*: such was Mainzer's success that the classes began to attract fashionable and musical visitors, among them George Sand, Lamartine, Meyerbeer, Berlioz and Liszt, who had already identified himself with working-class political movements, particularly on the occasion of a Socialist revolt in Lyons in 1835, when he interrupted his journey to Italy to play concerts in the beleaguered city, subsequently writing *Lyon*, a turbulent piece of piano music.[110]

However, the lower-middle-class menfolk of Norwich had other pleasures at a distance to contemplate and these were more crudely appealing than the attractions of the greatest living pianist and a handful of Italian vocal 'stars'. A local newspaper, during Liszt's passage through East Anglia, was advertising intemperate competition for Norwich travellers to and from London:

A.H.L.T.H.

To the Lovers of Harmony
The Best Room
The Best Spirits, etc., etc.,
The Best Singing
The Best Company, and
The Best Attention

Are all to be met every Evening, at a quarter before Nine, at Beck's (late of West Lexham, Norfolk), the Doctor Johnson's Tavern, Hotel, Chop and Steak House, Bolt-court, opposite the Bolt-in-Tun Coach-office, Fleet-street – Gentlemen supplied with Beds at all Hours – Ring the Bell![111]

The well-informed Norwich critic attacked the Italian singers for their 'insolence' to the audience in not singing even one recitative in a long programme of arias. Liszt's concerts, he said, were not 'fully

---

110. Ronald Taylor, op. cit., 116.
111. *Norwich Mercury*, 19 September 1840.

attended', and, risking the displeasure of those who were not among the 130 members of county families present at the morning concert, he suggested that 'pianoforte-playing is not sufficiently understood or appreciated by the public to make the performance of even so great a man attractive, except to the few'. Remarkably, he provided as preliminary, a thumbnail sketch of Liszt's early career, including his first visit to Britain in 1824; and he compared the juvenile performer of the 1820s with the nine-years-old George Aspull who, having played once at Norwich, had then 'sunk into the early grave prepared for him by over-excitement acting on a susceptible organization'. Liszt, however, had 'weathered the storm' of a prodigy's life and embarked upon a mature career. His tone was inferior to Thalberg's, but this was of little account; the latter's technique was 'adapted to the end of making the most of the INSTRUMENT ... but Liszt's object is to make the instrument do all it can for HIM ... he appears totally to forget the vehicle through which he is giving utterance to his unusual conceptions, and the natural impulse is to wish he had an instrument better fitted to do him justice'; it was surprising that he was able 'to force wire and wood to the performance of such wonders'. He was not one of those 'mannerist' players whose success depended upon one technical device: 'he has at his command every possible means by which effect has ever been or (we should think) ever can be produced'. But this marvellously perceptive moralist detected a psychological weakness: 'a little less love for common admiration would enable him to rise to far truer greatness – and we look forward to the time when a more certain judgement shall ensure a consummation devoutly to be wished, both for the sake of himself and his hearers'.[112]

For the rest, it was thought that Parry was at his best as a mime, rather than as a serious performer. Yet even here a note of censoriousness was sounded: a song which, to be sure, Parry treated as a frothy, amusing ditty, was discovered as a true satire on contemporary mores. And so it was:

A Governess wanted, well suited to fill
The post of tuition with competent skill,

112. ibid., 26 September 1840.

In a Gentleman's family highly genteel,
Where 'tis hoped that the Lady will try to conceal
Any fanciful feelings or flights she may feel,
For this Gentleman's family's so *very* genteel . . .
Superior attainments are quite indispensible,
With ev'rything too that's correct and ostensible,
Morals of pure unexceptionability;
Manners well formed, and of strictest gentility!
The pupils are five, ages six to sixteen,
All promising girls, as ever were seen:
And besides (tho' 'tis scarcely worthwhile to put *that* in)
There are two little boys, but they only learn *Latin*! . . .
The Lady must teach all the several branches,
Where into polite education now launches;
She's expected to speak the FRENCH tongue like a native,
And be to her pupils in all its points dative;
ITALIAN she must know (of course) nor needs banish
Whatever acquaintance she may have with SPANISH!
Nor would there be harm in a trifle of GERMAN,
In the absence (that is) of the master, Herr Hermann . . .
As the Salary's very MODERATE none need apply
Who more on THAT point than on COMFORT rely!
But perhaps 'twere as well, to make matters shorter,
To mention the terms, namely Five Pounds a Quarter . . .

The Norwich critic certainly believed that such pedagogical ver-satility should be properly rewarded. George Dubourg's words, set to Parry's music, 'touched upon the cupidity that but too often expects every accomplishment aided by every virtue under the sun, and surmounted moreover by the utmost stoical forbearance, all for a miserly £5 a quarter'.[113] The tone of the musical comments on Lavenu's party in Norwich even found an echo in the streets of the city, for, on their way to perform at the morning concert, Liszt and his companions passed a Temperance procession.

Tuesday 22 September was a 'shocking wet day'. After thirteen miles of their journey to Ipswich they breakfasted at Scoles' Inn near Diss, one of the great coaching houses of eastern England, with its remarkable heraldic sign suspended from a massive wooden gantry

113. ibid.

across the main road. Ipswich at this time was a town of character
rather than of Victorian gentility, and was being roused from its
eighteenth-century somnolence partly by Robert Ransome's local
innovations in agricultural technology. It was a political town;
Chartism and even Owenism were abroad in the streets when Liszt
came.[114] A few years earlier Dickens had stayed at the Great White
Horse to report on a local election for the *Morning Chronicle*. He
liked the town – it figured prominently in *Pickwick Papers* – but his
depiction of the hotel caused the landlord to contemplate suing him
for libel. Since there was also a garrison, prostitution was one of the
leading local service industries. In a missionaries' report in the early
1840s it was written that there were 'fifty-two houses of ill-fame in
Ipswich. Some of these are brothels of a first-class description; the
furniture and general appearance showing that means have not been
spared to render them in the highest degree attractive to the licen-
tiously disposed.'[115] Ipswich was also the place in which David
Garrick had begun his professional career.

The downpour continued before and during their evening concert
at the theatre in Ipswich, but it hardly dampened the enthusiasm of a
large audience. 'The only disappointments', reported a local
newspaper, 'were felt by those whom the rainy weather, or their
own apathy, hindered from being present.' Liszt again accompanied
Parry delightfully in *The Inchcape Bell*. His coming had been
heralded in an elaborate 'puff' studded with quotations, not just
from *The Times* and the *Musical World*, but also from the *Morning
Herald*, whose London reviewer had avowed: 'He may be compared
to the rarest of beings, a reader of superlative feeling and good
taste, by whom the poetic masterpieces of literature may be *recited*
with all the truth of meaning and touching eloquence of original
conception'.[116] This was the nearest approach yet made to solving
the difficult problem of how to explain that new phrase, 'Piano
Recital'.

114. John Burke, *Suffolk* (London, 1971), 187.
115. John Glyde, *The Moral, Social and Religious Condition of Ipswich in the Middle of
the Nineteenth Century* (Ipswich, 1850), 56. Glyde was a former Chartist and
Owenite.
116. *Ipswich Journal*, 19 September 1840.

The wild applause which greeted Liszt there suggests that Ipswich was a little in advance of Norwich in its appreciation of piano-players: '. . . many here will be almost ashamed hereafter of their own performances on their favourite instrument'.[117] Or was it, perhaps, that the theatricality of his platform manner, in their theatre, excited the crowd? Another local critic noted that,

> at the conclusion of his last performance, an elderly gentleman who sat in a stall at the side of the stage, in the heat of his excitement, rose, and catching a firm hold of the skirt of the performer's coat, pulled him back, in order that he might have the gratification of shaking him by the hand.

The Wizard was evidently on top form in Ipswich, for poor Miss Bassano was described as being 'as effective as under the circumstances she could be, the *genius loci* being the superlative Liszt'.[118]

At this successful Ipswich concert, Liszt also played three 'songs' on the piano, and Parry expressed surprise that such material was encored. Perhaps these were selected from among the Schubert lieder transcriptions which he had been making, sporadically, since 1835; he might also have included his piano version of Mendelssohn's *On Wings of Song* which he probably put on paper during this English tour. It has been implied that Liszt never used his great public appeal to popularize good 'new' music as energetically as he ought to have done: this is certainly a view which has recently been advanced by, for instance, Wilson Lyle in his *Dictionary of Pianists*.[119] The slender evidence available about his repertoire on this tour would seem to confirm that judgment. But, given the context of his provincial performances – the patter-songs of Parry, the flute fantasias by Richardson and the Italian flourishes of de Varny, which made up the bulk of Lavenu's programmes – there were few appropriate opportunities for systematically extending the range of his audiences' musical experience. In any case, despite the prior publication of what he might include among his *Morceaux Choisis*,

---

117. ibid., 26 September 1840.
118. *Suffolk Chronicle*, 26 September 1840.
119. Wilson Lyle, ed.: *A Dictionary of Pianists* (London, 1985).

we have no precise knowledge of what he may have included among his spontaneous encores in England – Chopin, Schumann, Mendelssohn, Beethoven? The probable performance of Schubert in transcription at Ipswich may be seen as both an act of considerable aesthetic daring, and an instance of his throwing off the constraints imposed by Lavenu's régime. Before an audience of three hundred, near the end of a long tour, he may have felt that he had nothing to lose, financially or artistically, by including works which his audience might not have expected to hear.

On Wednesday 23 they were up by eight and, having breakfasted on potted shrimps, they trotted the 18 miles to Colchester. It was a 'capital concert', for Lavenu made nearly £40. Next morning Parry bought books for himself and a five-guinea shawl for his wife. Evidently he thought that his stipend from the tour was assured. The concert at Chelmsford on the 24th was a dull disaster – only 45 came. Then they sped through London, without halting overnight, to play two final engagements in Brighton, which almost perfectly completed the circle of their long journey of 1167 miles in six weeks, since the beginning in Chichester. On the way south Parry sat outside on the box, and the weather continued dreadfully wet. They supped at Croydon. The first Brighton concert, on Friday the 25th, provided some recompense for the dismal coach-ride: about four hundred people attended.

Brighton's location south of the chalk Downs had posed very serious problems for railway engineers, and this helps to account for the surprise of finding that Lavenu and party had to travel by coach from London. Brighton did have a railway station in 1840, but this merely provided a connection with Shoreham to the west; the through-line, via Hayward's Heath, did not open till the summer of 1841, and even then, a stage coach service operated to link two sections of the route.[120] Despite these difficulties of access, or perhaps partly because of them, Brighton was a magnet for the confident, fashionable upper classes; the Pavilion and the opulent terraces, the sea-bathing and the ozone had already guaranteed its reputation as an exclusive seaside town. Liszt arrived at the very last moment of social exclusiveness: after the advent of the London

120. Cecile Woodford, *Portrait of Sussex* (London, 1972), 153.e.

railway the place quickly became a resort for the metropolitan lower-middle classes. In 1840, then, Brighton had not yet reached its bourgeois nadir.

Lavenu's two concerts comprised climax and bathos. The Brighton 'room' was stuffed with polite people, but the tour as a whole now had to be reckoned a dreadful financial failure. Parry noted, but did not describe, a heated business argument among Liszt, Lavenu and Frank Mori. They might have been discussing the fact that the two young entrepreneurs had made no profit from Liszt's exciting reputation. The pianist was beginning to understand what a thrillingly marketable quantity he was, even in temperate England; and he surely realized how ineptly Lavenu had tried to prepare the way for his triumph. In London, the previous summer, Liszt had drawn the crowds: his 30-guineas-an-evening there had led the novice impresario-publishers into a speculation which was based upon ignorance of the cool, conservative response of provincial concert audiences, on a lack of appreciation of the need for the consistent application of publicity, and upon the belief that genius would will audiences to attend, even in out-of-the-way places.

The three men must have discussed, in Brighton and earlier in the tour, how misconceived this initial adventure had been. The argument which the English promoters might have proposed would have been based on the notion that, because much had been learned from the tour through August and September, a second fiasco could not possibly occur, and that therefore another, even longer tour was feasible. At some point during September, despite the accumulating evidence of current financial failure, Liszt agreed with Lavenu upon a contract for a second tour. In Brighton, at the end of his tether, and denied the confidential advice of a manager with European vision, the pianist could have panicked, thinking possibly that his energies might be better employed in concerts in the Rhineland, Austria–Hungary, or even Russia. But he had earlier reported to Marie that English audiences and knowledgeable critics in the provinces had received him enthusiastically; the first tour could be seen as a trial run in the wealthiest country in the world, and more promising pickings were not to be culled elsewhere. So, by the time Parry was reunited with 'dearest Anne' in London, on Sunday 27 September, Liszt had probably been persuaded that it was worth his trying to woo English – and Irish and Scots – audiences with his unrivalled brilliance. Wherever he played during summer and autumn in England, he had been told that Thalberg was vanquished. Perhaps he and Lavenu, however, still underestimated how disconnected were the musical worlds of the metropolis and even the larger provincial towns. Parry, as a seasoned traveller through middle England, might have been able to offer cautionary advice; but probably, as the comedian of the party, he was never seriously consulted.

At the Ipswich concert Liszt had played Schubert. Perhaps one of the transcriptions he performed was his 1838 version of *Erlkönig*. The demented gallop of that song's accompaniment had much in common with the hectic rapidity of Lavenu's itinerary on this first tour.

CHAPTER FOUR

The Second Tour

Reading — Oxford — Leamington — Birmingham
Wolverhampton — Newcastle-under-Lyme — Chester
Liverpool — Preston — Rochdale — Manchester
Huddersfield — Doncaster — Sheffield — Wakefield
Leeds — Hull — York — Manchester — Dublin
Cork — Clonmel — Limerick — Dublin — Belfast
Edinburgh — Glasgow — Newcastle
Sunderland — Richmond — Bradford

IN 1983 ALAN WALKER PUBLISHED the first part of a monumental triptych in which he intends to depict the whole sweep of Liszt's career as personality, pianist and composer. *The Virtuoso Years, 1811–1847* has already established itself as a triumph of meticulous research and profound understanding of the man and the artist; in it, myths are dismissed and doubts resolved. But there are one or two minor fissures in the edifice when Professor Walker comes to deal with Liszt's English excursions in 1840–41. Particularly, he states that the first tour, of 'the south of England', finished 'at Bath', having made its way 'along the south coast through Brighton'; this, on the evidence of the previous chapter, is an inaccurate description. Of the second tour he says that the 'concluding concerts took place in Glasgow and Edinburgh':[1] this, too, is incorrect, as a glance at the top of this page will confirm. The detailed source for determining Liszt's itineraries, in England, Ireland and Scotland, exists in the diaries of John Orlando Parry, from which Walker quotes at some length. Parry's account of the second tour is, moreover,

1. Alan Walker, *Franz Liszt: the Virtuoso Years, 1811–1847* (London, 1983).

much more lavish and humorous than his shorthand record of the
first one.

Lavenu's planning had been seriously at fault in August and
September. In his haste to make money for and from Liszt he had
contracted for too many concerts in too many places. Had he
reserved him for the major provincial towns only – Plymouth, Bath,
Cheltenham, Leicester, Cambridge, Bury St Edmunds and Norwich
– then he might have achieved a considerable *coup*. From his friend
and partner, Frank Mori, he ought to have learned that, when
Mori's father, Nicholas, had accompanied Paganini on some of his
British journeys in the early 1830s, the great violinist had never
played more than one concert a day, and rarely more than three per
week.[2] When he came to prepare Liszt's second tour, then, though
his geographical aspirations were even more expansive than they
had been in the late summer, Lavenu made sure that the great
pianist would not have to give concerts morning *and* evening on the
same day in widely separated places. Nevertheless, their journey
this time was to take them through the Midlands, industrial
Lancashire and Yorkshire, across to Ireland (north as well as south),
to the Scottish Lowlands, and back into the north-east of England.

Between his two British tours Liszt had to fulfil some engagements in Germany during October and early November. He began
to plan a cantata for the unveiling of the proposed Beethoven monument in Bonn. For the time being, away from English enterprises,
he could afford to be altruistic, and he chose also to defend himself
against some mischievous attacks made upon his honour in the Paris
journal, *Revue des deux mondes*, while he had been in England. Liszt
was undoubtedly vain; but he was also genuinely proud that, at
Pesth, he had been presented with a ceremonial sword by a group of
Hungarian noblemen. He wrote to the editor of the *Revue* on 26
October 1840:

> In Hungary, sir, in that country of antique and chivalrous
> manners, the sabre has a patriotic significance ... when six of the
> chief men of note in my country presented me with it among the

2. Gerald Norris, *A Musical Gazeteer of Great Britain and Ireland* (Newton Abbot,
1981), e.g. 221–7, 232–4.

general acclamations of my compatriots, whilst at the same time
the towns of Pesth and Oldenburg conferred upon me the
freedom of the city, and the civic authorities of Pesth asked His
Majesty for letters of nobility for me, it was an act to acknowledge
me afresh as a Hungarian, after an absence of fifteen years ... I
agree with you, sir, that it was, without doubt, going far beyond
my deserts up to the present time. Therefore I saw in that solemn
occasion the expression of a hope, far more than of a satisfaction.
Hungary hailed me as the man *from whom she expects* artistic
illustriousness ... Be so kind as to insert these few lines in your
next issue.[3]

While he was away, the smart Parisian readers of the *Revue* had
probably been sniggering at Liszt's supposed vanity; but his
renewed pride in belonging, spiritually, to Hungary, at a critical
time of national aspiration, was genuine, as the remainder of his
career was to prove. At this point, however, between the two
punishingly unsuccessful British tours, his sensitivity to a
supercilious slight to his honour does seem rather incongruous. In
November the would-be Hungarian nobleman found himself trun-
dling over uncongenial English roads amid a distinctly bourgeois
party.

Liszt's successes in Germany served to efface some of the worst
memories of the earlier tour. He began again with renewed optimism, despite a stormy crossing from France. He had set out from
Calais on 23 November in an English steam-packet. Although he
much preferred a jolting coach to a rolling vessel, he seems to have
been in good spirits when he wrote to Marie from Dover:

Thanks to the English boat I took only three-and-a-half hours to
cross from Calais. The rotten French one which followed us
probably took twice as long, because, after half-past ten in the
morning it was out of sight astern. What a handicap it is to be
French, but similarly to have to trust everything to a foreigner. I
shall leave here at half-past eight this evening; it's seventy-five
miles from here to London. While waiting I'm reading *Faust*, my

3. Quoted in Walker, op. cit., 328.

mind still dwelling on the pale white figure I saw drifting away in
the morning, my heart full of woe . . .[4]

But though he had crossed the Channel quickly, his departure
from France had been delayed, and this ensured that the second tour
got off to a chaotic start. Lavenu's little party assembled at Pad-
dington Station on the 23rd for the journey to their first concert in
Reading; but Liszt was still aboard his steamer. John Parry was
typically excited:

> Miss Steele, her mother, Miss Louisa Bassano, Mr. Lavenu and
> self left by the Great Western Railway at 9 o'clock; my wife
> Anne, Miss Brooks, Miss Mori, and Mr. Steele came to see us off.
> Arrived (in Reading) at half-past ten, and went to the Bear Hotel.
> M. Liszt had not yet arrived from Calais in consequence of the
> winds which prevailed. We went to the Town Hall – 140 people.
> When they heard Liszt had not come a great many left ! We were
> obliged to go on with the concert, though to only a few persons. I
> was very glad when it was over. Lewis Lavenu gave up the
> concert we were to have had at Newbury in consequence of Liszt.

Lavenu dashed off to Newbury to deal with that part of the crisis,
then went up to London where he tracked Liszt down.
     In London one item of criminal intelligence might have been a
minor embarrassment for Liszt. A homophonic namesake, one
Alfred List, a warehouse foreman at St Katherine's Dock, had been
examined on a charge of plundering from his employers a considerable amount of teas, coffee and spices, and sentenced to two
months' hard labour.[5] More seriously, London musical enthusiasts
were enjoying good news and bad news. On one hand Giulia Grisi,
the Queen's favourite, was consolidating her reputation as the leading operatic singer, at Her Majesty's Theatre: 'she is still the same
yet ever new'. On the other, Tamburini was behaving like a prima
donna at the same theatre, and it was only through the intervention
of Liszt's friend, Count D'Orsay, that he was persuaded to forget
his argument with the manager, Laporte, and perform before the

4. Daniel Ollivier, ed.: *Letters of Liszt and Marie d'Agoult* (Paris, 1933), 53.
5. *Oxford City and County Chronicle*, 2 May 1840.

Queen and Prince Albert. Liszt disliked singers in general, not simply as gilded competitors, but as unpredictable animals, and the Tamburini story, circulating in the provincial press, may have confirmed his opinion.[6]

Meanwhile the rest of the party travelled to Oxford for next day's concert, and there Liszt caught up with them. The university town was a lively musical centre, by contemporary standards. For Liszt's concert it rustled up a competent orchestra led by Marshall. A week before they appeared, Oxford had been delighted by a vocal concert at which a local singer, Miss Lockley, had been supported by Lablache and his wife, by Marshall, the London violinist Blagrove, and by Parry's friend, Joey Richardson. After Lavenu's concert a local newspaper offered a suitably stiff-backed, academic report:

> By his pianoforte recitals, M. Liszt has obtained a degree of celebrity never acquired by any other individual; and this, we think, was fully exemplified by his performances, which were perfectly astounding, and which were not only distinguished by great power and rapidity of execution, but by correct taste and judgement ... The Countess of Jersey and the Ladies Villiers were prevented from attending in consequence of the death of the Hon. Mrs. Cavendish.[7]

The party which now accompanied Liszt differed in two particulars from the earlier one. Mlle de Varny had disappeared, perhaps to marry the whist-playing M. Lemoine, and Miss Bassano was promoted to undertake the formal role of première vocalist and the informal task of comforting Lavenu. His interest in Louisa Bassano during this tour does not seem to have been purely musical; and it is interesting that the only new member of the party, the soprano, Miss Steele, took the precaution of bringing her mother with her.

John Parry was still engaged in singing and selling his songs. But now he was also being asked to give a trial to some vocal pieces by Joseph Augustine Wade, one of the many characters of Dickensian disreputability which this period disgorged. In 1840 Wade was

6. ibid.
7. *Jackson's Oxford Journal*, 28 November 1840.

roughly 45 years old, a walking rag-bag of experience, constantly just the wrong side of the line of success. The son of a Dublin dairyman, he claimed to have studied anatomy at the Irish College of Surgeons, though there is no record of his having done so. Nevertheless, after marrying, then abandoning, an Irish heiress, he did practise for a while as a surgeon. Also, though he was a self-taught musician, he tried to become Professor of Music at Trinity College, Dublin – a predecessor had been the Duke of Wellington's father – and failed. Bur soon after his arrival in England, his oratorio, *The Messiah*, was performed at Covent Garden, and an opera, *Two Houses of Granada*, at Drury Lane. In 1826 he published a song, *Meet me by moonlight alone*, which achieved popularity to the point of parody. By the time he picked up with Parry and Lavenu, however, he had become a notorious drunkard and an opium addict. This tour was to be the last throw for Wade: his subsequent, final decline was swift; and his intermittent appearances during their journey seem to have disturbed the other artists in the party. Lavenu probably thought he would be useful to them when they got to Dublin.[8] At Oxford, besides Wade's duet, *The Wrong Serenade*, Parry sang a new piece of his own, *A Wife Wanted*; he said that the bell-effects in the accompaniment at the beginning 'tickled the ladies' fancies'.

On Wednesday the 25th, a lovely sunny morning, they left at 10 a.m. for their second visit to Leamington. Parry was very impressed by Liszt's attire:

> M. Liszt brought his great Hungarian coat with him, composed of skins and ornamented with different coloured leathers: it is a most enormous concern, and weighs at least as heavy as three great coats.

By contrast with their earlier railway journey, the trip by coach from Oxford to Leamington, only 46 miles, lasted eight hours; though they did have trouble with stupid post-boys who took them on a detour through Warwick. They arrived less than two hours before their concert, which went well. Parry tried the experiment of

8. *Grove* (1927 edn); *DNB*.

beginning Wade's duet by walking from the auditorium up the orchestra stairs, but he judged that this had produced rather an odd effect when he began to sing. The concert ended with a deeply felt rendering of the National Anthem: Victoria's first accouchement was imminent, and the future security of the realm, through a hoped-for male heir, was on everyone's mind. After supper the men returned to the concert room, in the company of the local leader of professional musical activity, Mr Elston (thought Parry called him 'Elliston'), and Lavenu, Liszt and Parry each tried the organ. But the most amusing feature of the Leamington visit seems to have been their discovery of an advertisement for a rival, 'Master Taylor, who', it was announced, 'would perform the *whole* of Rossini's Opera of "Guillaume Tell" on the *Harp* – divided into three parts'.[9]

Next morning the town was very busy with departures for a great steeplechase at Northampton. The musicians left Leamington at noon and passed Warwick Castle for the second time; Liszt was most impressed. They arrived in Birmingham at three o'clock and put up at Dee's Royal Hotel. The thriving town was a cornucopia for purchasers of presents and knick-knacks. Liszt and Parry walked abroad and visited several shops, buying toothpicks – indispensable travelling equipment for a hearty trencherman like Parry – and 'razors with a flexible edge' – essential instruments for a casual dandy like Liszt. Then Parry went to the post office to collect letters from his wife and daughters. Back at the hotel he replied to 'dearest Anne' and enclosed gifts of two books 'for my little girls'. The whole package weighed over three ounces and he had to purchase eight stamps. Later, the newspapers revealed that, while he had been in Birmingham, the local police (in the person of Superintendent Stephens) were investigating misappropriations on a large scale from that same post office; this was finally discovered to have been an 'inside job' by one Blakey, 'a young man holding a confidential situation' at the GPO.[10]

Birmingham was on its way to becoming one of the foremost centres of provincial musical activity. The Festival, which had

9. *Royal Leamington Spa Courier and Warwickshire Standard*, 22 August 1840.
10. *Liverpool Chronicle*, 12 December 1840.

begun as a charitable event in 1768, was about to reach the peak of its celebrity. The town did not yet possess a permanent orchestra, but in 1840 the Festival Chorus was reconstituted as the Birmingham Musical Institute, with 300 singers and 60 largely professional instrumentalists imported from London. There were frequent concerts throughout the winter season, and a week before Lavenu appeared, there had been a soirée in the Mechanics' Institute at which Miss Hawes and Mme Caradori Allan, singers with nation-wide reputations, were soloists.[11] Later, in December, at the six-year-old Town Hall, where Mendelssohn had recently conducted the first British performance of *Hymn of Praise*, there was the 76th Anniversary Concert for the Benefit of Aged and Distressed House-keepers, the orchestra led by Blagrove, with Lindley as leading cellist, and a local man, Mr Munden, conducting. Munden, Shargool the viola player, and Fletcher (double bass) were in fact the agents for selling Lavenu's concert-tickets.[12] Like Elgar's father in Worcester a few years later, they evidently combined music-making with music-selling. The newspapers contained a straight-forward 'puff' which told music-lovers that the object of Liszt's performances was to 'represent on a single instrument the effect of a full orchestra', not a bad description of one of his intentions. Far more extensive publicity, however, was afforded Benjamin Haydon's lectures at the Birmingham Philosophical Institution, which had begun in the first week of November and were repeti-tions of his classes at the Cadogan Institute in London. Haydon then was the most controversial British epic painter, constantly in debt, formerly committed to prison, and now charging fifteen shil-lings for admission to his lectures.[13]

None of the Birmingham papers seems to have bothered to review or even record Liszt's concert at Dee's Hotel, and there were barely 130 present. But, according to Parry, everything else went well: he had a *double* encore for *A Wife Wanted*, and he recognized his father's old friend Mr Munden in the audience. Liszt played exhilaratingly, 'broke three strings on one note', and then retired to

11. ibid., 16 November 1840.
12. ibid., 9 November 1840.
13. ibid., 2 November 1840.

bed, ill. Next morning Parry went downstairs to the concert room and played for an hour on Liszt's Erard. Lavenu came in and played him excerpts from his latest opera. They lunched on bottled porter and sandwiches, mounted their coach at two o'clock, and set off for Wolverhampton.

> At three we found ourselves in dense fog, and with the smoke and the *desolate* appearance of the villages and the whole country covered with Shafts which lead to the Mines, we were one and all perfectly miserable. It was so slippery that the horses were obliged to walk, so that we were two hours and a half going fifteen miles.

They dined at five in The Swan Hotel, Wolverhampton, off bread, cheese and celery, took some wine, smoked, and dressed for the concert. The Black Country evidently offered few genteel pleasures for travellers. But after the concert Parry took supper with a musical friend, Mr Hay, and enjoyed scalloped oysters, sage and cheese. Mrs Hay, said Parry, had been 'imitating the Queen !!' – Mr Hay would soon have 'an Illustrious Royal'. Even in the privacy of his diary, a *bourgeois* like Parry could not quite bring himself to use the word 'pregnant'.[14]

Next morning was bitterly cold, and after a huge breakfast, they set off for Newcastle-under-Lyme. Tantalizingly, their coach several times threaded over and under the railway from Birmingham to Liverpool, which was not yet convenient for their itinerary, and they saw the locomotives as they paused at Stafford. Parry knew the Potteries quite well, having played there five or six times. Earlier, in January 1840, with Blagrove, Lindley and Miss Bruce, he had taken part in evening concerts at Lane End, Shelton, Burslem and Newcastle, spending altogether a week in the vicinity, so he was hailed by the locals as a familiar celebrity whose *Buffo Trio* had delighted audiences before. On this occasion Lavenu's concert was billed to take place in the Assembly Rooms of the Roebuck Inn at Newcastle. The party arrived at 3.15 p.m., and Parry discovered, after collect-

14. Parry had played here, under Hay's management and direction, in 1839 and earlier in 1840. See John Orlando Parry Collection, newscuttings, Cardiff City Library, 3.358.

ing his London letters, that the Roebuck had 'horrible dirty bed-rooms'. Their dinner at 5.30 was also unsatisfactory:

> Queer Fish, Bad Pork, underdone Pease Pudding and Potatoes – Horrible Veal Cutlets ! – Decent Tart and Sago Pudding !! Dined on Sage, Cheese and Salary.

The programme of the Newcastle concert was typical of many on the English part of the tour:

PART I

Trio, 'Mi lagnero tacendi', *Miss Steele, Miss Bassano* and *Mr. J. Parry*	MOZART
Aria, *Miss Bassano*, 'L'amor suo mi fe beata'	DONIZETTI
First selection from the Celebrated Recitals, Piano Forte	M. LISZT
Aria, 'Che piu dirvi', *Miss Steele*	BENEDICT
Prize ballad, 1840, 'Fair Daphne', *Mr. J. Parry*	PARRY
Ballad, 'Memory's Dream', *Miss Bassano*	LAVENU
Second selection, Piano Forte	M. LISZT
New duett, 'The Muleteers', *Misses Steele and Bassano*	WADE
Mr. J. Parry will sing (by desire) his popular song, 'Wanted a Governess'	PARRY

PART II

New duett, 'The Wrong Serenade', *Miss Bassano and Mr. J. Parry*	WADE
Ballad, 'They tell me thou'rt the favoured guest', *Miss Steele*	BALFE
Third selection, Piano Forte	M. LISZT
Duett, 'The Sisters', *Misses Bassano and Steele*	WADE
Ballad, 'I've left a sweet home', *Miss Steele*	
Fourth selection, Piano Forte	M. LISZT
Song, 'The Last Adieu', *Miss Steele*	PARRY
Mr. J. Parry will sing his new Song, 'A Wife Wanted'	PARRY
Finale: ''Tis a very merry thing', *Misses Steele and Bassano and Mr. J. Parry*	WADE

Conductor, *Mr. Lavenu*
The Piano Forte is of Erard's New Patent, and is brought expressly from London for the occasion.[15]

15. *North Staffordshire Advertiser*, 21 November 1840.

The concert was poorly attended – only 80 present – despite Parry's local reputation.[16] And the room had certain inconveniences. The stage was too high, and several sets of steps had to be tried before the ladies could decorously reach it; this caused much mirth among the audience. Parry whiled away his time between the items by writing letters; and Liszt, having mislaid his spectacles, had to borrow Parry's so that he could sight-read the last piece in his part of the programme. One local newspaper offered some apology for the thin attendance: a Saturday, it said, was not a popular 'leisure evening' in that part of the world. But Liszt had 'completely electrified and delighted' those who had bothered to buy tickets. Afterwards the artists had toasted cheese ('mauvaise', said Parry), porter and egg flips; and Lewis, overcome by alcohol, blithely announced that he had lost £112 on the week.

They spent most of Sunday the 29th travelling, lunching at the Crown in Nantwich, and arriving at the Royal Hotel, Chester, at 5.15. Marchant, with the Erard on its waggon, had gone ahead and arranged for them to dine at 5.45. The bedrooms here were 'capital', and Parry was amused to find that a favourite chambermaid acquaintance of his, aged 50, had just married a man of 25. After dinner they entertained a notable local inhabitant, Mr St Albin, whose wife, a pianist, enjoyed the distinction of having played in Paganini's Chester concert in 1832.[17] Liszt spent part of the evening in Parry's room, smoking and writing, and then went downstairs for sherry flips at Lewis's expense.

Next morning Parry wrote out the words of Wade's *Wrong Serenade* so that they could be printed in the book of next Tuesday's Liverpool concert. Then he took a short walk with Liszt who, in his Hungarian coat and cap, 'astonished the Welshmen'. They both looked over the red sandstone cathedral, then much in need of restoration: '. . . very old', said Parry, 'but nothing to some I have seen'. Dinner, before the concert, was sumptuous, but rather spoilt by a protracted argument between Liszt and Bassano on the subject of birth and education. For the concert the large room of the hotel was only half full, and there was hardly any applause: '. . . all went

16. ibid., 5 December 1840.
17. *Chester Chronicle*, 27 January 1832.

as flat as possible'. A century earlier, Chester had welcomed Handel in his full-bottomed wig, on his way to Ireland for the première of *Messiah*; in 1840, it seems, the city was more interested in Liszt's strange strolling attire than in his musical accomplishments. Perhaps Lavenu's 'puff' in the *Chester Chronicle*, which stressed his 'serious' repertoire – Bach and Handel fugues, transcriptions of Beethoven symphonies – drove away all but the most committed musical enthusiasts.[18] The St Albins looked in after the concert to greet Liszt, while Parry and Lavenu hastily cobbled together some new verses for the *Musical Wife* – topical references to Liszt, Lavenu and 'young John Parry'.

On Tuesday morning they drove through the Wirral: did they admire Tranmere's new gaslights?[19] At Birkenhead in a riverside hotel, they lunched, as Liszt's treat, on oysters, pickles, bread and cheese '*in the open air* at the hotel gardens!' During the ferry crossing to Liverpool, Liszt was 'all alive', swaggering about the deck in his great Hungarian coat, 'everybody thinking he was a little touched – great fun though'. The hotels in the dynamic port were full to bursting; finding no rooms at The Rainbow they put up at The Feathers in Clayton Square. Their evening concert in the nearby Theatre Royal was a benefit for a local musician, Mr Ashton, though Lavenu was hoping to scoop some of the receipts to cover their expenses. While the ladies rehearsed with Lavenu, Parry and Liszt walked the two miles to the Coburg Dock to see an immense American steamer, *The President*, recently arrived after a much-publicized voyage. On returning they slept on sofas, 'being tired'.

At the Royal Amphitheatre, Great Charlotte Street, Liverpudlians were then enjoying a powerful mixture of theatrical pleasures. The evening began with *Jane of the Hatchet; or, The Women of Beauvais*, a 'Gorgeous Spectacle' in which, it was advertised, '*One Hundred Female Warriors* will appear in full costume of the period and go through *a Variety* of Military Evolutions'; the performance ended with Dibdin's Extravaganza of *Don Giovanni; or, A Spectre on Horse-back*, with Miss Daly as Don Giovanni and Mr Hammond as Leporello. The entr'acte of this extraordinary programme was 'a

18. ibid., 20 November 1840.
19. *Liverpool Chronicle*, 12 December 1840, 'Lighting Tranmere with Gas'.

new and laughable Burletta, *The Railroad Station*, starring Hammond as the first-class passenger.[20] Lavenu and the others may have regretted that the railway network was not yet extensive enough to make their journeys from concert to concert less arduous. But while the Liverpool audiences laughed at the Burletta, an atmosphere of anxiety was pervading Britain. A leader in the *Liverpool Chronicle*, November 1840, outlined the pressing cause of concern:

> The increase of *accidents* on the different railroads has, of late, become so awfully terrific, that it behoves the Legislature forthwith to enact some stringent measure for their prevention ... Human life is much too valuable to be trifled with as it now is, and an average week's consumption of it at present upon the railroads exceeds the whole losses of the army and navy in the conquest of Syria by Lord Palmerston.[21]

Another paper noted a fatal accident on the York and North Midland Railway: 'If the engine-driver should be convicted of carelessness, he will no doubt be tried for manslaughter.' Parry, constantly alert to the perils of travel, was probably grateful in the current circumstances for the relative safety of the stage coach, and was possibly tense with excitement during their short, infrequent railway excursions. Perhaps to reassure travellers of the measures being undertaken to guarantee their safety, George Stephenson, no less, spoke publicly in Liverpool in December 1840, on the subject of 'The Railway Talking Machine'. He described the miracle of the telegraph, 'constructed of galvanic wires', by means of which conversations could be held between railway personnel in London and Blackwall. Soon, he claimed, such dialogues would take place in seconds over hundreds of miles.[22]

Ashton's concert was part of a Liverpool subscription series.[23] The orchestra was led by Mr Herrmann, and, like other members of the band, the leading cellist, Mr W. Lindley, had been specially imported from Manchester. This use of 'foreigners', more particu-

20. ibid., 21 November 1840.
21. ibid.
22. ibid., 19 December 1840.
23. ibid., 28 November 1840.

larly of specially hated Mancunians, was seen by some as an affront
to Liverpool's musical dignity. 'A Musician' wrote vehemently to a
local paper on the subject of cellists at Liszt's concert:

> I think the subscribers ought to know why Mr. *Jackson* is not
> engaged. It is not right, in my opinion, to prefer strangers to
> those who are 'native here', when such persons are not only
> competent but *superior to any foreign aid*.[24]

Liverpool was beginning to test its muscle as a provincial city
worthy of respect, under the patronage of the feudal Lord Derby
and the commercially powerful Gladstone family, among others,
with intellectual middle-class leadership of a high order. But despite
its booming imperial trade, great new proprietary schools, and
public buildings (St George's Hall was being projected at the time of
Liszt's visit), the nagging rivalry with Manchester – reputedly
Lancashire's Athens – was still causing jealousy.

The Liverpool concert was a roaring success and raised
everyone's spirits. It was the fashionable highlight of the winter's
entertainment. Subscribers were given advice beforehand about
proper access to the theatre: 'Carriages to approach the Theatre by
way of Basnett Street; to drive off through the streets on the lower
side of the Square, and to take up in the opposite direction.' The
presence of an orchestra again gave Liszt an opportunity for dazzling the clients with Weber's *Concertstück*.[25] Parry had mixed feelings about the occasion: Liszt was 'tremendously received', and *A
Wife Wanted* 'told capitally', but was not encored because the concert had gone on too long. Most upsetting was the fact that some of
the audience left to find their carriages and avoid the traffic jam as
soon as Liszt had played the Weber, and thus they missed Parry's
last items. He vented his pique first on someone else – '*The Wrong
Serenade* [written by Wade] was hissed !!! We do not sing it again –
It will never do in its present form', – and then on their hotel – 'bad
Double bed room – no fire place, low windows, etc., etc., *male*!
male! – *Warming Pans*.'

24. ibid., 5 December 1840.
25. ibid., 28 November 1840.

Next morning, 2 December, Lavenu, Bassano, and Mrs and Miss Steele left by rail for Preston, with Marchant, the Erard and its waggon stowed on a railway truck. Lewis had deputed Parry and Liszt – the former, perhaps, for his gaiety, the latter for his intimidating celebrity – to stay behind and try to wring some cash out of Ashton; but that gentleman pleaded illness and 'Grazioso' and the 'Piano-centaur' had to leave empty-handed. Nevertheless, they used their remaining time in Liverpool profitably. Parry, who had already gained a reputation as an artist in oils, took Liszt to see an exhibition of paintings from London at the Royal Institution. They went also to Weiss and Himes's music warehouse, where *Governess* and *Wife* were 'being much asked for !!' Parry saw a lady buying a copy of the *Wife* while they were there: great excitement. Liszt had not found his spectacles, and so Parry helped him to purchase new ones. A local newspaper was warning short-sighted shoppers to beware the new gas-lighting in shop windows: it was becoming the practice for shopkeepers to place lights beneath eye-level, so as to dazzle the customer in the street and prevent him from seeing the goods on display clearly.[26]

They caught the 2.30 train and were in Preston by 5 p.m. This concert made up for Parry's Liverpool disappointments: he had a triple encore, and thought it worthwhile making a neat speech: 'I felt the honour they did me on my first appearance in Preston – but that I was so exhausted – I could sing no more'. Before bed they had egg flips, and Liszt became 'excited' (Parry's code-word for 'tipsy'). The ride next day from Preston to Rochdale was depressing. The concert began too early – at seven o'clock – but the attendance was astonishing: all the boxes were taken and there were 200 in the gallery alone. Everything was twice encored. Afterwards their carriage was late, so Liszt and Parry passed the time playing the concert piano. At the hotel they had toasted cheese and egg flips with sherry: 'All concerts *above* £40 – "Sherry Flips" . . . not in bed till late – bad.'

In Manchester, on 4 December, they stayed at The Moseley Arms. The first gentlemen's concerts in the city had begun in 1744, but despite the strings and harpsichord playing Vivaldi and

26. ibid., 12 December 1840.

Geminiani, these had probably been a 'front' for local Jacobite meetings.[27] The important German–Jewish community in Manchester, already established by 1840, was, on the other hand, genuinely and passionately in love with music, and when Hermann Leo enticed Charles Hallé to the town after 1848 – the year Chopin appeared there – its cultural exfoliation really started. But already in 1840 it was enjoying concerts whose qualities were probably unique in the English provinces. In the late 1830s in London, the pianist Moscheles had initiated chamber-music soirées at which the 'serious' quartets of Beethoven, Mozart and Mendelssohn were performed alongside the more accessible, fashionable works of Ferdinand Ries and Georges Onslow. Manchester imitated Moscheles, and in November 1840 we find a quartet series taking place at the Athenaeum, where Liszt was to play. The violinists Seymour and Couran, the violist Sudlow, and Liverpool's detested 'foreigner', Lindley, joined Mr P. Johnson, the pianist, in performances of Mozart's G minor Piano Quartet, Haydn's D minor Quartet op. 73, Beethoven's Cello Sonata op. 69, and Mendelssohn's E flat Quartet op. 44. The interludes – songs by Weber and Henry Bishop – were provided by a soprano, Miss Graham.[28] Of course, Manchester had also received the great operatic 'stars'; but it earned a particular footnote in operatic history by becoming the place where John Parry's friend and professional guide, the greatest mezzo of her day, Malibran, died. In London she had suffered a riding accident; later, and in consequence, she was taken ill in Manchester and expired at The Moseley Arms after lingering for a few days. Liszt and Parry probably appreciated that they were spending their first Manchester evening in a shrine to one of their indisputably great colleagues.[29]

After the short journey from Rochdale Parry was again out and about among the music shops. At eight he was in the Athenaeum Large Room which, though half empty, contained an audience of

27. *New Grove* (1980 edn).
28. *Manchester Guardian*, 28 November 1840.
29. See April Fitzlyon, *Maria Malibran, Diva of the Romantic Age* (London, 1987), 248, for the notion that Liszt actually slept in the room in Manchester where Malibran had died.

400. Manchester outdid Liverpool: Liszt was encored three times, and there was no room for Parry's encores. They returned to the hotel at eleven: 'Egg Flips – *Two* bottles of Sherry !! Dozen eggs and Sugar, etc., etc.' They quenched their exuberance with what was surely, in a pre-Freudian age, quite an innocent little game – ' "The Boots", "The Chambermaid", "Landlady", "Ostler", "Head Waiter", etc., etc.', which sounds as though it was typical of Parry's preoccupation with the eccentricities of the inn servants encountered by blasé musicians on tour. They were joined by a German friend of Liszt: 'Great fun (the concert was half composed of Germans)', said Parry. They went to bed at 1.30, and Parry had 'Queer dreams' – about eggs.

Liszt's German friend may have caused him to remember his erstwhile domesticity with Marie d'Agoult. As parents they were affectionate rather than attentive; consequently their three children – Blandine, Cosima, and Daniel – were often placed in the care of others, particularly when Liszt was absent from Paris. Sometimes they were with Liszt's mother; on this occasion Daniel was entrusted to the Lehmann family; and it was one of the Lehmanns, an artist, whom Liszt met in Manchester. 'He is handsome and seemed very capable', he told Marie. 'He was the only truly human person with whom I've exchanged words for eighteen days.'[30]

The syndrome of the first tour was beginning to repeat itself: Liszt was becoming dreadfully bored. The animated meeting with Lehmann, and perhaps with other interesting Germans, in Manchester, served ultimately to darken his ennui. He wrote to Marie:

> The only pleasant happening in my life at present is a letter from you. Write to me voluminously: talk of politics and literature. For two months now I shall know nothing of the outside world but what you tell me. Our company is about the same; only that the 'seconda donna' has become 'prima assoluta'. It is a notable improvement. Parry, Miss Bassano and Miss Steele are all persons of conservative, calm disposition. There's no Ecarté or

30. Ollivier, op. cit., II, 67. Lehmann had recently painted portraits of Liszt and Marie.

Whist; one becomes bored more pleasantly, when one has the
time; but, so far, that time has not presented itself.
    Of all ways to get money, this suits me best. I am completely
set apart from everything. I read, write, and play the piano,
rendering to everyone, according to the occasion, indifference for
indifference – and, when necessary, contempt for contempt – by
always doubling the ordinary dose of rationality.

There was probably as much frustration as boredom in Liszt's
reaction to the aspect of England he was seeing: surrounded by
audiences who responded to him with staid enthusiasm, and companions who treated him as a being on their second-rate level, he
must often have been bewildered into silence. Ironically, he seems
to have found conversation even about financial and artistic affairs a
matter of indifference:

> Perhaps there will be forty people – perhaps three or four hun-
> dred at the next concert – a heavy subject of preoccupation and
> parley for my travelling companions, who plague me violently in
> this way, as you may imagine. I lack nothing, provided that the
> bags are loaded and my cravat-pin is properly attached; that is all I
> need.[31]

English drinking habits provoked his irony further: he advised his
countess to 'try mixing Porter and ordinary beer: it's something like
"half-and-half". At 23 Place Vendôme you will find the best
ingredients, on the word of "Grazioso" ' – he meant Parry, who had
lived in Paris for several months in the early 1830s. He begged her
to send him some reading matter to fill the intellectual void around
him: Montaigne's *Essays*, *Childe Harold*, which he must have known
very well already, and *Don Juan* in Charpentier's French edition.
Later he thanked her:

> . . . I sigh, after reading Montaigne and Byron. They become two
> pillows, one for repose, the other for sleeplessness. Do you
> realise what a joy it is for me to receive them from you![32]

31. ibid., II, 54.
32. ibid., II, 61.

Liszt's performance in Manchester was the cause of such enthusiasm that Lavenu, perhaps reflecting on his failure to make capital from similar situations on their first tour, quickly arranged a second concert for a week hence. Next morning Parry 'walked about a little', and in Pickering's music store he sat down at the piano and sang *The Wife* for a lady who had missed his Athenaeum performance. Lavenu needed a few hours to arrange their second concert, and so the coach did not leave for Huddersfield until 3 p.m. The steep, twisting journey, only 26 miles, lasted until 7.15, and the concert had been due to start at seven. They dressed 'like lightning', and were in the Philosophical Hall by eight o'clock. The audience of intelligent Huddersfield music-lovers – £15-worth of them in Lavenu's terms – had been in their seats since quarter-past six. But they were, on Parry's estimate, 'very good natured', and greeted the conductor's apology with applause. From that moment everything went swimmingly. Liszt was encored, and, at the special request of a knowledgeable member of the audience, he played his *Erlkönig* transcription. After punch and charades with a select group of local inhabitants, they retired to bed at one.

Huddersfield hospitality had kept them from bed till the early hours of Sunday; at half-past nine the same morning they were roused by Huddersfield church bells. They travelled to Doncaster through 'very hilly country'. Louisa Bassano was quite poorly, and she surely avoided the bread and cheese, pickles and bottled porter which was their lunch. The journey continued after dark, and Parry read Grimms' Romances by candlelight in the coach. By the town clock they arrived in Doncaster at ten past seven. 'Liszt and I took a little stroll – met people coming *out* of chapel – all looked and laughed at Liszt's hair and cap !' They were staying at The New Angel, and there was a Collard square piano on hand for practice. Liszt's bedroom was superb. Parry had arranged for his friends, in the places where they had recently played, to send on newspapers. At the post office in Doncaster he collected a copy of the *Pottery Mercury*, whose florid language – Miss Steele 'eloquent', Liszt 'Prometheus' – they all found very funny. Looking ahead, Lavenu and Parry decided upon the programme for the first Dublin concert in a fortnight's time.

Liszt was not the only piece of exoticism to assail Doncaster in these few days. At the New Betting Rooms, High Street, the citizens could see Ponte's Celebrated Theatre of Arts, a coloured 'moving' picture show, with views of Smyrna and Verona, followed by 'the Exhibition of the Wonders of Creation' revealed by 'that splendid Optical Instrument, the Oxy Hydrogen Microscope'. The performance ended with a foretaste of the musicians' intended crossing by sea to Dublin: '. . . a faithful representation of a Storm at Sea, with its characteristic phenomena'. Front seats at 2 shillings; second seats at one shilling; back seats sixpence; children under ten, half price.[33] Added piquancy was provided by long accounts in the local press of the history and geography of China; for the first Opium War was the current focus of attention in internatonal affairs.

More prosaically, Lavenu had arranged that three of their Yorkshire concerts, here at Doncaster, at York, and later in Hull, should be collaborations with a noted young local musician, Mr Lockwood, pianist, conductor, composer, and formerly fellow-student with Richardson at the Royal Academy. He inserted an advertisement in the press which might be taken as a measure of Lavenu's anxiety about audiences and receipts:

> In order to meet the wishes of friends, and to give additional facilities to all parties to avail themselves of the opportunity of hearing not only the most celebrated pianist, but also the most eminent flutist [sic] of the present day, Mr. Lockwood has reduced the price of tickets of admission.[34]

The 'flutist' was, of course, Joey Richardson. Unfortunately he had to delay his departure from London and did not appear in Doncaster. This may have been cause for genuine disappointment since, as Lockwood said, he was 'an old favourite in this neighbourhood', where 'his performances at an early age elicited the highest commendation'.

Unusually, the party had two travel-free days in which to prepare for their concert. But because of her illness, Miss Bassano sang only

33. *Doncaster Chronicle and Farmer's Journal*, 5 December 1840.
34. ibid.

Lockwood's 'new ballad', not yet published, *There is no beauty*, and in Mozart trios which began and ended the programme. Parry therefore bore the main burden of the vocalizing and sang six solo songs. Liszt displayed considerable magnanimity to his greatest rival by joining Lockwood in a performance of Thalberg's Fantasia on *Norma* for piano duet. In describing Liszt's playing the local critic, as was now customary, dipped into his bag of metaphors taken from classical meteorology:

> The effect of M. Liszt's performance on the mind of the listener is most surprising; he feels himself borne away by a whirlwind of melodious sounds, at first calm and gentle as morning zephyr, and then rising into the tempestuous roar of the hurricane.[35]

It does seem that Liszt, the musical dramatist, avoided the obvious ploy of immediately threatening his provincial audiences with a barrage of *fortissimo* playing: almost invariably he screwed up the tension by starting quietly, making them wait for his most exciting displays of power and rapidity.

Next day, 8 December, their journey was shockingly wet, 'the first real soaker we had', and Parry consoled himself by reading 'The Bottle Imp' in his Romances. They stayed at The Tontine Inn, Sheffield, where he received a letter from Anne, 'the million and twoth'. They were at the Music Hall by quarter-past eleven after a delay caused by the driver of their fly's having delivered them to the Methodist chapel by mistake. Two hundred came, and Liszt was encored three times. Despite being dosed with sal volatile and peppermint, Miss Steele took her turn at being ill, and could not sing one of her songs. Parry's contribution was greeted unsympathetically by one local lover of musical profundity:

> When the *Governess* was encored, some wretch of a man hissed in the Room. But however [*sic*] I did not mind – 1 to 200 – so sat down to sing *Fanny Grey* as usual – and this vagabond (whoever he was) – *hissed* on every verse and sometimes in the *middle* – quite out loud !!! I could hardly sing for *rage* ! I spoilt the Song – and

35. ibid., 12 December 1840.

was within an inch of addressing the audience (who quite sympathised with me) had not the great applause at the end drowned the miscreant. It made me quite ill.

Parry now began to suffer from the bug which had laid the Ladies low. But his indisposition did not prevent him from indulging his usual Sheffield weakness: whenever he performed there he visited the cutlery showrooms. On this occasion he went to Rodgers' in Norfolk Street and bought, as a present for Anne, a very handsome smelling bottle in a morocco case, made to hang on the finger, and costing £1. 5s. 6d., with an initial 'A' inscribed on it. Then he caught the train, a slow one, for Wakefield. When they arrived,

> Loo [Louisa] and Lavenu went off in [an] Omnibus to Wakefield *two miles* (!) and left us four waiting in the Carriage for more than three quarters of an hour – while they went to the Hotel to send two pair of horses for the Carriage and the Van ! Liszt was in such a passion – he got out and walked all the way ! However, at last we saw the horses coming and were at the Stafford Arms by 5.

The Wakefield concert went very well. Afterwards Liszt tried out his new Fantasia on Meyerbeer's *Robert le diable* and his arrangement of *God Save the Queen*, having written down the latter probably in hasty tribute to Victoria who had just produced her first child. There was a 'beautiful' chambermaid, 'like a stick of sealing wax, with the head of a trout or Cod Fish!' – a description which neatly blended Parry's love of letter-writing and good food – and he was greatly entertained by an argument between her and Marchant, the driver of their Erard waggon. They had to do without their egg flips, for Lavenu had gone off to supper with a Mr White. He returned to the hotel at 3 a.m., 'rather Whiskeyish'. Parry hardly slept: through the night he heard the church clock opposite perform its whole repertoire of chimes.

They rose at twelve next day and started on the coach for Leeds at two, arriving at the Scarborough Hotel at three. Liszt's *Guillaume Tell* was encored, and they celebrated with egg flips, but 'with *musty* eggs'. Next day they took the railway to Hull, but much time was wasted, nevertheless, in putting the waggon on the train. The

journey along the side of the Humber engaged their interest, but
Parry thought the train was shabby, and the musicians sat in their
own coach mounted on a truck. After leaving his luggage at The
Kingston, Parry was out in the town:

> Saw *little* boys laughing at the title in a Music Shop – 'John Parry
> Wants a Wife – Who's he, I wonder?' 'Ha, ha, ha,' etc. etc. 'Jack
> Parry Wants a Wife – he, he, he.'

Parry had anticipated good food in Hull, and he was not displeased
by beautiful codfish, turkey and jellies. His pleasure was not disturbed by an argument raging across the table, between Liszt and
Bassano: ' "You ugliest piece" – "Speak when you're spoken to !!"
– "Ugly, uglier, ugliest !" – "No persuading Ladies" '. The young
contralto was evidently not the type of swooning young thing who
might throw herself under the spell of the Don Juan pianist. The
concert in Hull at the Jarratt Street Rooms was another collaboration
with Lockwood and was under the patronage of Sir Clifford and
Lady Constable. There was an audience of 160 in a hall designed to
accommodate 800. Liszt accompanied *The Inchcape Bell*, but Parry
sang, according to his own reckoning, 'miserably'. His spirits were
raised once again by Joey Richardson's arrival; he had dashed up
from a concert in Brighton, bringing with him his latest trick, 'Find
the Lady'. Liszt's visit seems to have coincided with new develop-
ments in Hull's musical life: the Choral Society, aided by Blagrove
and Lindley, was about to hold its inaugural concert; and two piano
and music dealers, George Atkinson in Saville Street and J. Fagg in
Whitefriargate, opposite the Custom House, would have hoped to
benefit from the publicity created by Liszt. The *Hull Advertiser* had
prepared the public for his coming by reprinting, in full, the
Athenaeum's review of his Philharmonic appearance the previous
May.[36]

They breakfasted on lobster. Parry bought three Leeds papers
and was disgusted that all of them had ignored Liszt's concert there.
Then by rail to York – they were among 2186 passengers that week
on the Hull and Selby Railway – where they arrived in The White

Swan at five. After reading in a Doncaster paper an excellent report of his singing, Parry went to stay with local friends and enjoyed their good soup and 'plenty of capital Port Wine'. The party had two concert-free days in York. Parry went to the Minster on Sunday morning with his friends the Barbers. In the evening he dined with them again and, in lieu of a concert, entertained their guests with 'all sorts of funniments – "Fra Diavolo" with *Tambourine* obbligato !!' On Monday he spent most of the morning writing letters to Anne in Mr Barber's silversmith's shop. He discovered that Miss Bassano was again very ill, and went on to the Great Rooms in Blackwall Street where the other musicians were rehearsing. What Liszt was doing while Parry was indulging in his discreet pleasures we may never know; but, at a guess, he might have been anticipating the kind of nocturnal excursion to which he later introduced his companions in Cork.

Lockwood was again the promoter of their concert, and he was now guilty of a breach of etiquette. His invitation to Liszt and Lavenu must have been delivered during their late-summer tour, but in the meantime dates had had to be rearranged and the concert was advertised to take place on a day which would cause Lockwood some embarrassment. As at Liverpool, the York concert was part of a subscription series. On 10 December two advertisements appeared in the *York Courant and Original Advertiser*. The first was for the second subscription concert, under the patronage of the Organist of York Minster, Dr Camidge, at the Great Assembly Room, on 15 December, to be followed by a ball. There was to be a band and three guest singers, Miss Hawes, Lieutenant A. Sobolewski de Braunhelder, and Mr Pearsal, 'the new tenor'. The second was for Lockwood's concert on 14 December, under the patronage of Lord and Lady Wenlock, J. H. Lowther, MP, and the Hon. J. C. Dundas, MP, also with a band of forty players. To his advertisement Lockwood judiciously appended a footnote:

> Mr. Lockwood is extremely sorry, that in consequence of *M. Liszt*'s Country Engagements, he is obliged to have his concert in the evening previous to Dr. Camidge's, having no *alternative* but that of cancelling M. Liszt's Engagement. Mr. Lockwood had originally engaged M. Liszt for *November*, but he, Mons. Liszt,

was obliged to defer his engagements in England *for some weeks*, having pressing ones on the Continent.

It is clear that Lockwood had not been at fault, for Liszt's letters to Marie and to his friend von Schober at the beginning of the first tour in August suggested that he had been expecting to return to England at the beginning of November. The collision of the two York concerts seems not to have perturbed the two sets of patrons, for the local newspaper reported that both events, and the balls which succeeded them, were very well patronized. Parry recorded that Liszt's concert was 'brilliantly attended : 650 at least !!! The Ladies were mostly in Ball dresses.' His songs were not as enthusiastically received as he had hoped:

> I played and sang the *Governess, encored*; then *Fanny Grey* – Miss Bassano being ill, I sang my *Singing Lesson* for her – great applause. Then *The Wife* – but this went very flat indeed !! They *laughed* but did not applaud – Wanted to Dance, I believe – that's the truth – A *Ball.* always ruins a *Concert* – I was completely fagged out – the Room was so *immense*.

The instrumentalists came from the Band of the 4th Dragoon Guards, stationed at Leeds. Liszt did not, however, play the *Concertstück*, and the orchestra simply offered the overtures to Weber's *Ruler of the Spirits*, Auber's *Masaniello* and *Gustavus*, and Hérold's *Zampa*. Liszt had brought his own winds with him: the local report mentioned 'zephyrs', 'a roaring gale' and 'softest breathings' as features of his performance.[37]

In order to get to Manchester for the second concert there, they had to be up by seven. The van, with the Erard, had to be left in York, and so their coach was carrying an extra passenger, and all the luggage, some of which usually travelled in the van. At 'Hempsdon Bridge' (Hebden Bridge? – Parry's calligraphy was far superior to his orthography) – 'a beautiful place in summer' – Liszt walked to The White Lion, enjoyed a 'countrified' meal of ham and eggs, and became 'touchy' about Napoleon. It was at this time that

37. *York Courant and Original Advertiser*, 17 December 1840.

the ashes of the French emperor arrived in Paris from St Helena, and Liszt's friend, Berlioz, was involved in the musical celebrations associated with that great social and political event; two of the singers in the Mozart Requiem which was sung over Napoleon were Grisi and Lablache.

Marie, perhaps hoping to kindle some jealousy in Liszt, wrote to him giving her account of the scenes at the Paris ceremony. From Yorkshire he responded tetchily at first:

> I am beginning to get angry and to feel offended. How ridiculous! You have been to the Champs Elysées for the Ashes ceremony. You were surely not alone. Why didn't you say who was with you? Isn't this to treat me like a husband? I feel I am beginning to look absurd, and dread that my brain will become distracted once and for all . . .[38]

That letter tailed off into a succession of short, broken sentences, which suggest that strong wine had taken charge of his pen. Later he wrote, of the current state of their relationship:

> After further reflection I have arrived at the idea of a kind of balance between our two natures. Please do not take offence; it is all to your advantage. I have always been susceptible to physical temptation, you to temptations of the heart and spirit. Neither of us knows how to reach the target. The eternal thirst for thirst [*Ewiger Durst nach Durst*] will consume me eternally.[39]

The Manchester concert was in no way remarkable, except for Liszt's playing on a Broadwood, their Erard being already on its way to Ireland. Afterwards, while the rest supped on egg flips downstairs, Parry had bread and cheese and 'Gin and Vater' in his room.

Next day, 16 December, they were joined by Wade from London, then left at eleven for Liverpool. Parry, Mrs and Miss Steele, Joey and Marchant sat in their carriage mounted on the train. The journey took an hour and a half. At the Dockside they put their

38. Ollivier, op. cit., II, 82.
39. ibid., II, 67.

luggage aboard the *Prince*, one of five vessels plying for the City of
Dublin Steam Packet Company, 600 tons burthen and 200 horse-
power.[40] Then they prepared themselves for the trials of the overnight sea-crossing. Lewis, Joey and Parry went to the shops: Lewis
bought a pea-jacket for 6/6d, and they had fun making Joey try on
all sorts of hats. At The Queen's Hotel they had cups of tea and
went down to the Quay at 6.30. All of them were 'making long
faces about the voyage tonight'. And so they might well have done,
for the local papers were full of numerous reports of gales and
storms. Recently the Dublin-to-Bristol packet, the *City of Bristol*,
had sunk off Swansea with the loss of 35 lives – and a cargo of 200
pigs. The sole survivor was an Irish pig-driver who had saved
himself by clinging to one of his animals, and who, for a long time
after his dreadful experience, had been able to articulate only 'City
of Bristol'! The Liverpool papers were littered with such stories of
terrible wrecks during recent storms.[41]

The wind was getting up as they arrived at the dock. Their ship
was now at anchor out in the Mersey, and with seven or eight other
passengers the nervous party of nine had to cross to it in a small
boat in pitch darkness: 'we were a tremendous boatload'. This
experience provoked a reminiscence from a frightened Mrs Steele:

> I understood she was crossing a plank once at *Margate* from a
> steamer and the vessel gave a lurch and she fell into the Sea ! Was
> caught by the *neck* and *side* by a Sailor – which dislocated her
> collar bone ! So poor lady it is enough to scare an elderly person
> from getting into more boats !

They scrambled up the ladder at the side of the steamer in the
darkness and found their berths, which were divided among four
rooms, four bunk-beds in each, 'very close work'. They had to wait
an hour and a half for the mail train to deposit its cargo. The
crossing to Dublin had often been perilous, and could last up to
twenty-three hours. Lycidas had been by no means the only victim
of the waters off Liverpool. It was in 1840 that the attempt to

40. *Liverpool Chronicle*, 28 November 1840, advertisement.
41. ibid., 21 November 1840.

shorten the sea-crossing began; but it was not until 1850 that Robert
Stephenson's extension of the railway from Chester to Holyhead
offered a measurable improvement.

Once the *Prince* had cast off, they enjoyed the night-time
shorescape: 'The view of Liverpool, with its thousands of gaslights
– the fires from the neighbouring mines, etc., formed a most beautiful tableau.' Liszt decided not to go below: shared close quarters
were not his style. Their carriage was tethered on deck, covered in a
sheet; and he spent the night there reading by candle-light. 'It
looked so odd', said Parry, 'the light shining through the yellow
tarpoline.' Joey and Parry walked up and down, arm in arm, for
some time. In their cabin they found a capital supper: they 'demol-
ished some fowl, beef, and beautiful haddock'. Then the boat began
to roll; Joey walked quietly to his berth, and Parry read a little in his
German Romances. He went to bed:

> Saw Joey and Lewis – laying on their backs – looking very queer!
> I hadn't been in my cabin for two minutes before ... 'Oh! my!
> Oh! lor!' – I was dreadfully ill, for ten minutes or so. Then lay
> down again on back and tried to sleep. But 'twas 'no go'. There
> was a little boy in his bed opposite me – and about 11 o'clock I
> heard him in a very feeble voice screech out, 'Steward, Steward,
> St-, St.-'. I being very humane was up in my little bed and called
> out 'Steward' pretty hard – but had no sooner done so – than the
> vessel gave a terrible lurch and the former scene was enacted
> again !! That's all I got by being civil. The Steward gave me a
> White brandy and asked if I had eat anything – I told him I had
> had a good tea – then he said that it was much better for me than
> being ill on an empty stomach – Bah! – Nasty man! The vessel
> rolled dreadfully – and what with hearing the surrounding
> neighbourhood, etc., 'cashing up their accounts', etc., etc., I
> never passed so miserable a time.

Nevertheless, in the morning, summoned by the same steward,
Parry went up on deck to see the Bay of Dublin: '. . . the hills were
clouded over with mist occasionally – but this rather added to the
imposing effect – when they passed and lifted – a fine mountain –
bathed in gold from the brilliant morning sun'. And he saw several
porpoises 'jumping quite *out* of the water'. At nine o'clock the

paddles were stopped for the first time since leaving Liverpool. On the quay of Kingstown Harbour, five miles from Dublin, they waited for the carriage and the van to be unloaded. Four horses drew Joey, the Steeles, and Parry to Dublin. Liszt, Lewis and Wade went by the Kingston-to-Dublin Railway (founded in 1832), which ran every half hour. Its little carriages were painted in different colours – Prussian blue, purple lake, yellow-green – to denote the class of passengers. It was Parry's first visit to Ireland, and he savoured the idiosyncrasies of the names over the doors they passed: ' "The M'Sheen", "Docheros", "Shea", "Sullivan O'Shocklmee's", "Blarney's" ', and so on. At ten past ten they were at the door of Morrison's Hotel.

Dublin was still full of good hotels. In 1840 Morrison's, at the bottom of Dawson Street, was perhaps past its best. But the 30-foot-long sitting room overlooking College Park was impressive, and it had an array of coffee parlours and a tavern. According to Peter Somerville-Large, the waiter's customary greeting was, 'Well, gentlemen, I shall be putting on a bottle of sherry and another of sauterne while you're thinking of what you'll have besides!' The food traditionally was delicious, salmon a speciality. Much later Parnell was to choose Morrison's as the place of his arrest, ensuring for it a footnote in the history of the Irish struggle for liberty.[42]

A local newspaper announced the new arrivals at Morrison's; the inaccuracies suggest that some mischief may have been hatched by one of the parties during registration:

> ... Major M'Lintock, family, and suite; Mrs. and Miss Steele; Miss Bassano; Augustus Stafford O'Brien Esquire; Sir Richard Nagle, Bart., M.P.; Fitzstephen French Esquire M.P.; Arthur Blennerhassett Esquire M.P.; Col. Smith; Lieut. Col. Fielding; Capt. Price; Lieut. Smith; 22nd Regiment; the Masters Hume; Mons. Liszt; Hugh Morgan Tuite; Daniel H. Ferrall; Thos. Danier; Robt. James; Geo. Armstrong; Wm. Reilly; John Parry; John Waters; John Knight; John Wills; John Lavenu; John Wade; John Richardson, Esquires.

42. Peter Somerville-Large, *Dublin* (London, 1979), 210.

The city may have impressed Liszt as being more beautiful than even Bath or Cheltenham. It had an aristocratic pedigree but had been in decline since the Union of 1800. In the first two decades of the century, it is reckoned, the value of houses had fallen 30 per cent. The cultured elegance and high living of the eighteenth century had changed into a more comfortable, bourgeois style. The last Dublin duel had been fought in 1838, and even then one of the participants shot himself in the leg; and in the same year a smart municipal police force came into being. The town also became more than a collection of habitations, and started to develop an industrial belt beside the Liffey and the canals. The roads connecting Dublin with distant parts had been improved lately: a doubtful blessing, as Liszt and his colleagues were soon to discover.

Lavenu's party had a splendid sitting room of their own at Morrison's, its walls covered with titillating French paper: 'Cupid and Phisbe', and 'Diana Bathing'. Parry went immediately to the post office in Sackville Street for news from Anne:

> This street is the principal, and is much wider than Portland Place ! I never have seen such wide, such splendid streets. The Bank of Ireland is very fine – far superior to our own exterior – the Nelson Column is very high, and being in the centre of the great [street] thus looks particularly well – There is a fine bridge over the Liffey.

But his commercial as well as his aesthetic eyes were open wide:

> Passed four or five music shops – one had on the *outside* ' "A Wife Wanted", – "A Governess Wanted", – "The Musical Husband" – all new by *Parry* – just out!'

Such enthusiasm proved, if any further evidence were required, how bourgeois Dublin had become. He went to Piggott's, the main music-seller, and met one of his rivals, the ballad composer, J. P. Knight, who took him to see St Stephen Green.

At seven, on the evening of the day they arrived, Liszt went to the Theatre Royal to see Charles Kean in *Macbeth*. He left early to go down to the Rotundo for a rehearsal of their first concert which was to take place next day, 18 December. Parry arrived later: 'We met him there – he played his *Concertstück* (Weber) with a very fair band . . .'. This orchestra was quite extraordinary in its social composition. The Duke of Leinster played principal double bass, and others among the players were only a little less distinguished in rank: knights and baronets, colonels and captains; though the bulk of the players came from Dublin-based regimental bands. Parry went back to Morrison's, pleased that there would be no rolling that night; though he nearly fell out of his narrow little bed. Next day he succeeded in getting himself a better room.

In Dublin there was a long-standing tradition of aristocratic participation in making good music. In the early eighteenth century, at the end of Swift's reign when Handel paid a visit, its chief musical venue had been the Bull's Head in Fishamble Street. Among those who played there regularly for the Charitable Musical Society were Lord Mornington, first violin, the flautist Lord Lucan, and the Earl of Bellamont on cello. The funds raised by their jolly activities helped to hide Swift's depressing poor from the fashionable gaze. Mornington, no mean musician, was an amateur of true Lockeian proficiency; and, for a time, his son, the great Wellington's father, was Professor of Music at Trinity College. Handel's invitation to Dublin in 1742 had been delivered from the Lord Lieutenant, the Duke of Devonshire.[43]

The Lord Lieutenant at the time of Liszt's visit was Earl Fortescue. A Devonshire grandee with a marked interest in learning and education at all social levels, he actively supported the arts in Dublin. In the week before Liszt arrived he had graced the Theatre Royal with an official attendance upon *Macbeth*, though the Lord Mayor received greater applause from the bourgeoisie when he entered the theatre. The Band of the 8th Regiment serenaded the playgoers as they arrived.[44] Some time after the Union, and in the relative lull before the ravages of the Great Famine, Fortescue's administration was attempting to heal and settle a demoralized, though still seething Ireland by means of gradual social and economic reforms. Before he played in Liszt's concert, the Duke of Leinster, with the Earl of Charlemont, had addressed a meeting 'of

43. *New Grove* (1980 edn), 'Dublin'.
44. *The Irishman*, 19 December 1840.

all parties' in the same Dublin Rotundo, on the subject of the promotion of Irish manufactures.[45]

But the poverty of greater Ireland could not be concealed beneath the gentle mask of well-intentioned reform. The gales which had lashed the musicians during their crossing from Liverpool caused far greater havoc among the impoverished lower orders in Irish towns and in the overcrowded countryside. In December 1840, *The Irishman* reported that the flooding in Cork, the worst since 1789, had been particularly damaging among the one-roomed dwellings of the poor in the Marsh.[46] Newspapers were making appeals for fuel to get rid of the most devastating effects of the floods. The chief item on the political agenda, voiced in numerous meetings by Daniel O'Connell, was repeal: a repeal of the hated Corn Laws, which action would, it was thought, release Ireland from economic bondage under the great absentee aristocratic landowners.

Liszt loved and envied aristocrats. In Dublin he was befriended by a man only a little less powerful than Fortescue, the Chief Secretary, Lord Morpeth. This young Anglican, like others among his colleagues in the Irish administration, did his best to ingratiate himself with common feelings in Ireland, even to the extent of attending Mass occasionally in a predominantly Catholic country. While Liszt had been in East Anglia on the first tour, the Tory *Cambridge Chronicle*, quoting the *Dublin Evening Mail*, had asked a question:

> Lord Morpeth ... occupies the high and important office of Chief Secretary in Ireland, and has always professed hitherto to be a staunch, unflinching Protestant. What will be said of the following notice, reflecting his Lordship's movements in that country? 'Lord Morpeth, after having heard High Mass yesterday in the Roman Catholic Chapel in Marlborough Street, suddenly took his departure in the afternoon.'[47]

He had even acted as 'Collector' after the sermon. Liszt was affected

45. ibid.
46. ibid.
47. *Cambridge Chronicle*, 3 October 1840.

more by the Liberal Morpeth's social grace than by his political tightrope-walking. He wrote to Marie,

> You ask for my impressions of Ireland? Alas, I scarcely leave my room, and have hardly any impression. However, I have met a most pleasant man, the brother of the Duchess of Sutherland, Lord Norpeth [*sic*], Secretary-of-State, and I know not what. He is the second most important person in Dublin. He invited me to a great banquet, and, in the evening there was a score of women, and music. We had a fellow-feeling from the first evening (at a concert). If I return to Dublin later, I shall visit him.[48]

Preparing for their first concert, Parry dined rather well; he was clearly very nervous about the most important occasion on the tour so far, and made a 'Tom Noddy' of himself 'by *Balletising, Ducroising, Pantomimising* – to slow music by Lavenu Esq.' He sobered up on soda water and lay on his bed reading. Then he went to Worn, the fashionable hairdresser, to have his locks curled: '. . . one shilling, just to turn the hair ! Nearly spoilt my hair he curled so tight.' Mistaking the time of the concert, he had to rush off in a car with Mr Knight to the Rotundo.

> The Concert was the most splendid sight I ever saw. 1200 persons at least, all elegantly dressed, and numbers of Officers, etc. Also the *Lord Lieutenant of Ireland* attended by a guard of honour ! 'Twas magnificent ! There was a fine band of 60 or 70 performers – the *Duke of Leinster* playing the principal double bass – *Sir George Gore Booth* violoncello . . . 'Twas superb effect – So brilliant . . . They began to the minute. 'Soave' did not go well – Ladies frightened – I stood my ground very well. Liszt was not so rapturously applauded as I expected from last night. But still it was a very good reception. He had a *new Grand* from Erard's expressly, but it was the worst Erard for *Public* I ever played on. Things went rather flat till Joey touched them up with 'Nel cor'. I think he had much more applause than the Great Gun . . . I made quite a hit ! – but it cost me a great deal of exertion – the Room was so very large and bad for sound. *Liszt* only played twice – 'Guill Tell' was tremendously encored. They seemed to like it

48. Ollivier, op. cit., II, 90.

much better than the Concert Stuck [*sic*] – which was his first piece. I ran away directly I had sung 'The merry thing' and arrived home as soon as the others. They having come in a Car.

Joey stoked up the fire in Parry's room; a letter to Anne; then 'Buona Sera'.

Next morning's papers had very favourable notices, said Parry, 'particularly of Liszt and I'. In the evening Mr Piggott took them to see van Amburgh's lions at the theatre in Abbey Street. Animal extravaganzas were the fashionable hit of the day: van Amburgh and his beasts had been Lavenu's chief competition during Race Week at Leicester on the first tour. In Liverpool, a few weeks before, Mr Carter's lions had taken up a good deal more space in the press than reports of Liszt's performances.[49] Parry was not impressed by the dramatic side of these bestial displays: '. . . the *gran piece* he placed was written in ten words *at most* !' Much more gratifying was their meal afterwards at the Oyster Room near Morrison's Hotel: though Parry chose kidneys 'underdone'. He was delighted by the Waiter's dialect. 'Had some Whiskey – very *strong* – returned home. "O' Gramachree o' doro ma Flanagan!" – Ireland for ever!'

Next day he had a bad headache: 'Come of "O Gramachree o' doro ma Flanaganizing" last night !' Mrs and Miss Steele went out to dine with friends, leaving Miss Bassano 'quite at the mercy of all the Gentlemen'. They anticipated that the second concert, on 21 December, would be a flop; theatrically they would be competing with Kean's night at the theatre, politically with a public dinner for O'Connell. The concert raised only £21, but lasted three hours. They got home, near midnight, to find there was nothing to eat. Wade lay on the sofa, 'angry because no one would speak to him. Lewis and he at loggerheads . . . Said I neglected him – Poor man ! Little crazed, I think.' It would seem that Wade, though he had been expected to lubricate the machinery of the Irish tour, had decided instead to dose himself with Dublin liquor. The long-term consequences of his carousing were to cause turmoil later, after New Year.

Tuesday 22 December was 'a whole Holiday!! . . . "Girls and

49. *Liverpool Chronicle*, 5 December 1840.

Boys go out to play" '. It was a brilliant, lovely day, and so the inseparable Parry and Joey went for a long stroll, dined, and read the papers at the Reading Room in a coffee house. They, with Lewis, took a box to see Kean that evening:

> ... very good in some parts – his *dying* scene was certainly the very best I ever saw on any stage – the *Lady* Macbeth was dreadful – a Miss Pelham, tall, very ugly, no mind or feeling – the Tradegy [*sic*] was followed by 'Deaf as a Post' – in which Mr. Compton sustained Liston's great part of 'Tristram Sappy' – not good tho' . . . Bed by ½12.

Their third concert was on 23 December, better attended, but still only raising £34. Liszt was applauded 'to the skies' for his performance of *Hexameron*, the variations written by him, Thalberg, Chopin and others on a theme from Bellini's *I Puritani*. He also played, for the first time in Ireland, extemporaneously; Parry was delighted:

> When Lewis asked the audience if they had any themes ready written – one was handed only – but Mr. Piggott gave him 'the Russian Hymn' in addition. This was not enough. So after *talking to the audience in a most familiar manner* – and making them *laugh* very much because he had got no *lively* air to work on – he turned round suddenly and said, 'I play de "Vanted Governess" ' – and off he started – with the Irish air and then the Russian Hymn and last my Song, which he played most wonderfully. Not all the way thro' tho', but the Waltz in the first Symphony. He played it at least 12 different ways and then wound up with the 3 together in a manner truly extraordinary! 'Twas received as it deserved with tumultuous applause.

Next day Liszt and Parry went shopping to buy presents for their respective 'wives'. After his lively transactions with the audience on the previous evening, Liszt must have become 'excited', for one of his Irish letters to Marie betrayed a certain lack of control:

> Do you like Irish poplins? Do you know what they are? They are probably very ordinary: I don't have the spirit of the explorer. However, I will send you 3 or 4 samples. If there is one to suit you, I'll send you a dress.[50]

50. Ollivier, op. cit., II, 82.

Parry, advised by Miss Steele, went to a shop in Grafton Street and

> 'then and there' I laid out for my own Sweet wife my money – for
> a *Superb Poplin Dress* – Pink with flowers in satin – It cost me
> £4. 16. 0., there being 16 yards at 6/- per yard. I gave every
> direction for it to arrive in London on Saturday *week*, as I wish it
> to be *my birthday* present to dearest Anne – I am sure she will like
> it – or I am very much mistaken.

Liszt delayed purchasing his poplins till later. In the meantime he
tried to apologize to Marie for his earlier, rather tipsy letter by
telling her how much work he had accomplished:

> I have set about half-a-dozen motifs from 'Der Freischütz'
> (Weber). It could be called a Fantasia. You love those tunes,
> don't you ? I am going to set as many from 'Don Juan' and
> perhaps from 'Euryanthe'. I have written the great organ-point
> (cadenza) for 'Adelaïde' (Beethoven), and significantly improved
> the piece on 'La Sonnambula' (Donizetti).[51]

Between his sojourns with Morpeth – and much else besides which
we shall never discover – and while Parry was parading through
Dublin and reclining on sofas with soda water, Liszt was working
hard at revising his transcriptions and arrangements, stocking up
with novelties for future Continental forays. It is easy to imagine
the patrons of Morrison's Hotel permitting a pause in their animated
conversation in order to eavesdrop on trials of some of the greatest
of re-creations in Romantic music.

Meanwhile, in the company of a musical friend of Joey, Parry
was being conducted around Trinity College:

> The Library, the first I ever was in, beats ours at the Museum –
> Oxford or Cambridge – 100,000 books and more, and all in
> beautiful order, and marble busts of all the great 'literati' ever
> known – the whole length of the room.

While Liszt was being received by Lord Morpeth, Parry was

51. ibid., II, 89.

enjoying middle-class hospitality in the suburbs. He went a short way by rail to Merrion to meet the family of Mr Slater, who had been their guide at the Library. At dinner he sat next to a nice girl with 'Good Eyes'; she flirted with him, not knowing he was a 'done Gentleman'. He sang for his supper and then returned to Dublin in a jaunting car, for the first time:

Later that night he went to Piggott's where he found some gentlemen playing quintets to a company which included Wade and Lavenu. Liszt came in later from Morpeth's, and Joey entertained them with 'Find the Lady'. All in all, it had been a most convivial way of celebrating Christmas Eve away from home.

On Christmas Day Joey, Parry and Lewis got together to prepare a 'Dramatic Effort' as an evening entertainment, rehearsing for nearly two hours their roles of 'Blowfluticus', 'Conductius' and 'Camilla Japonica', Parry, as might have been expected, taking the 'travesti' part. Then, on this day of goodwill, Liszt and Joey began a passionate quarrel: 'Speeches on both sides, hot and instantaneous. At last *the* Liszt very friendly gave his hand to Joey.' The ladies had been in tears, but now 'Much merrier than before – Miss Steele excited ...' Parry got himself up for the entertainment, 'all curls, night gowns, splendid legs, red slippers, etc., etc.' 'Blowfluticus' and 'Conductius' had perhaps overdone their imbibing of liquid

confidence. But the 'Tradagy' [*sic*] passed off well, and the performers '*crawled* off the stage (there being no curtain) amidst the loudest
applause'.

On Boxing Day the 'Boots' told them about the kind of dreadful
accident which morbidly excited Parry. The congregation in Frances
Street Chapel on Christmas Day had been frightened at 7 o'clock
Mass by a cracking sound; those in the gallery, thinking it about to
collapse, stampeded for the stairs. In the crush, nine people had
been trampled to death. There was no time for reflection upon this
real tragedy, for the party had immediately to prepare for their
huge, 160-mile coach-ride to Cork. They were venturing beyond
the Pale, into the friendliest, wildest and best-educated countryside
in Europe, wilder even than the most bandit-infested regions of
Calabria. Each of them took his own characteristic precautions.
Joey, for instance, possibly anticipating a wintry seat on the outside
of the coach, purchased a horse rug; Lewis, as the formal guardian
of the troupe, bought a brace of pistols, for which he paid a guinea.
The bill at the hotel, for eight people over nine days, was only £55.
Some of this must have been paid in recompense for the devastating
Christmas party: 'We (!) had broken several chairs, inkstands, etc.,
during our stay!' Evidently there are historic precedents for the ruin
caused by late twentieth-century touring pop-groups.

At noon Marchant and Joey took their places on the boot box.
The four horses were 'rough-looking, but "good 'uns to go"'.
They created a sensation as they dashed through the streets. Liszt
was inside with the Steeles, the 'lovers' [Lewis and Louisa] behind.
They left Wade in Dublin to prepare for the concerts they were to
give on their return. Parry's account of the journey is henceforward
accompanied by a linear road-map, running down the left-hand
margin of each page of his diary. By the time they reached Kingstown, Marchant and Joey were covered in mud. When they crossed
the Liffey at Kilcullen the massed beggars were dreadfully importu-
nate: 'I am sure since I have been in Ireland I have given away
nearly half a guinea in sixpences, etc., to get rid of these people',
Parry complained, though he quickly lost his pique during a lunch
of chops, eggs and porter. After dark in the candle-lit coach they
were comfortable. At half-past eleven they stopped for the night at
Kilkenny, where they had to knock up Mrs Walsh at the Hibernian

Hotel. The hotel fire impressed Parry: the waiter told him that Kilkenny coal neither smoked nor made a smell, and also that the streets of the town were paved, not with gold, but with black marble, 'which is a fact'. Here, there is a very tenuous musical connection. The first mineralogical survey of Ireland, which had identified the marble scientifically, had been conducted, two decades before, by Professor Sir Charles Lewis Giesecke of the Royal Dublin Society. This was the former Freemason, Carl Ludwig Giesecke, who, as a young man in Vienna, had played Second Moor in, and written a considerable part of the libretto for, Mozart's *Zauberflöte*.[52] The party were more interested, however, in the fact that Kilkenny was the most peaceful county in all Ireland, 'with the exception of a few Repealers *now* and *then*'. So they slept well, but largely because Lewis and Joey each had a pistol under his pillow, which probably also accounted for the flautist talking excitedly in his sleep.

When they set off beggars again crowded round, the women and children 'almost knocking each other down to try and get near the carriage'. Someone was attempting to give Parry and the others a lesson on the true human and economic condition of Ireland. By two o'clock, after a furious, hilly drive, they were in Clonmel, the county town of Tipperary. It was Sunday, and the chapels and churches were disgorging their congregations. During lunch in the Commercial Rooms, they met the keeper of a travelling bazaar – could this have been Abraham Rosenbaum, formerly of Weymouth, with his mechanical menagerie?

> He found us out and strongly recommended a Concert in this Town – He was a German Jew named ... [blank]. He talked to Liszt in German, said he knew Herz, Mendelssohn, Beriot [Malibran's husband], etc., etc., intimately (!) – Lewis run out and attacked the *Mayor* who was coming from church – asked him if he might give a Concert. The Mayor *very much affronted* walked on and did not speak !! However Lewis wrote an apology stating the *urgency* of the case and it was finally arranged that we come

52. See Henry F. Berry, *A History of the Royal Dublin Society* (London, 1915).

back this way on *Saturday* Jan 2nd 1841 – and give a *Morning* Concert. The Gentry are very numerous and highly genteel around this neighbourhood.

Lewis retained the Jew as their temporary agent in Clonmel, but his incompetence and the Mayor's injured dignity were probably causes of a comic episode on the party's return visit to the town.

The crowd of beggars which assembled to see them go numbered about 150:

> ... the scene almost baffled description : little babies under the wheels of the carriage almost, and screeching out for money. The lame and the halt and the blind ! I never was so glad to get away.

At 9.30 they had tea in The Queen's Arms in Fermoy. 'The waiter a most facetious fat man – everything was "illigant" – I had some "illigant" toasted cheese and Pickles, Porter, etc.' On the final leg, not far from Cork, in the pitch dark they met a man on the mountains carrying a large bough of a tree 'on fire' to make light for his way. At two o'clock in the morning they reached their target, the Imperial Clarence Hotel, Cork, having travelled, with one break for sleep, 158 English miles from Dublin. Their rooms were ready, and after 'a shade of Whiskey and Porter', they were abed. The journey, thought Parry, bereft of his usual buoyancy, was 'too long for the Performers, and too long for the "Conductor", for it can never pay to come such dreadful distances with a carriage and 4 – and 8 persons to keep'. Lavenu's desperate attack upon the Mayor of Clonmel had given some indication of the financial plight he was in; but if his schemes were too extravagant, at least he was learning to look for concert-giving opportunities.

There were to be three concerts in Cork. At one o'clock on 28 December they were dressing for the first of them in the Clarence Room. The audience was 280 – 'all money'. Despite a dark room and a dull day, it all went very well, though Parry was disgusted with his cracked voice and lack of spontaneity in the *Buffo Trio*, hardly surprising after the rigours of the previous two days. Liszt was on top form in *Guillaume Tell*, the *Lucia* Fantasy, and his *Galop*.

Parry tried to mend his voice by going to bed by one. But the rest of the party roistered on till three:

> Tricks, etc., downstairs ... Joey lost his Pin (!) – Lewis whiskeyish – Liszt promenading, etc., etc. Great hunting for Joey's pin – Noisy people woke me up slamming doors.

Next day all of them – except for Mrs Steele, who was poorly after being so friendly to Joey the previous evening – made an excursion to the Cork Cobh, and crossed to a small fort on the most beautiful part of the haven. Liszt, Parry and Miss Steele took a stroll, admiring 'the beauties of nature' – three pigs trotting ahead of them:

They arrived for lunch at The Navy Hotel, a small, snug inn facing the harbour. As at another waterside hostelry earlier, in Birkenhead, Liszt stood treat, this time cold turkey and oysters, with beautiful Irish bread and butter. From upstairs came the sounds of a concert. Forty people had assembled to listen to the remarkably fine singing of Signor Jacobowitz who, rather incongruously, was giving them 'Rule Britannia'. 'He has long black hair and looks something like Paganini – his voice', wrote Parry, 'is wonderful in its falzetto [sic], beats Mr. Trio Parry – as they call me in the Cork paper.'

It was obviously planned to give over the whole of this day, the
29th, to pleasure and relaxation. They returned to Cork and, after
tea, it was decided that the gentlemen should go to the little theatre
– boxes 6d., pit 3d. The play they were to see was Bulwer's
comedy, *The Lady of Lyons, or, Love and Pride*. First performed in
1838 this was still very popular – there was even a burlesque of it
and of animal extravaganzas, which had been given while Liszt was
in Liverpool, *The Lady of The Lions*[53] – and while Lavenu's party
had been travelling around Britain the original had been playing at,
for instance, Weymouth, Bath, Liverpool and Dublin. But so far
Liszt had managed to avoid being pressed into attending a performance. He may even have been irritated for emotional reasons by the
constant proximity of the play. Edward Bulwer-Lytton, its author,
had a brother, Henry, then a diplomat stationed in Paris, and during
Liszt's absences he had been paying court to the neglected Marie
d'Agoult, even offering marriage. Indeed, it seems likely that, when
Liszt had jealously speculated about the person accompanying
Marie to the Champs Elysées for the Ashes ceremony, he was
guessing that Bulwer had been with her. Therefore his action on
this evening in Cork may have been moved partly by his bottled-up
sense of mischief (and sexual frustration), and partly by a jealous
animadversion towards the Bulwer-Lytton tribe. In any case, as
soon as they left their hotel for the theatre, Liszt changed direction,
and the evening took a fantastic turn; Parry's thin sense of discretion
just conceals some of the coarser elements of a lively gentlemen's
party at a superior shebeen:

> ... when we were out it seems that the Eminente Pianiste was
> bent upon fun – he took us to a 'logement' he had found in Cork –
> I was quite surprised to see him take his patent copying machine
> with him – He introduced us to Miss Burke, and the 'Turk' was
> quite at home – the only fear was that he 'eat mice'!! *Bagpipes* for
> upwards of an hour – Dancing, Reels, *German* Gavots – Porter,
> Whiskey, etc., etc. *Eliza*, Ellen, 'Triste' – Mary, the Captain,
> 'The Clergyman', 'The dramatical Gentleman' and 'the Turk' –
> that lives on Mice ! No end to Fun – 'Bagpipes' second edition !
> Coffee, Riddles and Gran Finale – home by ½11. – Had some
> Bread and Cheese and Pickles – and at ½12 – Liszt, Joey and I

53. *Liverpool Chronicle*, 5 December 1840.

were in bed – a more unexpected event never happened to me – and it was truly *national* and rational – the Dancing of Joey was beyond all praise – the Bagpipe player was superb – Joey and Lewis had a try but could not get up the wind ! 'Twas the merriest party I ever was at !

Of course, this extraordinary account cannot be taken wholly at its face value. However, although some of its details defy accurate interpretation, it is possible to crack Parry's code in a number of particulars. Much of what happened was probably quite innocent, but it is reasonable to guess that Miss Burke's establishment was a superior kind of brothel: at least we can speculate that Peter Grimes would have recognized an 'Aunty' and her 'Nieces' there. It seems clear, too, that Liszt went with the positive intention of hearing, and writing down, some 'real' Irish music. He was always enthralled by the cultures of barbarous peoples living on the margins of Europe, and at Miss Burke's he came closest to the recent experience, in his native Hungary, of recording peasant music nearly in its raw state. Amid his relief at being temporarily released into unbuttoned gaiety after the captivity of the coach, the hotel and the concert room, he still retained his musical curiosity and sensitivity. The whirling Irish notes were fortunately the only mementoes he carried away from Cork. Yet he, the 'Turk', and Lewis, 'The dramatical gentleman', did 'eat mice': in London police stations 'mice' were 'ladies of the night'. Parry surely knew the term, and used it in this case with some precision. But it is impossible to be really certain what happened. Most of the existing evidence suggests that Liszt was a romantic, rather than a Priapic, Don Juan: the cloak of sexual promiscuity never fitted very comfortably around his shoulders. But who can tell what he accomplished during those few hours of freedom in Cork? It is unlikely that he wrote to Marie, or to anyone else, about what happened. The most intriguing question of all is how Liszt had found his 'logement'. Clearly, none of the other gentlemen knew about his investigation of the shady side of Cork. Perhaps, on the more leisurely second tour, this was not the first time that Liszt had ventured into the more dubious areas of Victorian towns.

It will have been noted that, in Parry's account, only he, Joey and

Liszt returned later that night to the Clarence Hotel. The three of them were up next morning for breakfast at 10.30. Soon Liszt was 'playing the Bagpipes on the Piano', while Joey and Parry attempted an Irish jig to entertain the ladies, all except Miss Bassano – 'Ah! whither my love', asked Parry tauntingly, 'Ah! whither art thou flown'. She was, he said, afraid that Lavenu had been '*Burked*!!!!' Lewis crept in about noon. Parry and Miss Steele discreetly took a walk, and met 'a limb of the Bagpiper'.

The evening concert was a success: 300 in the room. Liszt immediately put to good use the Irish tunes he had recorded the night before. He extemporized wonderfully, this time on 'Rory o' More', the March in *Norma*, and 'The Last Rose of Summer'. How extraordinary would be the effect of that musical mélange if we could hear it now. Intriguingly, it would seem that after the concert, the magnetic Miss Burke attracted some of her customers to return for a second evening of relaxation:

> Very tired indeed – went to bed directly after a bit of bread and cheese – *Some* of the party took it into their heads to go out at $\frac{1}{2}$12 !

And next morning, New Year's Eve, Parry's suspicions were confirmed:

> Mr. Roche very anxious to see Lewis – no where to be found! I *guessed*; was right; found them all at breakfast ($\frac{1}{2}$12 o'clock), brought them away.

Quite what the connection was between the musicians and Mr Roche is not clear. It is possible that he was the local figure prominent in public administration who was currently engaged in controversy over political appointments. The Lord Lieutenant, Fortescue, according to one local paper, was taking a long time over deciding whether to appoint a Mr Roche as Sheriff of Co. Cork. The *Cork Standard* reported that 'the only objections ... to Mr. Roche are – that he is a Repealer, and may probably be the returning officer in an electioneering contest in which his own son is a candidate'. His appointment would be 'the greatest Ministerial triumph' yet enjoyed by O'Connell's Repeal party in Ireland.[54]

Father or son – perhaps even a different Mr Roche – was instrumental in creating the scenario for the most macabre event to involve Liszt during the whole of his British enterprise. Roche obtained permission for Lavenu's little party to visit the new Cork Lunatic Asylum, accompanied by an officer and one of the governors. Parry's description is long, but it deserves almost complete quotation:

> I never yet beheld a sight which so fully impressed me with melancholy feelings – there are 460 inmates at present confined here – It is immensely large – kept beautifully clean – and [the] wards are full of poor wretched beings who stared at us, laughed, howled, grinned, screamed, and some made every possible distortion of the body., etc. The Women's Wards – were by far the most frightful. One poor creature (about 18) was confined in a straight-jacket – and tied to some railings ! She was crying and screaming for her Father and Mother – her hair was cut close and she [had] very little clothes on, always tearing them with her teeth and feet !
>
> Several asked me quite rationally for a halfpenny and for Snuff – Another whispered to me to let her know when she was to be let out – but not to tell anyone ! One was sitting on top of a dresser – with a *hood* she had made – with something immensely heavy in it, and there she sat without smiling or opening her lips day after day ! She was almost double. One was a very respectable person indeed and had not been there long – She became mad from jealousy ! Such a pretty woman. We saw her in bed first. We (the Gentlemen of the Party) went into the Female *Idiots* Room and where the *unclean* patients are kept – So dreadful a sight I never beheld – the place was more offensive than any Managerie [*sic*]. There were about 30 in the same Room – some howling – some bent up like animals – some scraping the walls – rolling on the stones, etc. One poor wretched being here was up in the farthest corner by the fire place (which is all iron rails from floor to ceiling) singing and rubbing the wall with her hand, her hair was cut short and she looked more like an Ape than a human being –

She had been there for six years (!) and had always been in the *same corner* and always humming with one unceasing moaning the following, which I wrote down at the time.

She took not any notice of us at all but went droning on – and so has continued for the last *6* years !!!

This room was altogether quite frightful ! Liszt was obliged to go away —

In the *Male* Wards we saw poor Mr. Keys, a once very respectable person in the *Musical* way in Cork – he had a beautiful voice and was in great repute as a singer – poor fellow he talked quite well for some time, knew Mr. Roche – but presently off he went about some £40,000 he was going to get out of the English Bank on Monday. It was dreadful to see him, so calm, so quiet – talked about his Wife and *Children* etc. (One of the latter a very pretty girl about 12 was at the door when we came away – She had brought something for her poor Father ! Oh! – how shocking – Sometimes he knew her, sometimes not !)

In a long Gallery by himself we saw a man rigging a beautiful model of a vessel which he had made entirely being the *second* ship of his workmanship since his confinement 8 years. We talked a very long while with this poor being – no one could even have believed him to be mad – and yet this being had been a Captain of a Vessel – by some means bound *9* of his men in different parts of his Vessel and then cruelly *butchered the whole – by beating out their brains with an iron crow-bar*!! – Most wonderful thing tho' this horrid deed was committed far at Sea – the Vessel floated into Cork Harbour without anyone to steer her or guide her helm – The Wretched man jumped overboard on her arrival – but was captured ! What a spectacle for those who went on board the Vessel – to see 9 mangled and putrid bodies ! – Horrible to think of ! – He was tried and brought in quite insane and ordered to be *confined for life* in this Mad House – After a lapse of time he was allowed to have tools and is now very quiet and harmless – always building ships etc. etc. – he makes every single part himself – paints and gilds etc. etc. This Vessel was about 6 feet long and 9 feet high – the name of this unhappy being is

– *William Steward*

I shook hands with him !!! Fancy shaking hands with a man who has *murdered nine* fellow creatures in such a horrible manner !

We saw also a man who had been an *Orator* once – and now his language was quite beautiful – and the manner he took leave of the Ladies by Kissing his hands and bowing, it was really worthy a first rate dramatic artiste. We left this place after seeing the Kitchen – tasting their oat bread, Cakes, etc. etc. – all so nice and clean – and went (by way of being lively) to the *Cemetry* [*sic*].

A visit to the cemetery epitomized this critical phase of Ireland's evolution. The Cork Cemetery had been a botanical garden, a symbol of the vain hopes raised by scientific inquiry and political and economic experiment in eighteenth-century Ireland – hopes which were now struggling to return to life. Of the Cemetery Parry recorded, ruefully, 'it is not at all well kept tho' – the walks are over-run with weeds . . .' He wandered into town and bought a print of Victoria, Albert, and the new Royal baby, sent it to dearest Anne, and then took Mr Roche to dinner in recompense for the experience of the asylum.

The Cork experience must have made Parry more sensitive to his own condition as a manic-depressive, swinging between public and private euphoria and the most profound melancholy. In his early forties he was to suffer an intense mental collapse which forced him to retire from concert-giving.[55] Mr Keys and his tragic little daughter very probably caused Parry to reflect on the darker side of his own outwardly merry nature. At this stage in his career Liszt was no stranger to melancholy; but his temperament was altogether more robust than Parry's. The great pianist's response to mental disability in others was, as his discreet behaviour in Cork would suggest, less voyeuristic and more positive than those of his companions. A few years earlier in Paris he had taken part in a primitive experiment with musical therapy: he frequently visited and played for an autistic woman who could achieve a measure of repose only while listening to music.

55. *Grove* (1927 edn).

Parry's vein of melancholy was not yet exhausted. That same evening he went alone – where were the other gentlemen? – to Collins Theatre in Nelson Square to see *Venice Preserved*. He was amused by the poor performance of this tragedy; but the pathos of one aspect of theatrical life did affect him:

> I had the daughter of the manager (who was walking about the Pit *alone*) – a child not 3 years old – in my lap a long while – We had oranges etc. – She was going 'to play a fairy soon' – poor little innocent . . .

This cry from a deep pit is one of the most resonant and suggestive moments in Parry's record of the tour. At the year's turning, far from home and family, in a chaotic country, with images of the madhouse still in his mind, he paused to look closely for once at the meretriciousness, the theatricality of the world he inhabited.

When he left the theatre and returned to the Clarence at eleven, he was in time to hear Liszt entertaining Mr Roche at the piano. Parry celebrated the entry of the New Year with oysters and whiskey. 'Great excitement prevailed on our going to bed – Whiskey triumphant ! – Fine Fun with (rooms) 27, 26–25, and 24. All quiet by half-past two ! And high time too !' Parry was restored to well-being in his true métier.

Because 1 January was a saint's day, their third Cork concert was poorly attended, though the Anglican Bishop (and his legitimate family) came. To suit the occasion the first half was uniquely devoted to a selection of religious pieces: Parry, for instance, sang 'O Lord have mercy'; then they returned to their usual miscellany in the second half. They were due to leave as soon as the concert had finished, having already abandoned the original plan for a final morning concert next day; but Liszt and Lavenu, who had met with a 'smoking friend', delayed their departure for over an hour. The bill was again very moderate: with concert room and servants it came to only £46. At seven the next morning they arrived in Clonmel. Liszt probably never knew it, but this had been the scene of an early tragic episode in the life of his London hostess, Lady Blessington. As Margaret Power, she had lived much of her child-hood in the town, where her father, 'Beau' Power, a debauched

henchman of the Dublin Government, had sold her in marriage to a
wastrel Army officer when she was 15. Clonmel in 1840 contained
elements which might have disturbed nervous travellers. While the
musicians had been in Yorkshire a month before, a local paper
carried the news that there were 326 persons confined in Clonmel
Gaol, 18 of them charged with murder. On 2 January, however, the
town was the scene of the most comic adventure on Liszt's tour.
When they all went to bed at 7 a.m., they expected to awaken for
the grand morning concert which, the German Jew had promised
them, was to be the pinnacle of their Irish success in gentry-girt
Clonmel.

When they arose they found that no tickets had been sold.
Perhaps the affronted Mayor had done his reproachful best to keep
the locals away. The room was filthy and there was no piano. But
Liszt's enthusiasm for public performance – tinged, on this occasion, with irony – was not to be subdued by such misfortunes.

> Liszt suggested asking 2 or 3 Ladies who had come in their
> Carriages – to the hotel – and *to come in our sitting Room* – where
> there was a little Square of Tomkinson – this being done we
> began and went thro' the *whole Programme* to 5 Ladies and Gentle-
> man – 'twas like a private Matinee – So funny to see Liszt firing
> away at Guillaume Tell – on his little instrument – but it stood his
> powerful hand capitally.

Thus was the whole nature of Liszt's British provincial enterprise
compressed into one small caricature.

Next morning when they awoke in marble Kilkenny, it was Parry's 31st birthday. They had travelled from Clonmel through an
awful storm, and it was still hailing and snowing and blowing. The
congratulations of his friends warmed Parry before their departure
for Dublin. Despite the hurricane conditions, Liszt insisted on
travelling on the outside of the coach. Those inside could not see
out, for the windows were covered in frost and snow. They arrived
at Morrison's, where Wade awaited them, at half-past midnight.
There was disappointing news: Wade had failed in his sole duty of
obtaining an immediate Dublin concert for them,

> after all our posting and *losing* the morning concert at Cork ...

This will be a dreadful loss to Lewis of course – Liszt and Lewis were very angry with Wade, as he had been left here expressly to arrange matters. We shall now have *nothing to do till Thursday* next – . . . 'All in the *downs* the *crew* were moored !'

Wade, possibly in his cups since their departure for Cork, had incidentally ruined Parry's birthday evening.

Next day the comedian cheered up after snatching a glance at a letter from Miss Burke to Lewis – ' "Love and affection" – "fond attachment" – "Pistols" ' – and in high glee he went to the Theatre Royal with Liszt and Miss Steele. Apparently the eminent pianist became embroiled in a quarrel ('quite French') about the position of their seats in a box, claiming that 'Little boys give way to *Ladies*' (a piece of gallantry which must have pleased Miss Steele); but he lost the argument. Nevertheless, he did succeed in getting better seats on the other side of the house. The opera they saw was *Fra Diavolo*, and Parry liked the acting of the principal, Miss Daley, better than her singing. In the pantomime which followed – *Harlequin and O'Donoghue of the Lakes* – he admired most of all 'Miss Chambers legs – fine woman'. Liszt and Miss Steele left as soon as the pantomime began. Their little affair – it must have been very innocent, even when Mrs Steele retired to bed discreetly early – seems to have centred upon Liszt's helping the soprano to learn some Schubert songs. When Parry was asleep Joey and Lewis burst into his room with their pistols, fought a duel using percussion caps, and were then ejected.

On Tuesday the 5th it was announced that Lewis had successfully negotiated for a concert engagement in Limerick, after which they would return to Dublin. Parry was horrified to discover that this would involve a round trip of 240 miles. At the Abbey Theatre that night he saw van Amburgh 'for the millionth time. Always the same . . .' On Wednesday he went to play the piano in Liszt's room. This occasioned the only extended description by Parry of Liszt's music and its effect upon him:

> He came up and to my great delight played to me *his* arrangement of 'Der Freischutz' Overture – 'twas gigantic! – quite wonderful and yet beautiful – he also played to me his arrangement from

'Don Giovanni' in which 'La ci darem' as [*sic*] been perceived by
him as a *duet*, the left hand playing the harp part and the right the
Soprano – it has a very beautiful and novel effect.

Earlier in the tour Liszt had grudgingly promised Marie some
poplins. Now, from Dublin, he wrote again:

> . . . I am going to buy two poplin dresses for you, one black, the
> other blue. The black one I took to for its plainness, but it was
> impossible to resist the blue one. I am overjoyed with them; you
> are sure to find them ravishing.[56]

She wrote in reply,

> . . . the rippling blue robe especially haunts my dreams! I assure
> you that I shall be not in the least despotic in the matter of dresses
> – no more than in any other matter.[57]

Perhaps Miss Steele had helped Liszt to select them. But on the
subject of poplins he may have spent more time and care in selecting
items for himself. Parry was most impressed:

> . . . he [Liszt] has bought two waistcoats – *of gold cloth*!! They are
> called poplins – but all gold thread – they are magnificent.

Wearing one of his glittering purchases, Liszt accompanied Parry
and Miss Steele on a tour of the Museum and Library of Trinity
College, with Parry, it may be imagined, animatedly introducing
Liszt to the treasures which he had already seen on Christmas Eve
with Mr Slater:

> Liszt much pleased – there is one shelf (very short) on which are
> modern books of the value of £50,000 – there is one very old
> 'missile' painted by Nuns and written on vellum – valued at £500!

At this stage of his life, Liszt was not by nature or training a scholar,
but even through the cloud of Parry's chatter, his fervid Romantic

56. Ollivier, op. cit., II, 105.
57. ibid., II, 108.

imagination must have been stirred by a glimpse of the Book of Kells. In Cork he had been charmed by Irish music; in Trinity Library he might have been overwhelmed by a brief vision of the primitive soul of Celtic Christendom. At such moments he probably became a colossus among pygmies. Busy little Parry interpreted his colleague's heightened condition by writing simply, 'I left *the* Liszt and Miss Steele.' But he uttered his respect for the great pianist, after leaving Trinity, by purchasing for him the gift of an English–French Dictionary, perhaps as a gentle lubricant for Liszt's pleasant musical relationship with Miss Steele.

The remainder of that day was taken up, first, by Parry's compiling the programme for their Edinburgh concerts. Then Sapio, the tenor and singing teacher, dined with them; he was to appear in next day's concert. Parry and Joey entertained the dinner-party guests, and Richardson put his foot in it by announcing one of the items as 'The sort-shited Gentleman'. Mrs Steele dined out; 'Miss "jined" her (went away in a Car with the *Erl King*!)'. All this excitement caused Parry, and everyone else, to forget that it was Twelfth Day; to his chagrin there had been 'no cake ! no nothing !! Bah !'

Liszt's proper affair with Miss Steele seems not to have prevented the continuation of another, darker relationship. On the day after he had dined with the Steeles, Liszt was discovered with Lewis at the hotel in the afternoon entertaining their lady-friends from Cork; Parry's encoded account did not conceal his glee:

'Follow, follow, over mountain !' – *Miss* Burke and friend. The 'eminent' and the 'unknown'! (Doors locked.) Liszt and 'Lis', Loo and his love – great affection 125 miles long ! – 2 for 1, small beds, single and 'family'!

All this – whatever it really was – may have comprised a very stimulating present for the 'unknown' Lewis Lavenu's 24th birthday. Before this assignation they had given a bad concert – their fourth in Dublin and the first of two that day – at the Rotundo: 160 present and takings of only £25. The response was so poor that Liszt flatly refused to extemporize. Otherwise, Parry was mildly interested by the news that Lablache, Tamburini, Grisi and the new sensation Mario were announced as coming for the opera at the

Theatre Royal later in the year. The second concert in the evening was far more significant, arranged in honour of the Anacreontic Society, at the acoustically more sympathetic Small Room of the Rotundo. Parry, despite hoarseness, created, by his own estimate, a 'sinsation'. Liszt was late arriving – perhaps delayed by 'Lis' – and so Bassano (who would have been enraged by Lewis's behaviour) filled in with Mozart's 'Batti, batti'. This item – quite appropriate in the circumstances – had been set out in the local *Saunder's Paper* as 'Air, – Miss Bassano – "Bath! Bath!" '

Liszt's contributions that evening were varied to suit the dignity of the occasion. In London the previous summer, he had played Beethoven's Kreutzer Sonata at a concert with the Swedish violin virtuoso Ole Bull, an artist whose musicianship he much admired. Now, in Dublin, he repeated the experiment in company with Herr Rudersdorff, leader of the local band. Parry's reaction to the event was almost predictable. For him, a musical item was the means of inducing laughter, quietening the audience, or provoking an instant sensational response either of tears or nervous excitement. He could not understand how a piece of chamber music, in several move-ments, could be treated as suitable matter for a miscellaneous con-cert: 'Liszt and Rudersdorff played a piece "Sonata of Beethoven" 20 minutes long ! 'Twas dreadful !' He might even have reused his pun about the 'Concert Stuck' from their first Dublin concert. Yet this attitude was surely another side of the critical vision which, in Bury St Edmunds, had occasioned the comment that Parry's comic songs were not worthy to be heard in concerts alongside Liszt's and Richardson's fantasias, and de Varny's and Bassano's arias. Parry, and his audiences in most cases, still wanted educating. The young Liszt had recently been criticized by one commentator for not using opportune moments to enlarge the musical experience and appreci-ation of a relatively uncultivated public, in England and elsewhere.[58] In Ireland at least he chose a moment, in front of Lord Morpeth, which one of his fellow-artists thought was inauspicious. We cannot know how the 'public', as distinct from the critics, responded on that occasion to his spirit of adventure. Hundreds of Dubliners had heard two considerable artists play a violin sonata of

58. See Wilson Lyle, ed.: *A Dictionary of Pianists* (London, 1985).

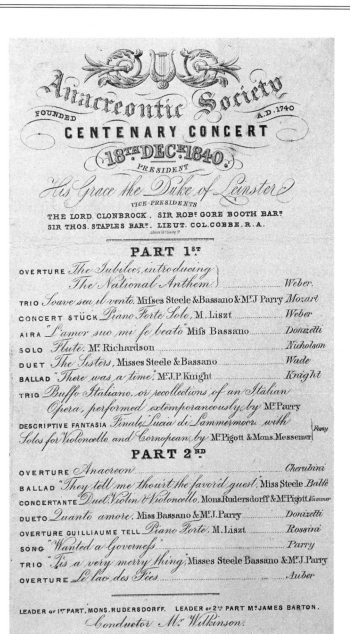

Anacreontic Society

FOUNDED A.D. 1740

CENTENARY CONCERT

18TH DEC.R 1840.

PRESIDENT

His Grace the Duke of Leinster

VICE-PRESIDENTS

THE LORD CLONBROCK . SIR ROB.T GORE BOOTH BAR.T
SIR THOS. STAPLES BAR.T. LIEUT. COL. COBBE. R.A.

PART 1ST

OVERTURE *The Jubilee, introducing The National Anthem* .... Weber.

TRIO *Soave sea il vento.* Misses Steele & Bassano & M.rs J Parry *Mozart*

CONCERT STÜCK *Piano Forte Solo,* M. Liszt .... Weber

AIRA *"L'amor suo mi fe beato"* Miss Bassano .... Donizetti

SOLO *Flute,* M.r Richardson .... Nicholson

DUET *The Sisters,* Misses Steele & Bassano .... Wade

BALLAD *"There was a time",* M.r J.P. Knight .... Knight

TRIO *Buffo Italiano, or recollections of an Italian Opera, performed extemporaneously, by* M.r Parry

DESCRIPTIVE FANTASIA *Finale Lucia di Lammermoor, with Solos for Violoncello and Cornopean, by* M.r Pigott & Mons. Messemer *Fessy*

PART 2ND

OVERTURE *Anacreon* .... Cherubini

BALLAD *"They tell me thou'rt the favor'd guest",* Miss Steele *Balfe*

CONCERTANTE *Duet, Violin & Violoncello,* Mons. Rudersdorff & M.r Pigott *Kummer*

DUETO *Quanto amore,* Miss Bassano & M.r J. Parry .... Donizetti

OVERTURE GUILLIAUME TELL *Piano Forte,* M. Liszt .... Rossini

SONG *"Wanted a Governess"* .... Parry

TRIO *"Tis a very merry thing",* Misses Steele Bassano & M.r J. Parry

OVERTURE *Le lac des Fées* .... Auber

LEADER OF 1ST PART, MONS. RUDERSDORFF. LEADER OF 2ND PART M.r JAMES BARTON.

Conductor M.r *Wilkinson.*

Beethoven, after routine performances of overtures by Mozart, Kal-
liwoda, Marschner and Rossini. For Liszt, the musician and public
performer, this fifth Dublin concert was the antidote to days of
idleness, during which he had an unwonted opportunity to reflect
on the flashiness of his run-of-the-mill concerts for Lavenu. Having
played the sonata, he went on, in the second half, to accompany
Miss Steele in Schubert's *Erlkönig*. This, too, marked a break with
the routine precedents of his other performances. We are faced with
two alternative interpretations of his behaviour: either, he grasped
the chance of enlarging the public's musical experience; or, confronted by their easy indifference, he was simply ignoring the canons of
accepted taste and practising in public. In Dublin Liszt could have
won plaudits with his transcription of *Erlkönig*. Instead he chose to
play the original with a young English singer whom he had been
coaching in the performance of German lieder. The Erl King was
willing to forgo the assured triumph of his solo pianism in order to
encourage a fledgling fellow-artist and to advertise Schubert's original composition.

On 8 January Lavenu's party left Dublin at 11 a.m. Incredibly,
their 120-mile journey lasted until 7.15 a.m. next day, with only
short breaks for meals and refreshment at hotels. They slept in and
on the coach:

> ... great trouble to make some of the turnpike-keepers hear –
> *Fired* a pistol at one place – most knocked his hut door down but
> it was an immense while before he came forth, and then in his
> shirt, *nothing on his legs*, and a large white Night Cap!

THE SECOND TOUR   155

Fancy having to turn out of a warm bed to walk in the Snow at 3 o'clock in the morning without any thing on but a shirt !! The moon was lovely all night and the Snow, and took rather away from the dreariness. We ran over a Pig (I understand about 6 in the morning) that was going to Limerick market – Poor thing – I heard a dreadful squeak once.

They slept well, at the Royal Mail Hotel, until noon, then rose to find that the concert was due to begin at one, not two. They arrived in Swinburne's Room at a quarter-past one. There were only a hundred present, and it was 'a poor, dirty place'; but the response was lively, with generous encores:

Joey not well – out in the cold all night – played very queer – threw his Flute down and nearly broke it after missing a Passage in 'Rousseau's Dream' (in which I accompanied him) – Joey very excited.

Limerick would seem to have been celebrated for eccentric, distracting events at entertainments in its rather inferior public accommodation. The previous year, Michael Balfe conducted his opera *Diadeste* at the Old Theatre, and during the performance members of the audience had kept their umbrellas up to protect themselves from cascades of rain through the roof. At Swinburne's Rooms in October 1831, while Paganini was playing, part of the floor quite close to him collapsed, and several listeners were surprised to find themselves suddenly deposited in the room beneath. Fortunately no one was seriously injured and, after a short pause, Old Nick continued his performance unperturbed. Conversations about the Deity, the Devil and foreign fiddlers must have been numerous and animated in Limerick for some time afterwards.

The dinner at the Royal was good but the potatoes were bad, '(as usual in Ireland)', reported Parry. At the post office he was amazed to find a letter from his wife: 'Quite astonished – how should she know I was here?'. Liszt, meanwhile, was being cultivated and entertained by the most important local official, the Police General, Mr Vaux; and Lewis caught up on his sleep. When Liszt came home to find him snoring, he placed two 'Queen's Heads' on his forehead, a mischievous compensation, perhaps, for the flagging receipts of the tour.

On Monday 11 January, Parry went shopping with Miss Steele and bought a pair of Limerick gloves 'which are so small they go into a Nutshell'. They played a much better second concert, then mounted the coach at 1 a.m. on the 12th and set off for Dublin, 'Liszt and I spitting misunderstandings for two. Joey came inside – awfully squeezed and cramped'. Despite all their discomforts Parry was still able to praise the breakfast butter during a brief stop in Roscrea. They arrived at Morrison's at ten to six – having suffered a journey of 16 hours and 40 minutes, with only two stops:

> I had some Tea, and some capital *Medley* pie – all sorts of good things – turkey, ham, tongue, ham. etc. etc. Directly after Tea, dressed and at 8 we were once more in the old Rotundo, ready for the CONCERT.

This time it was for the composer J. P. Knight's benefit. The star of the occasion was one of Sapio's pupils, Miss Catherine Hayes: 'Everybody was pleased and she was loudly applauded,' said Parry; 'her singing made *some people* look a little queer I think ... We all sang and played wonderfully well considering the fatigue we had undergone.' At Piggott's music store Parry was delighted to find that every copy of his songs had been sold; but this meant that he was unable to purchase one as a gift for Miss Hayes. Born in Limerick, she was only 15 in January 1841, but already a public subscription had been raised to pay for her lessons with Sapio. Later, she was to study with Malibran's brother, Garcia. For the next 15 years she had a brilliant career as a soprano, not only in Europe, but through tours in America, India and Australia. The most discerning connoisseurs, however, commented that, marvellous as was her vocal power, she remained musically insensitive to the last.[59]

On 13 January they gave their last Dublin performances, in the Rotundo for the Philharmonic Society. As at the Anacreontic concert,

> the Lord Lieutenant came in state ... There were at least 1,200

59. *DNB*; *Grove* (1927 edn).

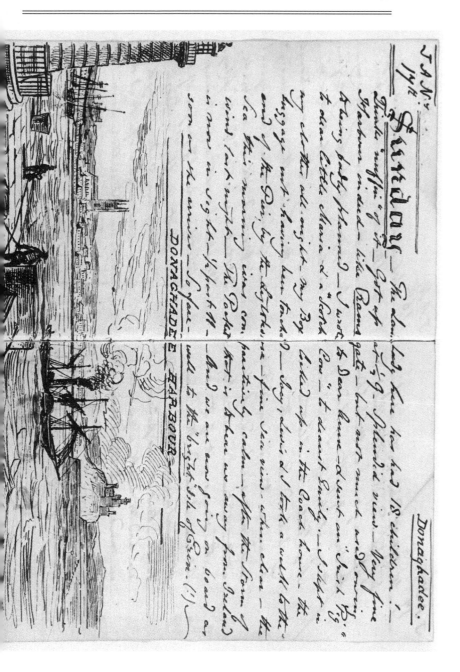

people!!! It was a grand sight. Miss Daley and Wilson sang in
addition to our party, also a very large Band ... The Lord
Lieutenant sent to say he was very much gratified with me
indeed!! ... I was not at all frightened or nervous, but I really
worked like a horse to fill that enormous rotunda with my poor
little lungs.

Next day they passed through Drogheda – 'dirty place' – and
Newry. They arrived in Belfast at quarter-past four on the 15th and
put up at the Donnegal Arms. The concert at the Music Hall was
'pretty well attended' – about 200 people at seven shillings each,
with seven encores. Parry declared: 'I never sang to an audience
fonder of fun'. A few days earlier he had been dreadfully homesick,
longing for a picture of his wife and children. Now he received a
letter from Anne with news which raised his morale in the best
possible way: the *Wife* had sold 1700 and the *Governess* 5700 copies.
Donaghdee, their Irish port of departure, had 'a very fine harbour
indeed – like *Ramsgate*, but not much used owing to being badly
planned'. As they bade farewell to 'the bright Isle of Erin(!)', he
made a charming sketch of the town and harbour, with the packet
boat on which they were to cross to Port Patrick on their way to
Glasgow. This time the Irish sea was in a more pacific mood.
    Once disembarked on the Scottish side they had trouble at the inn
about acquiring horses. They needed to get to Ayr quickly on
another boat so as to reach Glasgow for the morning concert next
day.

    Liszt went into the Carriage (which was in the Coach House (!)
    and slept – Lewis and 'Bread and Butter' [Bassano] went to sleep
    on the sofa in *picturesque* attitudes. It was now 12 o'clock (mid-
    night) ... Miss Steele wishes it put in genteel words that she is
    'suffering and labouring' most horribly (with the toothache). At
    $\frac{1}{2}$12 we called for some sandwiches (always eating!) and after a
    Glass of Whiskey and Water – the carriage was brought to the
    door, with Liszt asleep in it – and having got all our things we
    prepared for a start – 'twas now $\frac{2}{3}$3 and a fine starlight morning! –
    Freezing very hard – As the Quay was very near – (that is a
    quarter of a mile) the Ostler and Boots etc. put a rope to the
    Carriage and we proceeded without horses to the Quay – but as

our Carriage was very heavy – we leant a hand – and a funny procession it was – Miss Steele carrying a lantern and we all tugging the Carriage and the 'great Pianist' who was fast asleep all the while and knew nought of the honour being conferred on him:

Their anxiety now was whether they would reach Ayr in time to catch the 'steamer' [the train] for Glasgow. They began to dress for the concert while still aboard. Then,

we glided into harbour and to our dismay saw the Train just leaving !! Impossible to catch or stop it so there we were left in the lurch – No train till 2 !! (The concert begins at 1 !, 40 miles off.) However, on enquiry we found there was a *third class train* where they carried Pigs and Cattle and Luggage (!) – starting at 11 – and it was proposed we should go on this ! – So after taking Porter etc. at the King's Arms and leaving old Marchant in charge of the Carriage – which would be in Glasgow at 6 or 7 – by the 'Sir William' – we set off in the 'open train' this bitter cold day,

and went the (?) miles in three hours, which appeared an age owing to the intense cold.

In Glasgow they hastened to The George in George Square, but
found they were much too late for the concert – the audience had
gone away – and they arranged to give another one on Wednesday.
Stunned by the cold and lack of sleep (all except Liszt, who had
slumbered through most of the journey from Donaghdee) they
returned to the hotel. Parry snored over a half-completed letter to
Anne, awoke, but could not eat any dinner '(save Cranberry Pie –
which was capital)'. Half-past ten that night saw them aboard the
coach again – their 'moveable home' – on the way to the main
Scottish destination. They 'slept and woke and woke and slept etc.
etc. until 5 the next morning when we found ourselves in the great
and wonderful city of EDINBURGH'.

In journeying through Scotland Liszt was following a path similar
to one beaten by Mendelssohn in 1829; and he was making foot-
prints which Chopin was to use on his visit in 1848. Mendelssohn,
on his more leisurely excursion, had appreciated Scotland for its
savage Romantic splendours, in Holyrood for its historic associations, at Abbotsford as the habitation and inspiration for Sir Walter
Scott. Chopin, often not even on his last legs, was to be destroyed
by the climate. Liszt's hectic itinerary in 1841 barely gave him time
to complete all his professional engagements, let alone discover the
wonders of the Lowlands.

On their freezing ride from Glasgow, Lavenu's party slept in and
on the coach, Lewis and Louisa cuddled together on the outside rear
seat, covered by a makeshift awning: '. . . it keeps them from the
cold, and *they say* they are very warm and comfortable'. They
arrived at The Royal Hotel, Princes Street, at five o'clock in the
morning. Parry and Lewis were soon out visiting the local music
sellers, Robertson, Paterson and Purday, but commercial interests
did not efface from Parry's memory the first impressions of a
splendid city:

> It is impossible to describe this most ancient and beautiful city –
> the *fine Castle* – facing the Hotel on the right – then up Princes
> Street to the *Nelson monument* – the splendid river, land and sea
> view from Calton Hill and *Arthur's Seat* – the fine *Bridge* leading to
> the *Old Town* – houses 12 storeys (or flats) high !!

The public buildings are superb – verdure abundant everywhere.
This makes it splendid and in Summer it must be the most beauti-
ful thing ever seen – Fine Streets – Statues in every one almost –
The Shops are so splendidly furnished and all on a grand scale –
Everything in the best possible taste. Well may it be called the
Classical City and most worthy to bear the cognomen of

Modern Athens.

It was during the Scottish Enlightenment – in the Preface to
James Stuart's *Antiquities of Athens* (1762) – that modern Edinburgh
was first compared to ancient Athens. Early in the nineteenth century, some of Thomas Shepard's drawings of Edinburgh had been
published under the title *Modern Athens*. Shepard was then recording
the renovation of the old town and the growth of a new one, and the
titles of some of his pictures – 'Waterloo Place', 'Calton Hill', 'The

National and Nelson Monuments' – provide evidence that Parry
may have taken this book of recent 'views' as his guide. Evidence of
the bourgeois power of the city would have surrounded every step
of the walks he took through it, and the peculiar pride, part
national, part municipal, of its citizens – sterner than Irish ebullience
– must have impressed Liszt in each audience, at soirées, and in the
throng of respectable shoppers and sightseers.

Liszt, however, possibly viewed every passing parade through
spectacles tinted with considerable scepticism. He headed a letter
from Glasgow, on 18 January, with the phrase, '(After two steam-
boat journeys, and three hours in a railway train, third-class, frozen
and chilled to the bone)'.[60] Otherwise, he was anticipating his
return to Paris, writing – from one of the great centres of British
constitutional reform – about electoral changes then being
implemented in France. Amid the flurried concert schedule, he
found time to dine with the music publisher Robert Paterson, and,
like Mendelssohn before him, submitted himself to the cautionary
experience necessary for all musical visitors to Scotland: a tour of

60. Ollivier, op. cit., II, 108.

Holyrood Palace to see the chamber where Rizzio, Mary's Italian
secretary and minstrel, had been brutally stabbed to death by her
jealous husband's gangsters. Liszt was in sufficiently high spirits to
enjoy some 'fun' in Parry's room after their first concert, on the
19th. But later in the week, in a letter to Marie, he described the
itinerant torture of this hastily arranged part of their tour:

> Lavenu got up some very good concerts in Edinburgh and
> Glasgow. Consider the shape of my week. The day before
> yesterday, 7 o'clock in the morning, arrived from Glasgow in
> Edinburgh. Concert in the evening. Yesterday, 11 o'clock, left
> again for Glasgow (5 hours on the train, and we – in the coach –
> took 6); concert in the evening. Today returned at 5 o'clock from
> Glasgow; concert a few minutes ago. Tomorrow evening we shall
> set off anew for Glasgow; concert in the evening. And after
> passing the night in the carriage, morning concert in Edinburgh
> on Saturday![61]

It is worth comparing that fatiguing régime with the schedule of
Paganini's last tour in 1833. The violinist also shuttled about; but
andante rather than *presto*: Glasgow concerts on 23 and 26 September; Edinburgh on the 27th; Glasgow again on the 28th; and a final
concert in Edinburgh on 1 October.
Parry did have time to execute some pretty sketches of
Edinburgh, including a panoramic view of the castle, with the city
below. He accompanied them with his usual pattering descriptions.
On 23 January he wrote,

> We left Glasgow at $2\frac{1}{2}$ (this morning) (when the Whist party was
> broken up). It was snowing very hard and the fires from the
> different coal mines, etc., reflecting on the white ground was
> beautiful – the Sun rose about 7, beautiful frosty morning – I got
> a little sleep but not much. At 9 precisely we accomplished our 43
> miles for the last time.

Later the same morning he went for curling to his nicely named

61. ibid., II, 112.

hairdresser, Mr Truefitt, who had known Kemble, Charles
Mathews, Kean and Mme Vestris 'most intimately'; and then on to
their morning concert, the third and last in Edinburgh, at the
Hopetoun Rooms in Queen Street. There was a capacity audience
of 400: it was 'a lovely morning and all the ladies came out'. This
feature might have consoled Liszt amid the longueurs of his north
British adventure. Earlier, in Glasgow, Parry noted the pianist's
arrival at their second concert with 'some very dashing Scotch girls',
perhaps *écossaises* 'nieces' of Miss Burke. Whoever they were, these
charmers did not merit being mentioned in his correspondence with
Marie. At the second Edinburgh concert, perhaps to display his
most natural musical talents to the ladies, Liszt extemporized on
three or four themes handed up from the hall, among them 'Scots
wha hae'.

On Sunday 24 January, to the relief of all, they set off south-
wards, and were delighted to be in 'England' – Berwick-upon-
Tweed – for tea at half-past eleven. An hour later they were on the
road again, passing through Belford, Alnwick and nostalgia-induc-
ing Morpeth. At Alnwick, for an undisclosed reason – could he have
wished to survey his friend Morpeth's territory? – but probably in
part because of fatigue, Liszt left the coach and put up singly at an
inn, while the rest of the party proceeded to Newcastle, the end of
the 110-mile journey. Liszt caught the mail coach and rejoined them
next day. Arriving in Newcastle at 9.30 a.m., Parry had dinner in
the Coffee Room of the Queen's Hotel, went to bed before a blazing
fire – '(capital coals)' – was called at 6 p.m., had one cup of tea,
dressed, and went into the concert.

Feelings rather different from the Morpeth kind might have afflic-
ted Liszt in Newcastle, for at this time, local citizens were enjoying
yet another production of *The Lady of Lyons* at the Theatre Royal,
accompanied by pantomime performances of *Cinderella* and *Mother
Goose*, and interval entertainment from the 'Alpine Singers'. Mr
Carter and his lions were in town too, and they drew longer and
much more appreciative reviews in the papers than did Liszt's concert.[62] Some impression of the possible commercial effect of his
provincial performances may be constructed from advertisements in
the *Newcastle Chronicle* for 30 January, after his concert. Messrs John
and George Ewart – auctioneers, not music dealers – informed the
public that they had recently received a 'Consignment of PIANO
FORTES by Broadwood and Company, and other eminent makers',
and would be displaying them at the Newcastle Auction Mart, Grey
Street. The concert notice in the same paper was brief:

> His execution may almost be characterised as miraculous, but in
> taste and finish he is scarcely equal to Thalberg . . . We regret to
> say that the audience was not so numerous as was anticipated.[63]

But Liszt paid tribute, like Debussy much later, to Northumbria by

62. *Newcastle Chronicle*, 16 January 1841, advertisement.
63. ibid., 30 January 1841.

extemporizing on, not only 'Rule Britannia' and 'La Parisienne', but also 'The Keel Row'.

On reaching Sunderland next day they found they had mislaid their music, and so they went through their morning concert 'without a note of music !!!' The only comparison Parry could imagine for this phenomenon was with the Austrian group, the Rainiers, a sort of Trapp family who had toured Britain in 1838. The second concert of the day was in the theatre at Durham. For the moment some of the party might have thought they were reverting to the pattern of the first tour, with two engagements a day. On Wednesday the 27th, they kept their morning audience in Richmond waiting for two hours; by the time they arrived there were only 90 left, though the concert was patronized by the Countess of Zetland and her suite – 'a nice lady-like woman', according to Parry. During the evening concert in Darlington he thought the room smelt of new paint. On the 28th they left Darlington at 11.30, Liszt in his 'great Russian Cloak' sitting outside the van with Marchant. 'Lovely day – everybody staring at the extraordinary turn-out'. After 35 miles they halted for dinner at Borough Bridge – a marvellous meal with roast beef and tarts. They arrived in Leeds at 10.30 and were once more in their warm beds at the Scarborough Hotel by midnight. 'Read in bed. The wind blew and howled very much.'

Next morning they passed ruined Kirkstall Abbey, then up over 'fearful hills' through Bradford and on to Halifax. The roads were appalling, but Parry's mood was softened by two letters from Anne. He 'rushed to a public house and in a Tap [room] wrote a line back. The Mail cart was at the door.'

The last concert of their 'awfully long tour' was in Bradford to an audience of 400 in the huge Oddfellows' Room, not yet finished. It was Joey Richardson's birthday and so afterwards they had champagne which served for two celebrations. They left Bradford at quarter-past two in the morning, with their carriage now mounted on the railway truck and the van behind:

They arrived in Derby at 10 a.m. after a 'splendid breakfast' in the 'beautiful Station' – Parry had evidently forgotten being diddled out of twelve shillings there during the first tour. At quarter to eleven they departed in pouring rain for Rugby, joined the Birmingham to London train on Robert Stephenson's track, passing through the Kilsby Tunnel and Tring Cutting, and 'at a quarter to six, to all our hearts' content, stopt at *Euston Square Grand Birmingham Station*, London !' Taking a cab, Parry was at his house, 12 Tavistock Square, 'the long looked for haven', by quarter-past six. He had some tea, then began to tell his family about the Grand Tour, which had lasted exactly ten weeks, from 23 November 1840 till 30 January 1841. At the end of his second diary Parry summarized the events of those weeks:

> ... we sang together at 44 concerts during the 10 weeks – the previous 6 weeks tour with Mr. Lavenu and Liszt we sang at 50.

He totted up all his encores, and recorded their total mileage. In an excess of gratitude he praised – with an affixed Penny Black – 'the splendid arrangements of Rowland Hill, Esq., which enabled me to write so often to dear Anny !!!' (and, he might have added, which had enabled her to write so often, and with such unerring accuracy, to him as he sped about). He had spent £8 on sundries and £11 on presents. 'My salary was *16 guineas* a Week (both Tours) – making (four months) £271.'

Parry was tired but satisfied; Liszt was far less sanguine. The summary he sent to Marie was more caustic, but, remarkably, still coloured by hope:

> The end of Lavenu's tour has been very good, but it's impossible that, with 120,000 francs in expenses, he will not lose by it. The arrangements have not been well handled – far from satisfactory. For my own part, I leave with all the honours of war. It remains only for me to pocket the spoils.[64]

Nevertheless, with characteristic generosity, Liszt waived Lavenu's contract: he was not paid for all those miles, all that boredom, those

64. Ollivier, op. cit., II, 116.

many concerts, and the intermittent disappointments. The two
British tours were serious ruptures in the development of his career
as an internationally renowned pianist and composer. He had
managed to write and practise as he travelled about, particularly, it
seems, in Ireland; but his creative urge would have found greater
scope had he been closer to his Parisian base; and while his desire
for applause had usually been satisfied, his English, Irish and Scottish triumphs must have seemed petty and parochial by comparison
with what might have been his reception in Germany, Austria or
Hungary.

He may have learned a great deal about himself as he exchanged
tittle-tattle with Parry, watched Richardson's tawdry tricks, argued
with Bassano and encouraged the fledgling Miss Steele to explore
new repertoire. He had fleeting engagements with interesting
people, but outside London he generally encountered few with
whom he could enjoy challenging arguments or discussion of his
artistic intentions. To most Englishmen who saw and heard him he
must have seemed a character in a passing harlequinade, peacock-
proud, over-dressed, self-engrossed, and not the kind of pianist
they would have chosen to listen to every day. As the Newcastle
reviewer had implied, and others had earlier confirmed, Thalberg
was more suited to English taste: he had finish, cool charm, he
lacked the capacity to startle, and his style was a more realistic
model for aspiring amateurs to imitate. Thalberg was a dressage
pianist; and the English evidently distrusted Liszt's Cossack
manner. With his grand rhetoric, poetic temperament and wide
dynamic contrasts, Liszt was too large for the frame of English
concert-giving, as it was then constituted. It could be argued that, if
he had bided his time and made his assault perhaps five years later,
the tide of English taste, already on the turn in 1840–41, would
have borne him on to a much more successful shore. But on
balance, just as Thalberg and Moscheles were then England's
favoured pianists, so, throughout most of the Victorian era,
Mendelssohn and Sterndale Bennett were her beloved composers.
When Wagner and Berlioz visited England professionally in the
middle decades of the century, for the same purpose as Liszt, they
too encountered calm indifference and some hostility.

The most startling footnote to the second tour, however, was supplied in Liszt's last letter to Marie; in spite of all that had happened in the way of discouragement and mismanagement, he was still optimistic about making a reputation in London. In the back of his mind, perhaps, lay the festering thought that Thalberg had already enjoyed several seasons of real success in England.

> On the 3rd (of February) I play at a huge concert (25 items on the programme) in London, so as to find out whether I will return in May. It is probable I will do good business.[65]

A major step in the development of Liszt's concert enterprises during his tours of Britain was being taken in Paris. While travelling he had written forlornly to his friend von Schober, and for a time had hoped that their former good companionship might turn into a business partnership. This was not to be. One of his recent pupils, Hermann Cohen, had seemed to fit the role of manager; but he had absconded with some of Liszt's money. Then, at the beginning of the first English tour in late summer 1840, Marie, in the middle of a letter devoted mainly to gossipy information about Chopin and George Sand, mentioned the following:

> I have seen Belloni. I am completely happy about him. He has accepted with pleasure; without any ifs or buts. He will not hear of a contract, and leaves that entirely to you. He hopes to travel everywhere with you, and appears to understand, better than anyone else could, what he will be expected to do.[66]

Liszt's reply was positive. 'I am so pleased by what Belloni has agreed to do. I hope we shall be equally content with each other.'[67] Gaetano Belloni was to look after Liszt's affairs for the remainder of his career as a virtuoso. Italian musical taste, outside the opera house, may have been feeble in this period of its development, but Italian musicians knew better than anyone how to drive a profitable bargain. It was already clear in 1840 that Liszt could not continuously trust the vagaries of *ad hoc* planning. But it was the experience of British touring with Lavenu which sealed his belief in

---

65. ibid.   66. ibid., II, 13.   67. ibid., II, 16.

the need for a constant companion who would also be a disin-
terested, efficient manager.

The monster concert in which Liszt took part on 3 February was
given by two other pianists, Mme Dulcken and Julius Benedict. One
listener called their programme 'too liberal': it contained Weber's
First Piano Concerto, played by Dulcken; Miss Birch singing arias
(a critic wrote that she was 'totally inarticulate' in an extract from
Spohr's *Crucifixion*); Mme Caradori throwing away her gifts upon
Donizetti and Coppola; overtures by Beethoven and Sterndale Bennett; and the latter, as pianist, joining the other two in the Allegro
from Bach's Triple Concerto. The *Athenaeum* reviewer found it
totally indigestible, but commented:

> ... between the Acts was the best thing of the evening – the
> casual apparition of M. Liszt, and M. Liszt in all his glory, playing
> the *Hexameron*, as none save himself could play it; and when
> tumultuously encored by the audience, giving a fragment of a
> new fantasia, in which *God Save the Queen* was arrayed in a more
> dazzling magnificence than it has ever hitherto worn. Separate,
> however, from the work of which it forms a part, the air and its
> variations were on a more vast scale than is agreeable. We shall
> hear the whole during the coming season, for which M. Liszt
> returns in early April.

Of Liszt's reappearance in the spring, Alan Walker simply says
that he played at a Philharmonic Society concert under the handicap
of a sprained left wrist, which he had suffered in a coaching accident
between Norwood and London. This mishap, Walker writes, was
'somehow symbolic of his entire encounter with England'.[68] As a
general judgment this is unimpeachable. But Liszt's encounter with
London in the spring was hardly 'fleeting' – and professionally it
was by no means confined to the Philharmonic concert.

In fact he returned to London in the second week of May. His
first public engagement was an act of splendid generosity towards
one of the less eminent members of his recent touring party. Miss
Steele had learned from Liszt some appreciation of Schubert while
they were languishing in Dublin because of Wade's negligence. On

14 May in London, she was to give a benefit concert in the Hanover Square Rooms, at which she hoped to enlist the support of the leading musical artists then working in town. Both *The Times* and the *Athenaeum* thought her concert worthy of a long review. Henry Chorley, perhaps the most perceptive musical journalist of the day, wrote in the *Athenaeum* of Miss Steele's 'purity of tone and finish of style', which had enabled her to hold her own in duet with the great Belgian *prima donna*, Mme Dorus-Gras. Joey Richardson and Chatterton played duets for flute and harp, and John Parry, said *The Times*, sang *A Wife Wanted* 'amidst a great deal of laughter'. Lablache and his daughter and Miss Birch completed a long list of contributing artists: '. . . the room was crowded and the concert went off brilliantly'. But the star of the evening, according to both accounts, was Liszt. Chorley admitted that the pianist had never been heard to such advantage during his 1840 London season: 'either his tone has grown richer during his pilgrimage of the twelvemonth, or he is in peculiar force just at present'. Nothing more colossal than his performance on this occasion could be imagined:

> He is, if we mistake it not, better appreciated than formerly by his audiences, and they may appreciate him without misgiving – for the variety of resources with which he has to please them is next to inexhaustible.[69]

Liszt then played briefly in Miss Steele's concert on a Saturday evening. The following Monday he again appeared, at Julius Benedict's monstrously impressive event, where the beneficiary was supported by surely the most startling galaxy of vocal talent ever assembled on an English concert platform. It was as if Sutherland, Caballé, Janet Baker, Geraint Evans, Gobbi, Christoff, Domingo and Vickers had not only appeared during the same concert, but also sung together in chorus in the 1970s. Benedict managed to bring together the two Grisis, Persiani, Pauline Viardot (Malibran's sister), Dorus-Gras and the Austrian soprano Löwe, as well as Rubini, Mario, Flavio, Lablache and – Tamburini being unwell – our John

69. *Athenaeum*, 22 May 1841.

Parry as deputy baritone. Among the instrumentalists, Puzzi played the horn and Vieuxtemps the violin. Together all the vocalists gave the 'Preghiera' from Rossini's *Mosè*. Chorley wrote, 'It is impossible to imagine anything finer than the body of tone given out by these picked voices.' Yet, confronted by this stunning display of vocal brilliance, he singled out for special comment 'the magnificent accompaniment' which Liszt added to the Rossini. What an extraordinary performance that must have been! And in spite of the high esteem usually accorded to operatic singers, it seems that Liszt's playing of the *Hexameron* in the interval of Benedict's concert 'roused up the most crowded and coldest audience of the season to something nearer a *furore* than English men and women often indulge in'.[70]

After this there was a pause of more than a week, in which Liszt seems to have given no public performances, but when it is more than likely that he played at private soirées for the *haut ton*. On Monday 31 May, he joined forces with Mme Dulcken again, to make her concert go with even more than its expected success. The lady first played a duet with her brother, Ferdinand David, who was to give the first performance of Mendelssohn's Violin Concerto three years later. Once more, however, by Chorley's account, Liszt stole the principal's thunder; he noted

> the force and fervour with which she kept pace with Liszt in a grand duet for two pianofortes, arranged from the *Hexameron*. To keep pace with Liszt on Monday was no child's play. It was a race not only with mechanical omnipotence, but with fancy in its most excessive mood: he has never played so brilliantly in London.[71]

Given that Chorley was a social acquaintance of Liszt, and had long been a hearty advocate for his playing, it does seem that in the 1841 season the pianist was capturing the town; and that, in some ineffable way, his playing was even more astounding than it had been in the previous year. Audiences certainly flocked to see and hear him. And he won their attention gallantly as well as musically. The *Athenaeum* noticed that 'a thoroughly magnificent sacrifice' had been made by Liszt: finding that his planned solo recital was due on

70. ibid., 29 May 1841.   71. ibid., 5 June 1841.

the same day as a charity concert for Polish refugees, 5 June, he postponed his own performance. In the event, there may have been something of impure calculation in this apparently generous act, for, a few days after playing for Mme Dulcken, he had sustained the injuries to his left arm which are mentioned by Walker.

Nevertheless – and we may be sure that histrionically he would make the most of his indisposition, just as Paganini used to capitalize on breaking a string – Liszt appeared at the Polish matinée: playing a lightweight Cyril Smith to Benedict's Phyllis Sellick, he scored a professional triumph; one can now almost see the fashionable ladies pushing and craning to witness how he accomplished the feat:

> . . . and there was M. Liszt, placing another feather in his cap, as a man and an artist, by playing, in his disabled state, *with one hand*, with M. Benedict, and doing more, it may be added, than many a well-versed pianist with all ten fingers. After the sacrifice of a very lucrative week's engagements, the steadfast resolution to keep faith with Charity, seems to us even more worthy of honourable notice, than the wonderful skill which made the performance so surprising.[72]

He played single-handed again at the violinist Eliason's concert the following Monday. It was generally admitted that the two best features of this occasion were Herr Staudigl's singing of Schubert and Liszt's 'one-handed sorcery'. It is only fair to say that he was not the first in this particular field: for instance, Alexander Dreyschock, a staggeringly brilliant and impressively insensitive player, had already composed a very popular fantasy on *God Save the Queen* for *left* hand alone. And Liszt would have been aware of such competition.

By Saturday 12 June, Liszt had recovered sufficiently for him to give his postponed matinée recital at Willis's Rooms. Despite the lingering effects of his disability, this occasion, too, was an artistic and public triumph; though he wisely decided to enlist the intermittent support of other eminent performers, which made it, strictly speaking, not a 'recital' at all. He played the *Sonnambula* Fantasy, in

72. *The Times*, 10 June 1841.

which, according to *The Times*, he produced 'the effect of four hands', against all the digital odds. He introduced to London his bubbling transcription of Rossini's *La Danza*; and the concert closed with 'an unlooked-for treat': Liszt and Benedict played Thalberg's *Norma* Fantasy. Between these two performers 'there almost appeared to be a galvanic circle which electrified the audience'. In addition, Mme Löwe sang Beethoven's *Adelaïde*; and Staudigl (the great Viennese baritone) Schubert's *Wanderer*, 'in which he was, as usual, encored'. The audience was vast and of the most fashionable kind. Its leader was that famous Hanoverian soldier, the Duke of Cambridge, Victoria's uncle, 'who appeared to be highly delighted with the performance. Indeed, no laurelled conqueror could have had a more complete triumph than M. Liszt was granted on this occasion.' All this despite the coincidence between the hastily arranged recital and the Flower Show.[73]

Chorley's comments on the 'recital' comprise the most comprehensive contemporary analysis of Liszt's powers as a pianist by any writer in Britain. The English, Chorley admitted, were perhaps 'slow to move'; but they were neither perverse nor unjust:

> As a musical illustration to this text, we have but to point to the career of M. Liszt. He came among us as a wonder – and some of the graver musicians, repelled by such reputation, set themselves, in the first instance, to magnify his individualities and extravagancies, ere they had time to discover whether or not they had aught to rest upon by way of basis. Hence arose criticisms of a wider discrepancy than we remember in the case of any other artist.

Chorley had never thought that Liszt's initial success in 1840 was 'meteoric'; the pianist's more profound qualities were, he was sure, bound to disclose themselves 'during a long-continued intercourse and experience'. Their existence was now, 'with homeopathically small exceptions', universally admitted. Since the summer of 1840, his technical accomplishment had become more wonderful; but 'there is less, if we may say it, of fever in his playing'. Can Chorley have been reminding the English public, obliquely, of Liszt's illness

73. ibid., 14 June 1841.

at the beginning of the first provincial tour? So convincing were his current performances, thought Chorley, that 'not one in twenty' of his enthralled audience at Willis's Rooms would have known that he was playing at three-quarters of his power (though many of them must have read of his accident in the newspapers). Because of the injury, he had sacrificed the most demanding part of his intended programme. Yet, by Chorley's account, Liszt seems to have played instead a most extraordinary pot-pourri of extracts from his most popular pieces: '. . . he combined such themes and snatches . . . as were within his power, with a grace, fancy, and execution so rare, that it was hardly possible to conceive that anything was lost, or could have been superadded'.[74]

There now remained only Liszt's last public engagement in England before his return in 1886: an appearance at the Philharmonic Society concert on Monday 14 June. The orchestra played Weber's Overture *Der Freischütz* and Beethoven's Second Symphony, conducted by Moscheles. The second half consisted of a Beethoven quintet, led by Vieuxtemps, and the Chenonceaux Scene from Meyerbeer's *Les Huguenots*. Into this grave farrago, perhaps in order to prove the quality of his classical pedigree, Liszt chose to insert his piano transcription of Hummel's septet. This, *The Times* said,

> was played from memory – an effort prodigious enough, with anyone else, to have absorbed all that animation, force, and brilliancy which must belong to the moment's enthusiasm, or they become formal and fatiguing. Yet . . . the artist was never more at ease in the most whimsical drollery thrown off on the spur of the moment, than when infusing new vigour of life and vividness of character into Hummel's fine, solid composition, and enough cannot be said of his performance, without praise trenching upon the boundaries of extravagance . . . The reception given to it by the audience will, we hope, open a way to our hearing other master works of the classical composers for the pianoforte, rendered with a like splendour by the same matchless interpreter.[75]

Unfortunately for British audiences during the next 40 years, this was not to be so.

74. *Athenaeum*, 19 June 1841.   75. *The Times*, 16 June 1841.

CHAPTER FIVE

Later Careers

IT IS EASY to overlook how young were the members of Lavenu's touring parties. Perhaps the whole enterprise ought to be viewed as a youthful *jeu d'esprit*. Parry was 30; Richardson 26; Bassano a mere 17; Miss Steele a demure 22, and of course Lavenu himself – impatiently ambitious – 23. Only Wade, their intermittent companion, was tottering into premature middle age. Like a successful pop-group of the late 1960s, they had style, some panache, temperament and considerable stamina; and they were making up much of their experience as they went along.

Not surprisingly Liszt came to find his companions boring, though he remained loyal to them in public, and never commented in writing on their particular musical failings. It may seem extraordinary that they were not overwhelmed by him. Parry had felt honoured by Liszt's several times accompanying him in *The Inchape Bell*; but, remarkably, through all the manuscript diaries covering many of the remaining 30 years of his career as a popular entertainer, he did not mention Liszt again. In one respect this is hardly strange, since during that time the great pianist never visited London, nor did his burgeoning musical reputation throughout Europe impinge upon English concert life in ways which Parry might have noticed.

It is impossible to know what Parry's small baritone voice was really like. On the other hand, the tone which rings through his diaries is vivacious and nearly always lightweight. He appreciated Liszt's phenomenal piano playing in much the same way as he enjoyed Joey Richardson's party-tricks with flute and dice. Only once or twice, in all those months of touring, did he attempt even a short description of Liszt's performance at the piano; and it is remarkable that there is no detailed account in his diary of the pianist's unique public manner. 'Tom Crotchet' had provided a lively picture of Liszt's behaviour at Parry's London concert during the 1840 season, and in the Cheltenham man-about-town's gay words there is a clue to Parry's indifference. The comedian – who clearly spread delight whenever he took the stage – saw Liszt as a rival. For Parry, public performance comprised equal parts of nervous energy, flamboyance and fun. In the first two of these elements he was eclipsed by Liszt, as was anyone who had the courage to share a platform with one of the greatest public performers in musical history. Parry could enviously measure Liszt's charisma; but he did not possess the means for assessing his musical or pianistic significance. He judged the 20-minute duo performance of the Kreutzer in Dublin to have been just so much tedium before *he* got down to the real business of tickling the audience's fancy. Liszt's performance of a transcription was little different, to his ears, from the brilliant effects of other pianists like Thalberg, Döhler and Herz.

Parry played no part in shaping serious musical taste in England, which was gradually improving during his career. In the 1840s he undertook further extensive tours with Camillo Sivori, Paganini's celebrated pupil, with Mme Grisi, and, for comparison's sake, with Thalberg.[1] He appeared a few times as baritone soloist at Philharmonic concerts in 1841, but that side of his career withered away, and he became the comic darling of miscellaneous programmes. The 1840s were his heyday. As the legitimate theatre continued to be attacked by guardians of bourgeois morality, so the star of Parry's innocent gifts rose. His humour remained in the best possible taste.

F. C. Burnand, born in 1836, a Catholic and one of the great editors of *Punch*, recalled his childhood experience of seeing the young Parry at his best:

> 'Boy and man' I have literally writhed with laughter at his fun; indeed, as a boy, hearing John Parry for the first time in my life at the Hanover Square Rooms when he pretended to give an even-

1. The other Parry Diaries are in the National Library of Wales, Aberystwyth. The Thalberg Tour, e.g., is NLW MS 17719B.

MR. JOHN PARRY—THE ARTIST.

ing party all by himself, whereat he was host, hostess, friends to
guests, young ladies, young gentlemen, the waiters, and even the
supper, my 'risible faculties' were put to so severe a strain that I
must have 'died o' laughter' had I not been judiciously removed
by my father and taken out to air in the invigorating atmosphere
of a draughty passage. John Parry was wonderful! and of course
an immense attraction to all classes of the community who love a
laugh, so long as they have not to go inside a theatre for it and see
'a profane stage play'.[2]

Parry's enthusiasm for private and public performance was
indomitable. After a concert he happily continued to expend energy
into the small hours. We first met him in a Moscheles 'at home' in
1836. In 1843 they still found him amusing. According to Mrs
Moscheles,

without him no party would be complete; ... he sings a trio all
by himself; everyone laughs as soon as he sits down to the piano,
over which he has a perfect mastery; in his 'parlando' songs, which
are for the most part in verse, he generally satirises some folly of
the day. He may truly be called the musical Molière of our time.[3]

Despite his growing attachment to a species of theatre – he had
appeared unsuccessfully in the first performance of Dickens's *Village
Coquettes* in 1836[4] – Parry never really became a worldly man; and
that, ultimately, was his downfall. He was titillated by the Priapic
antics of Lavenu and Thalberg while he was touring with them, but
his own métier was firmly joined to his family – 'dear old Dad', and
his devoted wife and daughters. In recent times the most appropriate similes for his contribution to Victorian entertainment are the

2. F. C. Burnand, *Records and Reminiscences, Personal and General*, 2 vols (London,
1904), I, 62.
3. Charlotte Moscheles, *Life of Moscheles with Selections from his Diaries and Correspondence*, 2 vols (London, 1873), I, 170.
4. Edgar Johnson, *Charles Dickens, His Tragedy and Triumph* (London, 1977), 107:
'John Parry was Young Benson in rustic garb and a preposterous wig with long
ringlets that wobbled over his brow.' Braham, the tenor, produced the play and
took the part of wicked Squire Norton.

performances of Flanders and Swann. A bubble of nervous energy supported him on stage, but it was soon pricked. Burnand reported 'what fun he was at Christmas parties, when he came out strong in a quadrille or a country dance! On such occasions he was always in the best of spirits; but alas! he suffered from the reaction next day; and later in life from melancholia.'[5]

In the late 1840s he devised a very successful kind of entertainment modelled upon the single-handed performances of his friend, Charles Mathews, and of the chief collaborator in his songwriting, Albert Smith. Parry's 'Notes, Vocal and Instrumental' comprised a sequence of comic songs and scenas given in a room decorated with his own water-colour paintings. But his manic–depressive personality reached a critical moment at the height of his success in 1853. Recuperating from a severe nervous collapse, for a time he retired from the London mêlée to become organist of St Jude's, Southsea, and practised there as a teacher. In 1860 he reopened in London in the daytime family entertainments of Mr and Mrs German Reed. One of their scriptwriters was F. C. Burnand; another was William Schwenk Gilbert; some of their music was composed by young Arthur Sullivan.[6]

In 1869 ill-health again caused Parry to retire. Despite all the evidence of success, his life had a tragic declension. When he took leave of his public at a benefit before the Prince and Princess of Wales at the Gaiety Theatre in February 1877, he was penniless: his trusted financial advisor had absconded with the savings of a profitable lifetime. Parry died in his son-in-law's house two years later. *The Times* remembered him with considerable respect: 'His triumphs were not won, perhaps, on stricken fields, nor did he walk in that "fierce light which beats upon" those who would win the highest honours of the stage. But in his own career he was inimitable.'[7]

Joey Richardson remained the best flautist of his generation in England. He was famous for devoting many hours a day to practice,

5. Burnand, op. cit., II, 334. See also *Musical Standard*, 16 December 1871, 'The Gallery of Illustration'.
6. ibid., 332; and *DNB* (J. O. Parry).
7. *The Times*, 8 February 1877.

and though his technique was brilliant, the tone he produced was reputedly rather thin. However, in spite of his sustaining sense of fun, there were weaknesses of temperament which, perhaps, had caused the flare-ups with Liszt and the outwardly genial Parry on tour. He was always guaranteed steady work as first flautist in London orchestras, but in the early 1840s he quarrelled with a leading London conductor, Louis Antoine Jullien, and played out the rest of his career in the backwater of the Queen's Band.[8]

The two lady vocalists disappeared from public view within a few years. Miss Steele could at least reflect upon the experience of having been coached by Liszt in the songs of his beloved Schubert. Miss Bassano's short relationship with Lavenu, her encounter with the master teacher Domenico Crevelli, and her own good voice seem not to have ensured the smooth development of a public career. According to the *Athenaeum* critic, Henry Chorley, writing of Mlle Meerti's concert in June 1841 – where John Parry was in 'drollest humour' – Miss Bassano exhibited 'a very fine voice'; but 'where, save in England, do performers present themselves to metropolitan audiences on the mere strength of a crude voice? Everything else is wanting to her.'[9]

Lavenu lost faith, not just with Louisa Bassano, his 'Bread and Butter', but with all things English. Along with Joey Richardson, he had been an early student at the Royal Academy of Music. He published several songs and piano pieces of his own; and an operetta, *Loretta, a Tale of Seville*, had a successful run at Covent Garden in 1846. But his English career did not satisfy his ambitions, and, emigrating to Australia, he became music director of a theatre in Sydney, where he died in August 1859.[10]

His even younger publishing partner and collaborator in the Liszt escapade, Frank Mori, came to terms with his second-order place on the London musical scene. His father, Nicholas, soloist at an early Philharmonic concert, had studied violin with Viotti, and was the customary leader of London orchestras in the 1830s. The son became a reputable conductor in the 1840s, and in 1854 founded the

8. *DNB.*
9. *Athenaeum*, 12 June 1841.
10. *Grove* (1927 edn).

London Orchestra, the first briefly successful attempt to create a permanent ensemble in the capital. One of Frank's sons (another Nicholas) wrote the music for W. S. Gilbert's fairy comedy, *The Wicked World*, in 1873.[11]

According to even his most sympathetic biographers, Joseph Augustine Wade had shot his bolt long before he met Liszt. His commercial successes of the 1820s and the early 1830s may have persuaded Mori and Lavenu that his solo songs and duets might still earn money. But it was not simple anxiety about competition which caused Parry to criticize the Irishman's recent compositions during the second tour; and it is improbable that Wade was ever in a sufficiently sober condition to make revisions to the songs while the performers were on the road. After parting company with Lavenu in 1841 he lived in poverty, making a few pounds by cobbling together accompaniments for Chappell's *National English Airs*, and writing short articles for the new *Illustrated London News*. He was undoubtedly a man of various talents; but his final attempt to diversify was a tragi-comic affair. In 1844, a year before he died, he published an astonishingly funny musical manual. Its title, which probably cost him as much effort as compiling the rest of the book, deserves quotation in full:

> The Hand-Book to the Pianoforte; comprising An Easy Introduction to the Study of that Instrument and Music in General: The Art of Fingering according to the Modes of the Best Masters, exemplified in Various Exercises, Scales, etc., in All the Major and Minor Keys; and Interspersed by Relaxations from Study, Consisting of Popular Melodies and Romances, and Selections from the Pianoforte Compositions of some of the Most Celebrated Masters. Also, A Short and Easy Introduction to Harmony or [sic] Counterpoint, and a Vocabulary of Terms —— By J. Augustine Wade, Author of 'The Dwelling of Fancy', 'Songs of the Flowers', 'The Two Houses of Granada', an Opera, 'The Prophecy', an Oratorio, etc., etc.

The frontispiece of this remarkably short volume was a portrait-

11. *DNB*; also C. Humphries and W. C. Smith, *Music Publishing in the British Isles* (London, 1954).

engraving – quill-pen poised over manuscript; right profile – of
Liszt, 'to whom the following pages are dedicated by his Friend, the
Author'. Ironically, Wade's piece of pedagogical plagiarism suggests that he – alcohol and opium notwithstanding – was the only
actor in Lavenu's harlequinade who truly appreciated Liszt's potential stature in 1840–41. The beginning of his short essay in the 1844
treatise, on 'The Genius of the Pianoforte', indicates some understanding of Liszt as the embodiment of the instrument in its continuing development:

> The pianoforte, above all other instruments, is best calculated to
> form a musician; it is the epitome of an orchestra – an abridge-
> ment – a 'multum in parvo', which can enable the performer not
> only to conceive but express all possible harmonies and combina-
> tions by himself, independent of the aid of others.

During the two tours Liszt, perforce, had not been independent,
but neither had he been dragged down by his colleagues; and
whenever possible, he had risen to the summit of an occasion. It
cannot be argued that, in failing to return after his successful 1841
London season, he had rejected England. Probably he preferred,
until 1848, the nomadic Romance of wide-ranging Continental
experience to the railway-bound constraints of an offshore island. It
is intriguing to speculate that, if he cherished any memories of
English life, they were centred upon the genuine musical
enthusiasm he had met at Rochdale and Huddersfield, in the
dynamic industrial areas of Lancashire and the West Riding; that,
when he met the adoring George Eliot and her enlightened
paramour, George Henry Lewes, in his retreat at Weimar in 1854,
he could talk not simply of her great neighbour Shakespeare, but of
the bewilderingly seething communities of the Midlands which he
had traversed in 1840 and 1841.[12] Liszt was a child of the Industrial
Age only in the sense that he appreciated the advantage of playing
on an Erard with a cast-iron frame. For the rest, he was a noble,
east-European peasant who, in later years, was happy to smoke
cigars in plush railway-carriage compartments.

12. Gordon Haight, *George Eliot, a Biography* (Oxford, 1968), 154–7.

He did return to London, a benign Rip van Winkle, in 1886. But in the meantime he had not been artistically asleep. An outline of what had happened to him in the intervening years must have been known in England – through the pages of the *Musical World*, the *Musical Times*, and occasionally *The Times* – to an increasingly intelligent concert-going public. British musical apprentices had gone on pilgrimage to Weimar to learn something about piano-playing from Wade's 'Friend'. He was acknowledged, at first reluc-tantly, then with grudging enthusiasm, in the role of John the Baptist to Wagner's Son of God. His devotion to the Roman Church might have won him some fashionable sympathy in the apostate era of Cardinals Manning and Newman.

More pragmatically, his few constant admirers in England saw to it that Liszt's music was heard during his absence. Percy Scholes, in *The Mirror of Music* (1947), calculated that between 1841 and 1867 none of his compositions was played at Philharmonic concerts in London.[13] In the 1870s, however, a real interest in his works began to appear, though only one of them, the E flat Concerto, was repeatedly performed; and this new sympathy was engendered almost solely through the evangelical work of a Liszt pupil. Walter Bache was born into a bourgeois Birmingham family in 1842. He studied piano with Liszt – incongruously for a Unitarian – in Rome. Bache's earnest Midlands shoulder gradually pushed aside the bar-rier of resistance to his master's music. Using his own funds he promoted annual London recitals and orchestral concerts devoted entirely to Liszt's compositions from 1869 till his death in 1887.[14] But even in 1882 the critic of the *Musical Times* found Liszt's Piano Sonata 'somewhat affected' and 'ugly'; the rest of the works on that year's programme were characterized by 'rhapsodical diffuseness and pretentious incoherence'.[15]

This kind of comment was hardly a suitable anticipation of the hysterical reception Liszt enjoyed when he finally arrived in London in 1886. None of his former companions on the British tours was

13. Percy Scholes, ed.: *The Mirror of Music: 1844–1944* (London, 1947), I, 426.
14. *Grove* (1927 edn).
15. *Musical Times*, December 1882.

alive to greet him or to reflect upon his belated triumph. And he was
a notable survivor in other respects. Of the tallest trees in the
European forest of the 1840s, Mendelssohn had died in 1847, burnt
out, but in the full bloom of his high reputation and powerful
influence in England. Chopin had succumbed to tuberculosis in
1849, soon after a British tour in winter which had hastened his
end. Liszt had tried to promote his friend's music in London in
1840. Slowly, and despite that generous advocacy, Chopin posthu-
mously struggled free of Victorian prudishness about his sup-
posedly consumptive fantasies. Schumann, Moscheles's candidate
for the Pantheon, died rabidly in 1856, and then assumed his proper
place in English concert programmes, mainly because of a growing
appreciation of his wife Clara's conservative devotion to performing
his compositions. Moscheles's own life ended peacefully in 1870 in
Leipzig where, having been appointed to a teaching post by
Mendelssohn in 1846, he had continued to preserve the finest
aspects of the Classical tradition, while countering what he saw as
the worst excesses of the younger men.

Perhaps the most eminent instance of mortality, which made
Liszt's 1886 visit a moment of great significance, had been the death
of Wagner three years earlier. It is almost impossible to understand
now, in an age when his influence is recognized even by fervent
antagonists, the reasons why Wagner's early operatic works were
treated so vituperatively by English audiences and critics in the
1850s and 1860s. When extracts from his masterpieces were given
by well-schooled gangs of London players under Richter at the
Albert Hall and the Crystal Palace, there were still fusillades of
criticism. Perhaps, in spite of continuing resistance, the break-
through occurred with the first complete staging of the *Ring* in
1882, under Seidl, and of *Die Meistersinger* and *Tristan*, conducted by
Richter. There can be little doubt that Liszt came to London in
1886, not simply to receive compensatory homage in a country
where he had been largely ignored since 1841, but also to be saluted
as Wagner's inspirer. The *Musical Times* admitted,

> Had it not been for Liszt, the director of the Weimar Court
> Theatre, who can say but that the musical revolution in affairs

operatic had never occurred. Only by the light of Weimar does Bayreuth become a possibility.[16]

Just as Parry's innocent theatricality had been accepted in the 1840s, so now, in the 1880s, Liszt's clerical gabardine was seen as a suitably moral cloak for the excitement formerly aroused by his Mephistophelian reputation as a performer. In the realm of politics, Garibaldi, alongside Verdi, had been feted in England as a great liberal talisman; so perhaps Liszt could be greeted as a proponent of Hungarian nationalism, fighting, without bloodshed, against the despotic might of Habsburg Vienna.

Reports of his European activities had usually been confined to tit-bits and waffly anecdotes. In the second half of 1871, for instance, the *Musical Standard* devoted a sequence of items to Liszt. First, in August, there was a rave notice for a performance in Vienna by the beautiful Sophie Menter, who was called 'the pupil of Liszt'. Then, 'Dr. Franz Liszt has left for Rome, passing through Bavaria on his way south . . . He will return to Pesth in the winter.' In September the *Standard* wheeled out a dusty little story which might have revived memories of the early British tours:

> Liszt and Rubini agreed to give concerts in various European cities; having arrived in one, which shall be nameless, despite the tempting programme, an audience numbering thirty person only was secured. Rubini angrily declined to sing; but Liszt played his best; the public was enchanted, and endeavoured to encore the celebrated pianist; he, however, declined the honour, but invited the whole of the audience to dine with him. The dinner cost Liszt 1,200 francs, but the next day his salon was crowded with people, who came not so much to hear the music, but on the expectation of obtaining a dinner *gratis*.[17]

The anecdote said a great deal about Liszt's legendary generosity; but its waspish little coda embodied lingering English suspicion of his musical significance.

In October the same journal reported that the Hungarian authori-

16. ibid., February 1871.
17. *Musical Standard*, 23 September 1871.

ties in Pesth had settled a pension of £600 a year on Liszt: 'it is said that a title of nobility is to be conferred on him'.[18] And in the next month, under 'Foreign Notes', it promised that 'Abbé Liszt is coming to London in May, and will probably give some concerts here.' This must have been speculative comment: Liszt did not arrive for another 15 years.

Despite such tittle-tattle and prognostications, Liszt's growing European reputation was gradually acknowledged. In 1871 the passing of his great early pianistic rival was noted, with muted sadness: the *Standard* reported in May that Thalberg had died after a short illness, at his villa in Posilipo. His operas *Florinda* and *Christina of Sweden* were called 'failures', a benign comment. But much more damning were the revised judgments upon his playing and compositions for the piano, 'which are showy drawing-room transcriptions on other people's ideas'. Several of his 'most admired artifices' had been 'copied from Liszt and our great English harpist, Parish Alvars'. He had advanced the mechanism of piano playing, but his compositions 'astonish the ear rather than touch the heart ... They show no signs of genius.' His *Etudes*, however, might still prove useful as a gymnasium for aspiring pianists.[19] So effectively, by the time Liszt returned in 1886, Thalberg and all the other fashionable virtuosi of the 1830s and 1840s were dwelling, with their reputations, in oblivion.

Liszt's fortnight in London, in the second and third weeks of April, was a triumph of much greater magnitude than might have been expected; indeed, no foreign musician revisiting England ever enjoyed such hyperbole of praise, such uncritical acclaim. Bache, as might have been guessed, was the engineer of the visit. The excuse was the mounting of a grand performance of his master's oratorio *St Elizabeth*, and it must be admitted that, without Liszt's presence, it is doubtful whether that work would ever have been heard in London in the late nineteenth century. The oratorio, massive in scale and conception, was a product of his middle period, composed in the years 1857 to 1862. It represented threefold associations: first, his desire to make a noise as a composer in the Roman Church; second,

18. ibid., 7 October 1871.
19. ibid., 18 November 1871.

his love of country, expressed through the legend of Elizabeth, the patron saint of Hungary; and third, his attachment to Weimar with whose region, Thuringia, the saint was historically connected. Probably London audiences did not know that their initial enthusiasm was to be tested by a work which lasted nearly three hours in performance.

The *Musical Times* had announced in November 1885 that Dr Franz Liszt had accepted an invitation from Messrs Novello, Ewen and Co. to visit London for a performance of the oratorio:

> Considering that it is forty years since the great master was in this country, notwithstanding that repeated offers have been made to tempt him here, we need scarcely say that the utmost interest will be felt in the fact of his being amongst us; and it may be hoped that in the preparation of his oratorio, he may at least be induced to give the benefit of his valuable counsel to the artists engaged in the presentation of his work before an English audience.[20]

Liszt hoped to be welcomed in London as a composer rather than a pianist. Preparing for his visit he wrote to Bache from Budapest in February,

> My very dear Friend,
> They seem determined in London to push me to the Piano.
> I cannot consent to this in public, as my seventy-five-year-old fingers are no longer suited to it, and Bülow, Saint-Saëns, Rubinstein, and you, dear Bache, play my compositions much better than what is left of my humble self.
> Perhaps it would be opportune if friend Hueffer would have the kindness to let the public know, by a short announcement, that Liszt only ventures to appear as a grateful visitor, and neither in London nor anywhere else as a man with an interest in his fingers.[21]

Yet in spite of *St Elizabeth* and all the metamorphoses of his career since 1841, it was as a pianist that Liszt was still revered in England.

---

20. ibid., 6 May 1871.
21. La Mara, ed.: *Letters of Franz Liszt* (London, 1894), II, 484.

People wanted to see the legend; but they also desperately wished to hear the magic conjured by ancient fingers. And hundreds of English men and women were delighted that he did play several times in public and in private.

The Times, at the end of his first heroic week, recorded all the events at which he had appeared and played.[22] He arrived in London on Saturday 3 April. He had intended coming the previous Thursday, but, said the *Musical Times*, 'the pressing solicitations of Parisian musical circles' had induced him to remain there for a repeat of another of his massive choral works, the *Graner Messe*.[23] He went immediately to Westwood House, Sydenham, the home of Mr Henry Littleton, who was the representative of Novellos, the promoters of the main concert. Mr Forbes, Chairman of the London, Chatham and Dover Railway, arranged that the train should make a special stop at Penge, the local station; and there Liszt found a welcoming party of expatriate Hungarians.

On that first evening, after a musical entertainment laid on by Bache before three or four hundred guests at Westwood, Liszt went to a piano and played Chopin's Nocturne op. 32 no. 2, providing possibly a calculated echo of the unselfishness he had shown in performing the same piece – then freshly composed – at London concerts in 1840. On Sunday, for an enchanted circle of friends, he performed excerpts from his E flat Concerto. On Monday afternoon he attended a rehearsal of *St Elizabeth*, as *The Times* noted, 'giving now and then valuable hints to conductor and artists'. In the evening he was present at a choral rehearsal, 'when he played the piano to the delight of the singers'. On Tuesday he went to the Royal Academy of Music for a concert inaugurating the Liszt Prize, after which he played to the pupils and their friends one of his arrangements of Chopin's Polish songs. In his speech the Principal, Sir George Macfarren, felicitously compared Liszt to Wellington who, 'when he had no more battles left to fight, proved himself as great a statesman as he had been a warrior'. That evening Liszt battled through the crowds to hear the performance of *St Elizabeth* at St James's Hall.

22. *The Times*, 10 April 1886.
23. *Musical Times*, May 1886.

On Wednesday he travelled to Windsor where he played four
pieces to the queen: an improvisation; an arrangement of 'The
Miracle of the Roses' from *St Elizabeth*, '(this by Her Majesty's
special desire)'; a Hungarian Rhapsody, and Chopin's First Nocturne in B flat minor. In the evening there was a further performance of the oratorio, this time under the auspices of the Royal
Academy of Music. In the programme was printed the following
poem by Miss Constance Bache:

> We welcome thee, from southern sunnier climes,
> To England's shore,
> And stretch glad hands across the lapse of time
> To thee once more.

Full twice two decades swiftly have rolled by
Since thou wast here;
A meteor flashing through our northern sky
Thou didst appear.

Thy coming now we greet with pleasure keen
And loyal heart,
Adding tradition of what thou hast been
To what thou art . . .[24]

On Thursday evening at eleven o'clock, surrounded by artists, musicians, and men of letters, he performed for Bache at a reception in the Grosvenor Gallery presided over by Burne-Jones. (Those two days, Wednesday and Thursday, epitomized not only what Liszt might have chosen to remember from this visit, but also what he may have recalled most affectionately of his social encounters in the capital in 1840 and 1841.)

The next day, he went to hear the E flat Concerto played by Emil Bach at the Albert Hall, with an excerpt from another oratorio, *Christus*, and his symphonic poem *Orpheus*. Mr and Mrs Henschel and Mme Liza Lehmann sang some of his songs with orchestral accompaniment. The following afternoon, at the Crystal Palace, he heard Manns conduct *Les Préludes*, *Mazeppa* and a Hungarian Rhapsody. The vocal offerings, again from Lehmann, included *Die Lorelei*, *Angolin del Biondo Crin* (the first solo song he ever wrote, which was dedicated to his daughter Blandine), and *Es muss ein Wunderbares sein*, the subtleties of which must have been lost in the palace's huge galleries. The highlight of this occasion was a performance of the inevitable E flat Concerto by his favourite pupil, Bernard Stavenhagen. In the evening Liszt was the guest of the German Athenaeum, a literary and philosophical society, where he played two of his own pieces.

Of this first week *The Times*'s critic wrote, somewhat ironically:

A younger man might well have broken down under the weight of honour and excitement. But Liszt is prepared to brave the fatigues of a second week in London . . . Ovations such as those

24. ibid.

offered to Liszt have never before been witnessed in musical
England, and for the psychological student it was an interesting
phenomenon to see quiet and decorous persons mounting on
seats, waving hats and handkerchiefs, and clamouring with
unrestrained lung power. Even outside the hall the composer's
arrival was always waited for by crowds who raised their hats to
him as if he were a King, and the very cabmen on Saturday were
fain to raise a cheer for the 'Habby Liszt'. These humble admirers
have never heard a note of his music, and would probably not be
very much the wiser were they to have that privilege. What
impresses them, as with electric force, is the noble face and form,
and the bearing worthy of a leader of men, and denoting an
overpowering personality; and this fact at the same time accounts
for the phenomenal and uninterrupted success of Liszt's career
from his boyhood to his old age.

Just as Paris had detained him, so now London insisted on his
staying a week longer than he had intended. On his second Sunday
he attended Brompton Oratory, heard an organ recital there, con-
versed with Cardinal Manning, and took tea with the Duchess of
Cambridge who could even remember performances by 'Master
Liszt' in the 1820s. He went on to a reception given by W. Beatty-
Kingston, a man of letters, and improvised incomparably. Then in
the evening he attended a Hungarian reception in Earls Court where
his playing was listened to 'with almost greedy satisfaction'; and
from there he went to a 'Monday Pop', Joachim and Charles Hallé
playing the Kreutzer Sonata (surely 'by desire'). On entering the
concert room Liszt was 'obviously regarded as quite as much a part
of the entertainment as the music itself'.

On Tuesday the 13th he lunched with Baroness Burdett-Coutts;
then went to see the 99th performance of *Faust* at the Lyceum:

> Mr. Henry Irving graciously placed the royal box at the disposal
> of Liszt and his party ... The theatre was darkened when the
> Abbé and his retinue entered, so he was not at first observed, but
> at the fall of the first drop, when the lights were turned up, the
> conspicuous figure of the white-haired musician became the
> cynosure of all eyes, and a ringing cheer brought forth responsive
> salutations.

After *Faust*, Mephistopheles supped with Irving in the cavernous Beefsteak Club beneath the theatre, surrounded by benevolent ghosts of actors like Macready and Kean. The suggestiveness of this candlelit scene has been caught immaculately by Sacheverell Sitwell.[25]

On Thursday afternoon Liszt attended his Scottish pupil Frederic Lamond's recital; and on Friday young Stavenhagen's concert included *Funérailles*, *Sposalizio*, the two St Francis Legends, two Paganini etudes, and the Fantasia and Fugue on B A C H. The final Saturday bestowed the accolade of a hastily arranged third performance of *St Elizabeth*, taking the place of an intended Beethoven Symphony, this time at the Crystal Palace. The audiences for the oratorio had been prepared for their marathon experience by two extended analytical articles in the *Musical Times*. At the end of the concert Liszt was presented with a valedictory address from the London branch of the United Richard Wagner Society. He made his final appearance at the vocalist Countess Sadowska's concert on Monday the 19th; near the end Mr Charles Fry, 'the well-known elocutionist', emerged to deliver a 'Farewell to Liszt' specially written by Beatty-Kingston.

The sweep of Liszt's career – as 'the greatest living pianist' – had been described in several columns of the *Musical Times* on 1 April. The writer even recorded the fact, important to bourgeois Englishmen, that his last British engagement, to Lavenu, had seen the appearance of 'no less a deficit than £6,000 ... on the agent's books'; but it was noted, somewhat inaccurately, that Liszt, 'with characteristic complacency and good nature, bade the agent not to mind, that he himself would make up the difference'. It was also recalled that Liszt had been chiefly responsible for raising funds to erect the Beethoven monument at Bonn, and that, in Weimar, he had frequently sponsored the work of hitherto unrecognized musicians.

In 1886, while not remembering every detail of his far-off provincial tours, Liszt may have recalled their few dazzling highlights, and some of the bathos: the episode in Clonmel with the Tomkinson Square was perhaps balanced in memory against his Dublin meet-

25. Sacheverell Sitwell, *Liszt* (London, 1934), 323.

THE TWO GRAND OLD MEN, WHO DIVIDED THE HONOURS OF LAST WEEK BETWEEN THEM.

ings with Lord Morpeth, the Chief Secretary, in 1840–41. Ireland
impinged upon Liszt's last visit in at least two ways. The country –
Dublin, Cork, Kilkenny, Belfast – had been uncharacteristically
quiet in 1840 and 1841. By the mid-1840s it had become chaotic
through tragic famine and renewed terrorist violence. The Fenian-
ism of the 1860s propelled Ireland once again towards the centre of
the political stage. Five days after Liszt arrived in Dover, Gladstone
conducted the first reading of his controversial Irish Home Rule
Bill. Throughout the pianist's stay in London, therefore, the chief
counterpoint to the social excitement of his presence was provided
by the political controversy provoked by Gladstone's radical stroke

of policy. Some members of the audience for *St Elizabeth* had come straight from heated debates in the Commons and the Lords.

Gladstone was two years older than Liszt, and *Punch* could not resist making a graphic comparison between these remarkable Grand Old Men. Beneath a striking caricature of Gladstone, shamrock in buttonhole, trampling Rose and Thistle underfoot, the writer extolled the virtues of four men:

> Within one fortnight to have seen Cardinal Newman, aged eighty-six, officiating, to have shaken the wonderful hands of, and talked with the Abbé Liszt, aged seventy-six, and to have heard Mr. Gladstone's great oratorical effort, at seventy-seven, is indeed something to be remembered in a lifetime. And I may note that those who heard Mr. Gladstone finish at eight o'clock, could . . . have heard Canon Liszt play at Mr. Walter Bache's Reception at the Grosvenor Gallery – another memorable event – at eleven o'clock the same night. If I contrived to be in two places at once, depend on it I shall keep the secret of my mysterious power to myself . . . P.S. – How tired Liszt must be of hearing his own Music! Fancy PEARS being treated for a whole week to nothing but his own Soap! On second thoughts, this is an inadequate illustration, as PEARS actually lives on his own soap all the year round.
>
> NIBBS the LISZT'NER.[26]

But amid the soft soap which had lathered Liszt's hectic fortnight, there was some Irish coal tar – of the Dublin, not the Kilkenny black-marble variety – in the form of George Bernard Shaw's lively attempt at objectivity. In the *Dramatic Review* for 10 April, he wrote:

> If music be to you only a glorious dream, an unknown language transcending all articulate poetry, a rapture of sublimity discharging itself into your inmost soul with thrilling harmonious thunder; then for you especially the voice of man's innate godhead will speak in whatever Liszt plays, whether he extemporises variations on Pop goes the Weasel or faithfully re-utters for you the chromatic *fantasia* of Bach. The great player is to you no mere pianist: he is a host of associations – George Sand, Lamartine, Victor

26. *Punch*, 17 April 1886.

Hugo, Paris in the days of the Romantic movement, and what not and why not? Happy hero-worshipper! No generous infidel will grudge you your ecstasy, or untimely urge that it is intense in inverse ratio to your knowledge of music. Indeed if one feels disposed to throw cold water on such genial transports, it would be difficult to find any just now to throw, Liszt having the gift that was laid as a curse upon the Scotch laird (in Scott's *Redgauntlet*) who made icy water bubble and boil by touching it.

That sums up very appositely the dramatic unreality of Liszt's reception in 1886. For most of his London listeners he was simply a survivor from an age of heroes.

As he departed on the morning mail from Dover to Antwerp on 20 April, the critic of the *Musical Times* was making plans, on behalf of the English concert-going public, to assuage the guilt lingering from his treatment in Britain 40 years before:

> The year 1886 will long be remembered by the lustre thrown upon it by the presence of a truly great man, the most imposing figure in the musical world . . . now that he has tested the warmth of English feeling, we can only express the hope – wherein we but re-echo the wish of thousands – that he may long be spared to put our friendliness again and again to the proof. We welcomed him with pleasure; we part with unfeigned regret from
>
> FRANZ LISZT.

Liszt did indeed intend to return. But on 31 July he died in Bayreuth. The *Musical Times* commissioned Frederick Niecks, the first unsentimental biographer of Chopin, and a considerable musicologist, to contribute Liszt's obituary, a document remarkable for its judiciousness and wide range of reference. Niecks remembered Liszt's humour – Mendelssohn's comment upon him as 'a good hearty fellow' – and quoted George Eliot's remark: 'I never met with a person whose manner of telling a story was so piquant'. But above all he emphasized his generosity to fellow-artists. The final paragraph of the article drew Liszt back into the parochial circle of English experience:

> It must be a great satisfaction to the people of England that

among them Liszt closed his artistic career, and that he spoke to
everybody of the great pleasure which his visit had given him.
Another circumstance which will interest Englishmen is that the
last notes which Liszt put on paper were a few lines ... of a
fantasia on subject's from Mackenzie's *Troubadour* which the master had volunteered to write when he was in London ... Enough!
Liszt has lived a noble life. It is for us to honour his memory.[27]

One of the people closest to Liszt throughout his stay in London
was F. C. Burnand: he was the intermediary, for instance, who
arranged that Liszt should hear Mass privately at the Oratory, so as
not to attract too much attention. But much as he admired Liszt's
personality and genius, Burnand could not resist a note of censoriousness when surveying his career in England:

> His temperament had crossed his genius, and only in the last
> years of his life ... when 'repentant ashes' had been strewn upon
> his head in the shape of his long, thick, white locks, and when he
> had devoted himself mainly, if not entirely, to sacred music, did
> we in England see the gentle, amiable musician, whom all who
> knew him loved.

Perhaps, during evenings of fun in the 1860s, his friend John Parry
had told him some of the juicier stories from the Irish and English
tours.

Burnand saw and heard Liszt play at Littleton's house. His subsequent reflective remarks, had the 'Wizard' lived to read them,
might have seemed to offer some compensation for the complacency
with which he had been treated by British audiences in 1840–41:

> That was such playing as never before have I heard, as never in
> this world do I expect to hear again. It was in its way a realisation
> of Dr. Newman's well-known glorification of music. On this
> occasion Liszt did not descend from the platform to be con-
> gratulated, but while the last sweet notes of his playing were yet
> lingering in our ears, he quitted his seat, and, by a side door in
> the gallery, disappeared. Our host, on bidding us good-night,
> apologised for his guest's not being with him to receive our

27. *Musical Times*, September 1886.

congratulations, thanks, and adieux, but the playing had overcome him, and this truly 'grand old man' had bidden us, silently
but eloquently, farewell. That evening is indelible in my
memory.[28]

28. Burnand, op. cit., I, 61–2.

Select Bibliography

Books Specifically about Liszt

Ernst Burger, *Franz Liszt: a Chronicle of his Life in Pictures and Documents* (Princeton, 1989)

La Mara, ed.: *Letters of Franz Liszt*, 2 vols (London, 1894)

Zsigmond László and Bela Mátéka, *Franz Liszt: a Biography in Pictures* (London, 1968)

Ernest Newman, *The Man Liszt* (London, 1934)

Daniel Ollivier, ed.: *Letters of Liszt and Marie d'Agoult*, 2 vols (Paris, 1933)

Humphrey Searle, *The Music of Liszt* (New York, 1966)

Sacheverell Sitwell, *Liszt* (London, 1934)

Ronald Taylor, *Franz Liszt: the Man and the Musician* (London, 1987)

Alan Walker, ed.: *Liszt: the Man and his Music* (London, 1969)

Alan Walker, *Franz Liszt: the Virtuoso Years, 1811–1847* (London, 1983)

Alan Walker, *Liszt: the Weimar Years* (London, 1989)

Derek Watson, *Liszt* (London, 1989)

Other Works

C. B. Andrews and J. A. Orr-Ewing, *Victorian Swansdown: Extracts from the Early Travel Diaries of John Orlando Parry* (London, 1934)

Kathleen Barker, *The Theatre Royal, Bristol, 1766–1966* (London, 1974)

Julius Benedict, *Carl Maria von Weber* (London, 1881)

Henry F. Berry, *A History of the Royal Dublin Society* (London, 1915)

R. Brunel Gotch, *Mendelssohn and his Friends in Kensington* (Oxford, 1938)

John Burke, *Suffolk* (London, 1971)

F. C. Burnand, *Records and Reminiscences, Personal and General*, 2 vols (London, 1904)

H. C. Colles, *The Mirror of Music, 1844–1944*, 2 vols (London, 1947)

Robert Elkin, *Royal Philharmonic: the Annals of the Royal Philharmonic Society* (London, 1947)

John Ella, *Musical Sketches at Home and Abroad* (London, 1878)

April Fitzlyon, *Maria Malibran, Diva of the Romantic Age* (London, 1987)

Elizabeth Forbes, *Mario and Grisi* (London, 1982)

Reginald R. Gerig, *Famous Pianists and their Technique* (Bridgeport, Conn., 1985)

John Glyde, *The Moral, Social and Religious Condition of Ipswich in the Middle of the Nineteenth Century* (Ipswich, 1850)

Gordon Haight, *George Eliot, a Biography* (Oxford, 1968)

Arthur Hedley, ed.: *Selected Correspondence of Fryderyk Chopin* (London, 1962)

Edgar Johnson, *Charles Dickens, His Tragedy and Triumph* (London, 1977)

John Lawson and Harold Silver, *A Social History of Education in England* (London, 1973)

Ernest J. Lowell Junior, ed.: *Lady Blessington's Conversations of Lord Byron* (Princeton, 1969)

Wilson Lyle, ed.: *A Dictionary of Pianists* (London, 1985)

Charlotte Moscheles, *Life of Moscheles with Selections from his Diaries and Correspondence*, 2 vols (London, 1873)

Gerald Norris, *A Musical Gazeteer of Great Britain and Ireland* (Newton Abbot, 1981)

John Parry (Bardd Alaw), *A Trip to Wales, Containing much Information that Relates to that Interesting Alpine Country* (London and Caernarvon, (?)1840)

Nikolaus Pevsner and John Harris, *The Buildings of England: Lincolnshire* (London, 1964)

Bernarr Rainbow, *The Land Without Music: Musical Education in England, 1800–1860* (London, 1967)

H. C. Robbins Landon, *The Collected Correspondence and London Notebooks of Joseph Haydn* (London, 1959)

L. T. C. Rolt, *Isambard Kingdom Brunel* (London, 1970)

Harold C. Schonberg, *The Great Pianists* (London, 1964)

Jack Simmons, *Leicester: the Ancient Borough to 1860* (Gloucester, 1980)

A. Temple Patterson, *Hampshire and the Isle of Wight* (London, 1976)

H. Temple Patterson, *Radical Leicester: a History of Leicester, 1780–1850* (Leicester, 1954)

David Wainwright, *The Piano Makers* (London, 1975)

David Wainwright, *Broadwood By Appointment* (London, 1982)

George Weir, *The History of Horncastle* (1820)

Index

Mendelssohn, Felix (*cont.*)
  Prince Albert and, 28
  in Scotland, 160, 162
  works,
    Hymn of Praise, 107
    keyboard works, 13
    Midsummer Night's Dream
      Overture, 10
    'On Wings of Song', 28, 96
    Quartet in E flat (Op. 44), 115
    songs, 15, 28
    string quintets, 13
    Symphony No. 1 in C minor, 12
    Violin Concerto, 172
Menter, Sophie, 186
Metz, 82
Mayerbeer, Giacomo, 92
  Huguenots, Les, 175
  Robert le diable, 121
Milan, 34, 45
Milnes, R. M., 33
M'Lintock, Major, 128
Montaigne, Michel Eyquem de, 117
Mori, Frank, 19–20, 37, 44, 74, 75, 86,
    98, 101, 181–2
  reviews of, 49, 51, 73, 78
Mori, Miss, 103
Mori, Nicholas (father of Frank), 11,
    49, 87, 101, 181
Mori, Nicholas (son of Frank), 182
Morning Herald, 95
Morning Post, 43, 64
Mornington, Garret Wesley, Earl of, 130
Mornington, Richard Colley, Earl of,
    105, 130
  glee by, 28
Morpeth, 165
Morpeth, Lord, 131–2, 135, 136, 152,
    165, 194
Moscheles, Charlotte, 15, 34, 37, 179
Moscheles, Ignaz, 12–15, 17–18, 20,
    21, 23, 37, 67, 89, 115, 168, 175,
    185
  family, 26, 179
  and development of recital, 13–14,
    34
  works,
    keyboard works, 13

Piano Concerto in G minor, 15
  songs, 15
  Studies, 37
Mount Edgecumbe, 58–9
Mozart, Wolfgang Amadeus
  'Batti, batti', 152
  Cosi fan Tutte, 46
  Don Giovanni, 15, 51, 68, 135
  Exsultate Jubilate, 63
  'Mi lagnero tacendi', 109
  Nozze di Figaro, Le, 87
  overtures, 153
  Piano Quartet in G minor, 115
  Requiem, 88, 125
  string quartets, 12, 13, 115
  trios, 120
  wind serenades, 12
  Zauberflöte, Die, 10, 138
Munden, Mr, 107
Munich, 20
Music Hall (Sheffield), 120
Musical Standard, 186–7
Musical Times, 184, 185–6, 188, 189,
    193, 196–7
Musical World, 30, 83, 87, 95

Nagle, Richard, 128
Nantwich, 110
Naples, 42
Napoleon I, 24, 124–5
  Ashes ceremony, 125, 141
Newark, 81–2, 85
Newbury, 103
Newcastle-under-Lyme, 108–10
Newcastle-upon-Tyne, 165–6
Newcastle Chronicle, 165, 168
Newman, Dr, 197
Newman Ernest, 1, 7
Newman, John Henry, Cardinal, 184,
    195
Newmarket, 87
Newport (Isle of Wight), 47, 48, 51
Newry, 158
Newstead Abbey, 80
Niecks, Frederick, 196–7
Normanby, Lord, 33
North Staffordshire Advertiser, 109–10